UTAH

OTHER BOOKS BY THIS AUTHOR

UTAH

Toby Olson

*

MASTERWORKS OF FICTION (1987)

GREEN INTEGER
KØBENHAVN & LOS ANGELES
2003

GREEN INTEGER
Edited by Per Bregne
København/Los Angeles

Distributed in the United States by Consortium Book
Sales and Distribution, 1045 Westgate Drive, Suite 90
Saint Paul, Minnesota 55114-1065
and in England and the Continent by
Central Books
99 Wallis Road, London E9 5LN
(323) 857-1115 / http://www.greeninteger.com

First Green Integer edition 2003
©1987 by Toby Olson
Published originally as *Utah* (New York: The Linden Press/
Simon & Schuster, 1987)
Reprinted through agreement with the author and his agent,
The Ellen Levine Literary Agency

Design: Per Bregne
Typography: Guy Bennett
Photograph: Marion Ettlinger

LIBRARY OF CONGRESS CATALOGING IN PUBLICATION DATA
Olson, Toby [1937]
Utah
ISBN: 1-892295-35-0
p. cm — Green Integer 92
I. Title II. Series

For Joe and Linnea Fitschen

Too many conflicting emotional interests are involved for life ever to be wholly acceptable, and possibly it is the work of the storyteller to rearrange things so that they conform to this end. In any case, in talking about the past we lie with every breath we draw.

—WILLIAM MAXWELL

Book 1

RETURN

1 ❧ *The Heat*

The Heat stood at the window overlooking the Palisades, the Hudson running dark and deep in the twilight and the blocky figures of Manhattan's buildings beyond his shadowed profile. Lights reflected dimly in the glass, but near his brow I could see the spark of a bright pinpoint. He stood straight, though he was lounging, his legs crossed at the ankles.

"Boys," Melchior whispered, leaning toward me on the couch. His head moved from side to side, his hand pressed among the scatter of old photographs on the cushion between us. And though I don't think The Heat could have heard him, he turned his thin body and face into the light and smiled. I saw the post in his right lobe then, the tiny bright jewel of the earring.

Melchior pulled back and erect as The Heat moved, his shin striking lightly against the coffee table and his arms awkwardly at his sides. He seemed fully in his head and torso only. Just pushing out of adolescence, I thought, and his appendages haven't caught up yet. He nodded as he crossed the room and headed for privacy.

"It's that fucking earring," Melchior said when The Heat was gone. "And now it's the trophy. He's got his mother hassled. But you should meet his grandmother!"

I looked over at her, The Heat's mother. She had her hands in her lap and she smiled faintly.

"I can imagine," I said.

"She's afraid he's a sissy, and she's started to watch the ball games on TV; she can never get it straight that it's baseball and not football. Really, it's the clothes the kids are wearing, unisex. She's afraid it's faggotry, homosexual, but she could never think the words, let alone say them. Boy, if she ever saw that earring!" Barbara laughed and moved her hands to the chair's arms. She didn't seem hassled at all. Melchior looked at her, his face set and almost serious.

"*Your* mother?" I said.

"No." She pointed with a limp wrist at Melchior.

"His." I thought of Anson's earring and both wondered and knew what I was doing there.

"Hey, remember this one?" Melchior said. He held a photograph from the pile in his fingertips, a posed group shot taken in front of a gray building. There were seven sailors lined up in uniform; Melchior was in the center, grinning. I wasn't there.

"I'm not sure." I couldn't recognize anyone but him.

"Sure, at a smoker. There were four good bouts that night."

"Right," I said. "One of those smokers." Barbara got up and went to the kitchen to get beer. Melchior searched for another photo.

The package arrived three weeks before I visited Melchior and six months after Anson was probably in his grave. I knew it was a real grave, though he had wished for incineration and to have his ashes cast on the Hudson. Anson, atypically, a thwarted romantic at the end. But he was somewhere in Utah now, in a place I had only the name of. She had come and taken his body away, a woman named

Patty. She had papers of some kind. I hardly glanced at them. She was sure of herself, and I wasn't yet. Taken him, but nothing else. In our apartment, two days after his death, she wouldn't sit down or meet my eyes, and she avoided touching things as if she feared contagion. She left shortly with the information, the name and address of the funeral parlor, and only spoke to say they would bury him in Utah. There was no room for protest, and I let her go.

When the package came and I puzzled out the smeared return address and remembered it, I recognized that I had been setting things in order almost from the day of Anson's death. I'd changed credit cards and bank accounts of course, but I had also begun to release myself from my own part of our life together. Books had been sold off, boxes of clothing taken to Goodwill, and I had gradually backed away from the contracted therapeutic massages at the club, leaving myself with only individual appointments. The day after the package came, I gave my notice. There was money in the bank account, and the apartment was almost empty.

I could still feel Anson, in his cot at the side of my bed at night, but even the cot was gone.

The package was a used liquor carton, wrapped in butcher paper and tied awkwardly with twine. I found it at my apartment door, late one evening when I got back from the club. The return address was that of my ex-mother-in-law, someone I had had no contact with for over ten years. Reading the address in the vaguely remembered hand, an image of Lorca came back to me. She was sitting in a chair in her tennis outfit. Her long black hair spilled over the shoulder of her white shirt. Her legs were glistening with sweat, and there was a dust of red clay from the court at her ankles I was flushed in the image before it left me, and I felt perspiration rise in the residue of body oil still in my palms as I worked to loosen the twine. There was a folded paper on top of the contents of the box, a brief typed note.

Dear David,
    In cleaning out the little house, I came across some things I believe are yours. I've enclosed them

here. Jack died two years ago, a coronary, and I'll be leaving in a month to live with my sister in Riverside. Hollywood has changed, the neighborhood here not what it used to be. I hear nothing at all from Lorca. I hope this note finds you well. I acquired your address through the certification register.

Best,

Patricia Bowman

The note fought against emotion, which was appropriate. Who was I, I thought, to share her double grief, a dead husband and a lost daughter? And though it was a long time ago, writing the letter must have brought things back to her. Lorca and I living in the little house behind her own, the awkward resentment at our parting, the possibility that Lorca was lost to her because of me.

The box contained many things. There were Navy mementos, old photographs and unused postcards, a pen and pencil set, two blue military jumpers, stickpins and ties, and a brown envelope full of notes and school blue books. Rolled and stuck in a thin cardboard tube were two of Lorca's drawings, line drawings of gardenias. And at the bottom of the box, resting among paper clips and a few ticket stubs, was a small address book. The box also contained a pottery ashtray and a small vase. I put the vase to the side of the box on the kitchen table and lit a cigarette and put it in the ashtray. Then I picked up the old address book and began thumbing through it. Under the M's I found Melchior's name. The address was in Lawrence, Kansas, and there was a phone number.

"You got me through my aunt?"

Melchior already knew this; I'd told him when I phoned. An aunt had answered in Kansas and had given me his number in New York. But Melchior had gone quickly through what reminiscences we had in common, and he was reaching for things in his discomfort.

Barbara brought the beer in, found us sitting on the couch in silence, Melchior's hand shuffling among the photos. She put down a tray of crackers and cheese and then went back to her chair.

"So it comes down to getting his trophy," she said. "Paul really wants it, poor kid." She smiled her lovely smile. "And after tonight's hand-out they store 'em away until next year."

Melchior seemed relieved that she had come back to the subject. Here was something to break our awkward silence, something in his life now that he could share and talk about.

"Yeah, Paul's a pitcher. They call him The Heat! Can you imagine that? Six wins and only one loss in his senior year. He gets the most-valuable-player trophy. But that damn earring. I don't know." He shook his head, smiling a little this time, and Barbara laughed.

"I don't understand," I said.

Melchior raised a finger, and I heard a noise behind him. It was The Heat passing from his room to the kitchen, a tall wraithlike shadow against the window to my left. The refrigerator door opened and then closed, and The Heat passed by again. He was carrying a large tray brimming with bottles, jars, and packages of food.

"It's his coach," Barbara said when he was gone.

"A real hard-ass," Melchior said. "If he saw that earring, there'd be hell to pay."

"Why doesn't he take it off?"

"Oh, no," Barbara laughed. "He wouldn't do that!"

"And anyway," Melchior said, "his friends'll be there. They'd rag him for sure, show the coach the hole in his ear."

"A real drama," Barbara said. "You wanna go down there with us?"

"Where? Is there a ceremony?"

"Oh, no. It's somewhere down on the Lower East Side. The coach just hands out trophies."

I had no more than a vague recollection of smokers in San Diego. There had been one in boot camp—all of us pressed into a smoky hall; a bright, lighted ring; and a red-faced Irishman pummeling a dark Indian. The Indian kept his arms up, his gloves covering his face, and when the Irishman grew tired of hitting him, he lashed out with a stiff right and the fight was over in the first round. But at the Naval Hospital, later, I could remember no smokers. I remembered the building, the shape and facade in front of which the group of sailors in the picture stood, but I did not remember the use of it. Their faces had no names for me; only Melchior located that past.

Melchior and I. A trip to Tijuana to buy rum. We were both in our early twenties, a little older than our peers, moody and dislocated. Melchior had left his Kansas farmlife on a whim; he wanted to be back there. I had left nothing, work at a gas station and the gray winter of Illinois. We found each other in the morgue on a shift exchange. I'd been there longer, and it was my job to orient him, show him procedures, glass jars of preserved organs, temperature gauges, charts. And in a week Melchior was out of the place. He couldn't handle it and he searched me out. We both had a love for quiet jazz, Miles Davis and the MJQ. When the time came, Melchior opted for pharmacy as his advanced school. I took physiotherapy. He was short and stocky, arms like hard, smooth boards, and when he drank he got wild.

We bought the rum and drank a half bottle of it

out of a paper bag as we walked the streets of Tijuana in the early twilight, searching in various shops among trinkets and serapes. Melchior was half lit, loud and brash, and joked with salesgirls and dour store-owners. We stopped at a bar and drank Cuba libras and watched a lurid floor show. Women came up to us, but Melchior was too aggressive and energetic for them, his eyes slightly glazed, and they drifted away when they felt his hot turgid breath and saw the way his shirt stretched over his shoulders when he moved.

I had seen times when Melchior had gotten violent. His skin would flush, and he would have a broad smile on his face. The violence was always joking. He would grab a sailor, show him how a bale of hay was thrown, lift him above his head, and cast him up on a top bunk or, sometimes, even against a wall. He would laugh and grin then and we would all stay clear of him.

He was getting that way now. Large, dark men to the sides of the room were tensing; waiters were positioning themselves; even the girls on the stage were watching him. He knocked a drink over, and when I put my hand on his arm to quiet him I could feel the heavy hardness of his strength. I ordered a bowl of guacamole. He was rambling, but he ate it when it came, smears of the green fruit at the corners of his mouth, his fist on the table beside the bowl.

I managed to get him out, and when we reached the street he walked a little bowlegged, steady, but with his arms swinging and his path directly down the middle of the sidewalk so that anyone approaching us had to move to the side. I had to walk to the side too; when I got too close to him, his arms hit me, heavy and solid as cement tubes.

Close to the turn that would take us back to the border from the main street, Melchior pulled up. We were in front of an open shop, the interior full of glass cases of jewelry and Indian artifacts. Grave rubbings hung on the wall among blankets and carved masks. A small and lovely young girl stood behind a long glass counter, and there was an older man, dressed in a suit, sitting on a high stool at a cash register near the sidewalk. The girl smiled at Melchior, a wicked smile, and the man on the stool shifted and looked at her. He spoke sharp and briefly in Spanish, and the girl lowered her head. I reached for Melchior but only caught a touch of his shirt fabric as he moved, bowlegged and unsteady, into the store. The girl lifted her head again, but her smile tightened as Melchior bumped into one of the glass cases. The case shivered on its long metal legs, then slowly steadied as Melchior moved around it. I was behind him, my hands slightly elevated, hoping I might catch him if he stumbled or fell. The glass in the cases looked extremely thin, the bright lights in the store shining through it as if it did not exist. And the cases were close together; there was just enough room to get through.

Melchior reached the counter where the girl stood, grinning at him now; the man was rising off his stool. When Melchior put his hands on the case in front of her, the girl raised her finger, gesturing for him to stay put, and turned and walked to the rear of the store. I could see the imprints of Melchior's sweating palms on the glass when he raised his arms and rubbed his hands together. His back was broad as a door, and his neck was a thick column, flexed and as wide as his head.

The girl returned and stood in front of Melchior, smiling again. And then still looking into his face, she lifted her hand and snapped her fingers. Melchior watched her, but I turned to the rear of the store when I heard the sound. There was a curtain over a doorway. It parted, and I saw the top of a bent head, thick oily hair, and then shoulders turning, wider than the doorway. His head came up when he'd cleared the lintel. A dark mustache and a hammered forehead; he was monstrous, and like the girl he was smiling.

"Melchior," I whispered.

"Christ, he's a *big* fucker!" he said.

"Shut up," I said. "Let's get out of here."

But Melchior was talking.

"Do you speak English?" he said to the girl.

"Si," she said, nodding and still smiling. The man on the stool had settled back in and was smiling also now.

"Does *he?*" Melchior said, gesturing to the back of the store but looking into the girl's eyes.

"No," she said. "Only me."

He reached for his pocket, stumbling slightly but spreading his legs wider and steadying himself. His hand came out with a fist of bills, dollars and fives, and he threw them down on the counter. Then he turned to the back of the store and lifted his arm up, moving his fist and forearm from side to side.

"Here's all I got," he said. "Come on!"

"Melchior," I said. I was beside him now, tugging at his sleeve.

"Your friend?" the girl said.

"Right," I said, catching her smile with one of my own, rather sheepishly.

"My father will hold the money then, okay?"

"That's right, that's right," Melchior said. " You hold it." He grinned at the girl.

"Hokay," she said.

The big man had reached the counter now. He dwarfed both of us. Melchior was as thick as he was, for his stature at least, but half again as small. The man put his hand on the counter, over the sweat print Melchior had left; the print disappeared.

He turned his hand over, tapped the ring he wore against the glass, and shook his head and spoke something quick to the girl.

"He says, not here; the glass is too thin. This is my brother Paco." She laughed lightly, and Melchior raised his hand. Paco looked down at it for a moment and then took it. I could see Melchior's wrist, his thumb, and just the edge of his heel. His head was back; he was grinning up at Paco whose mustache twisted at the ends.

"Okay, hell! Let's find somewhere else!" Melchior yelled.

The girl translated quickly, and Melchior pulled his hand away and stepped back from the counter, looking around. Paco grinned at his sister, then looked up and smiled at the man on the stool. Then he brought his hands together, laced his long thick fingers and cracked his knuckles.

They found a place at the front of the store, a large metal cooler with sliding doors on its flat surface, but when they crouched over it their bodies were against one of the glass counters and they couldn't get a proper and safe stance. Melchior slid one of the doors open and looked in. There were Coke and Pepsi bottles inside, standing in a pool of water up to their tops, around a large block of ice.

Melchior shut the lid, shrugged, and said, "Well, shit." Then he hunkered down, his legs braced, and reached for the indentations at the ends of the soda cooler. His arms were relatively short, and he had to extend them fully, get his chest against the side of the cooler, in order to reach the handles.

We stood back, watching. The girl had one hand at her neck, the fingers of the other touching her lips. Paco was looking down, incredulous, his mouth slightly open, and even the older man had risen from his stool and was leaning out over the glass counter now.

Melchior pressed his chin to the top of the cooler as he got his fingers in the indentations that were the handles.

"This is impossible," I whispered.

He heard me and lifted his chin and looked up at us. He was grinning, his eyes sparking in the bright lights from the interior of the store, his face like a red moon.

Then he lifted the thing. Bottles fell, and there was a dull liquid sliding, heavy, as the ice shifted, shuddering against his chest as it came to the side of the metal case. He leaned back, squatting and turning, managed two duck-steps, and settled the case in the middle of the sidewalk, four feet from where it had rested. He came up from his crouch then, shaking his arms and pushing his face out at Paco and the girl.

"Is that fucking all right now? Is that good?"

The rest seemed only perfunctory. Paco had little heart for it. They got down, their elbows beside each other on the case. Paco had to move back some, his arm was so much longer than Melchior's. Their hands came together, Melchior's disappearing in Paco's palm. We stood around them watching, and Melchior looked at each of us and then looked into Paco's face.

"Any old time now," he said softly.

There was a moment's shudder down their arms, then the click of Paco's ring hitting sharply against the metal top of the cooler as Melchior quickly pinned him.

And in the light of all those bright days passing in San Diego, it was Melchior and I, I and Melchior. Until the others saw the permanence of our bonding, saw we were fixed and inseparable, and withdrew from us. It was in the days when such things were possible, unintimidating as anything beyond their actuality. The two of us together in the dorm barracks, Melchior suffering the slabs of his body to the practice of my massages, my learning of muscle groups and how to move them therapeutically. The two of us bent over books, pharmacological symbols and compounds, Melchior's ferocious concentration in learning, not noticing those who glanced in at the doorway passing.

And then the time of our tour of duty was passing. Melchior was the first to be transferred. We embraced briefly and awkwardly at the bus station, and then in a week there was a call from Philadelphia. He said it was a good command, a large pharmacy, and he liked the city.

I now had the bodies of new men under me,

and once a Wave recruit who was coming down with something the doctors couldn't figure. It was circulatory, and I handled her thin legs and arms, pressing the blood into them. She recovered without diagnosis, and I was taken under the instruction of a young doctor who said he saw promise. The bodies of the many men became isolate flesh, their skins only sheaths for the important anatomy that I was learning. Their heads rested on pillows, disembodied, and though I could feel what I thought was the pulse of life at times, it was small compartments of mechanical energy only that I was concerned with.

In my first year in Corpus Christi a card found me from Melchior. He was soon to be discharged and was getting married. I think I remember answering the card, but I heard nothing more. I was deeply involved in learning, gaining a new awareness in the small morgue in Corpus. Things I had only felt had now become visible, and I was like a blind man who has gained sight. I forgot about Melchior. He was then no more than an image who came back to me in occasional reverie, the two of us sitting on a bench overlooking the golf course in San Diego, Melchior smiling his open smile, my face slightly quizzical, squinting in the sun. I had no memory at all of who might have taken the picture. It was in the scatter on the couch through which Melchior's hands had searched.

It was dark now, and there was a light rain falling, a sheen on the grimy, oil-stained streets somewhere in lower Manhattan. The bite of a late-March wind tilted signs on their hinges, and the rows of warehouses were dark, only occasional dim night-lights on the upper stories. Melchior drove slowly.

"This is not the Lower East Side," I said.

"It's far enough down," Barbara said, "but a little west of that."

She had spoken of another West earlier. They would try a trip out there this summer. They traveled every summer, something about Melchior and grave rubbings.

"We're pretty close, I think," The Heat said, and when I looked over I could see, at the edge of his brown fedora, the bright, small glimmer of the earring.

Melchior's neck was still a short, thick column rising above his coat collar. He hunched forward over the wheel, checking the street signs through the rain-streaked window. But now the column had horizontal lines in it, small curves of flesh; he had gained weight over the years and had softened a little. He had most of his hair, and his heavy arms, but work at the pharmacy was not farm work and he had broadened considerably in the thighs. I touched my face and looked over to where Barbara was sitting beside Melchior in the front seat. She was half turned, looking back at The Heat and smiling. The Heat was beside me in an old overcoat, his fedora pulled down almost to his ears. His legs were crossed, and I could see the tapered heel and pointed toe of his Italian low-cut, the edge of a white sock below his jeans. Barbara laughed.

"You're a *sight,*" she said.

"I know it," The Heat said.

I saw Melchior's eyes in the rearview mirror, a slight crinkling at the edges; then his head dropped again, and he slowed to a crawl and made a right turn into another empty street.

In ten minutes the rain and wind had slackened and the dark buildings were sharper in their outlines through the drying glass. I had no idea at all of where we were; there had been so many turns down short and narrow streets that I wasn't even sure of direction. So many uniform buildings that they all began to look alike. Then I saw Melchior's hand come briefly up and felt the car slow and move to the curb.

"Around the corner," he said. "I think we're close."

"Right. I bet that's it," The Heat said, pointing high through the windshield.

Lowering my head, I could see, up above the buildings beyond the corner, a faint glow in the sky and then the beam of a wide searchlight's sweep across the water storage tanks and elevator housings. When Melchior rolled the window down we could hear the faint sounds of voices and instruments.

"Get set," Melchior said. "Here we go." Barbara laughed, and Melchior opened the door.

The street we were on was as dark and empty as the rest, and ours was the only car at the curb. We were parked in front of a row of medical-supply wholesalers, small window displays for the trade only, a mix of artificial limbs, bedpans and walkers. On the sidewalk together, The Heat was perceptibly taller in his fedora and Italian heels and towered above us. Thin and straight as a rod, his overcoat hung and bagged out from his broad, angular shoulders.

"Thrift shop elegant," Barbara said with a chuckle, seeing me looking. The Heat nodded with head and shoulders, almost a bow.

"You silly ass!" Barbara laughed again and moved up to him and struck him lightly on his padded shoulder.

Melchior shook his head and raised his arms up and then dropped them.

"Let's go," he said.

As we approached the corner, the sounds of music and voices got louder and light leaked into the intersection, making the manhole covers shine. Then a group of people entered the street we were on, pushing and carrying things. There were four of them, a man and a woman, a young girl, and a boy about The Heat's age. The girl was picking at the boy's jacket sleeve. He carried a small oblong box, and she was begging him to let her hold it.

"Let me *see* it!" she said, but the boy laughed and pulled it away. The man and woman were a little behind the two, the man pushing a larger box down the sidewalk on a rubber-wheeled dolly, the woman hovering beside him, directing his progress. String had gotten caught up in one of the dolly's wheels, and it wavered a little in its path, the box tipping slightly, the woman reaching out tentatively to keep it steady. All four were laughing and talking. When they passed us, the boy glanced sharply at The Heat for a moment. The Heat touched the brim of his hat, hiding his face. The boy stared hard at him; then his sister grabbed at his arm and he looked away. Then we reached the corner and turned into the street.

There were police barricades at the ends of the long block, and there were cars lining the street, bumper to bumper for the full length of both curbs.

In the middle of the street, at the far end, there was a temporary scaffolding holding a high platform. It had a bright-colored canopy over it, and there were people standing on the platform, a grouping of metal chairs, and tables with rows of sharp-edged glittering objects. A crowd had gathered in front of the makeshift stage, and groups of people moved over the whole length of the street, some gathered in small clusters around vending wagons with broad umbrellas.

We had pulled up at the shock of it, the size of the crowd, the bright canopy, and the small band that we now saw to the side of the platform. We could hear them tuning up, a flute and a saxophone, the honk of a tuba and the heavy thud of a bass drum.

"Can this be *it*?" Melchior said. "Good Christ!"

"This is it," The Heat said.

To the right of the stage and the milling crowd in front of it, and halfway between us and the end of the street, there was another crowd, this one more fluid, moving in and out of the only open shop on the block. The storefront was brightly lit, objects displayed in its windows, and above it was a large neon sign blinking *Ideal Bakery.* People were going into the store, crowding each other, and at times people popped out from the crowd and into the street. They were pushing large boxes on dollies, carrying boxes, steering cellophane-covered pyramids as large as a small boy.

"Did you put an order in?" Melchior said dryly.

"Oh, hell no! I didn't know about any of this," Barbara said. She looked quickly and accusingly at The Heat, who smiled down at her.

People were coming at us down the street. A man and a woman squatted close to us, maneuvering a huge cake draped with cellophane up over the curb. The dolly it rode on was small and precarious, and the cake was in danger of falling. I counted seven ten-inch tiers that grew smaller as they ascended. The cellophane was held in place, away from the soft, creamy surface, with thin toothpicks. Only the dolly itself was a safe purchase. The man yelled out at the boy standing beside them, clutching a small shining object to his chest as he and his wife struggled with the dolly and the wobbly cake.

"Give us a hand, for Christ sake!"

There was a small figure at the cake's top, a boy in a loincloth with a feathered headdress and a bow and arrow.

He was in a kind of bower of small sugared rosettes, red and blue against the cake's yellow frosting, and he was aiming, his bow taut.

"Some sort of letter in archery," The Heat said.

"No shit," Melchior said.

The boy moved toward them, still clutching the object, but they had negotiated the curb before he could find a way to help.

"A little guy, he is," The Heat observed, and Barbara laughed again.

Then the threesome went by us, steering the cake as best they could, crouched down and weaving along the sidewalk as they rounded the corner from which we had entered the street.

The searchlight scanned the facades of the buildings, and now the band was playing, a rousing fight song from somebody's high school. Barbara grabbed Melchior by the arm.

"The bakery first!" she said.

When we got to the front of the bakery, the crowd had ebbed a little, and Barbara, motioning for us to wait, ducked between people and went inside. We could see into the windows now. They were full of cakes, each over a yard in height and each spotlighted from above or below. The windows were draped with white satin, and the cakes stood on various elevated pedestals so that each seemed special. They were gaudy and exciting, fragile and like melting architecture, hanging heavy in their fat icing, ready at any moment to slump and collapse.

"Look at that one!" Melchior said.

The one he noted was white and festooned with small autumnal trees around the circle of each layer. There were images of women in various athletic postures embossed in the layers' sides and at the base small naked female figures, at intervals, holding a limp, dipping chain of sugar daisies between them. There was a frosted plaque on the pedestal that held the cake. *Conference Champs,* it read.

"What's the sport?" I asked.

"There, at the top," The Heat replied.

There were five small women standing in a row under an archway. They wore short skirts and high, thick socks. One of them held a ball under her arm. To each side of the five, and on small rocklike objects, sat two angels with large, arching wings. They were turned in slightly, watching, possibly protecting the team. On a higher rock, and behind the row of players, stood a woman with a halo in a long robe. The faces of the five team-members were too small to be distinct, but they seemed to be smiling. Their legs were thick, their bosoms abbreviated. The surface on which they stood was a bright green, their uniforms black and gold.

"Saint Agnes Rugger Champs!" The Heat said.

And there were hockey cakes, and cakes with whole football teams on them. And there was a dark brown dour cake with two chess players at a small table. Baseball and soccer cakes. And there was a spelunking cake, tunnels in the openings of which figures with ropes and lanterns squatted.

Barbara popped up at our side, carrying a box.

"Got one!" she said.

"Let's have a look at it," Melchior said.

"Later. We better get over to the platform." The crowd surged around us again, and we backed off the curb and down into the street.

When we reached the back of the gathering that milled around in front of the stage of the platform, we could see the rows of tables glittering with trophies and the line of heavy men sitting in chairs to the side of them. The Heat pulled his fedora down a little, shadowing his face, and hunched over a bit in his coat, getting himself as inconspicuous as he could; he was still a head taller than anyone else in the crowd in front of us.

One of the men on the platform stood and moved to the front. Raising his arms above his head, he grasped his hands together and yelled out the name of a school. There was a drumroll and a surge of applause and yelling from the crowd. Then he called out a sport, honor, and name. There was more yelling, and a boy jumped up the steps to the platform, waved to the crowd, and moved to where the man stood, now holding a trophy cradled in his hands. It looked like a wrestling trophy; the boy looked squat and thick enough for that, but I couldn't make it out for sure. The coach shook hands with the boy, who looked up at him in a serious way. Then he thwacked him on the shoulder and grabbed him by the back of the neck and shook him. There was laughter from the crowd. When the boy reached for his trophy, the coach teased him, pulling it away, and shifted his body into a wrestling pose. The boy mimicked his actions for a moment, and then the two straightened up, laughing, and the coach extended his arm and handed the trophy over. They shook hands again. The boy waved to more applause, then left the platform.

"Is that your coach?' I said, turning up to look at The Heat beside me.

"That's the fucker," The Heat said, his earring bobbing as his lobe shook. "Oh, Jesus! Look there, Mom!"

Barbara stretched up on her tiptoes, her hand on The Heat's shoulder.

"Oh, no!" she said.

"What is it?" Melchior said.

"Your mother."

"Oh, shit!"

She was moving up the steps to the platform, a small woman who looked to be in her seventies, in an old fur coat and fur hat. When she reached the stage, the coach at the front looked over at her, pausing in the middle of his next announcement. She moved to the chair he had vacated, and when she sat down with the other coaches they leaned forward in unison, turning and looking down the line at her. There was tentative laughter in the crowd, and a few boos. Then The Heat's coach raised his arms up, quieting the spectators, and continued. Another boy worked his way through the crowd and bounded up to the stage.

"This is a pisser!" The Heat said, cocking his head down to look at me, just the hint of a smile crossing his otherwise darkened face.

The boy came down the steps holding his trophy, and the coach went to one of the tables and got another.

"What'll we do?" Barbara said.

"Fucked if I know," Melchior said. "Can we leave?"

The coach came back to the front of the stage again. The trophy he held was very large this time. He had it in both hands, his left at the base, the other grasping one of a number of shining cylinders rising to its complex entablature. He pushed it out in front of his chest and shook it. He was smiling, somewhat intensely now, and the crowd caught the occasion. A few isolated cheers broke out, an expectant buzz of talking. He stepped forward then. His face grew serious, and we heard the fearful words.

"And for the most valuable player—six wins and only one loss, and that on a field error—a boy...no, a *man*...of such tough, wholesome, American skill and hardness, that he has become a legend in his own time. They call him *The Heat!*—a name whispered fearfully in the dugouts of opposing teams.

"Now he's had a few problems in school—academics—"

The Heat's grandmother stiffened in her chair.

"—but he's toughed it out ... toughed most of it out anyway. And tough is what he is! For most

44

valuable player—a man who any man would be proud to call a son! The Heat! Paul Melchior!"

On The Heat's name, he raised the trophy above his head and shook it. Applause swelled up in the crowd. Melchior's mother shifted in her chair and looked sharply out at the gathering below her. Melchior backed up a little, bumping into me.

"What the hell!" Barbara yelled above the clapping. "Go for it!" And The Heat shook himself in his long coat and pulled the brim of his fedora down tight again.

I stayed back in the crowd and watched Melchior reach the stage ahead of the other two. He glanced at his mother, then moved up to the coach, falling, I thought, into a slight and bowlegged crouch. His mother followed his movements, then looked away and back to the steps. Barbara and The Heat reached the platform together, and I saw Melchior's mother lean forward in her chair, blinking. Melchior was now standing next to the coach, speaking up at him. They were both squat and stocky, but the coach had almost a head on him. After he spoke intently for a few moments, Melchior stepped to the side, and the coach moved forward a little, raising the trophy again. It was at least twice as large as any he had passed out previously. It had numerous columns, American eagles at their tips, flanking what looked like a pitcher in midstretch.

"The Heat couldn't make it!" the coach yelled out, waving the trophy and shaking it. "Brought down—temporarily, I'm sure—with a touch of flu! This is The Heat's father!" He flung the trophy out in an ark toward Melchior. "A man proud of the man who is his son!"

The coach was half turned toward Melchior when he paused. He was facing Barbara and the tall, lean apparition beside her. Even from where I stood, I could see the shine of The Heat's earring blinking under his brim.

"Wait *just* a minute!" the coach said, holding the trophy high up and stationary in the air, craning his neck and staring at Barbara and The Heat.

Melchior reached for the coach's arm as he was beginning to move toward the odd pair. The crowd grew silent, and though he spoke in a voice just above a whisper, we could all hear the coach distinctly.

"Who the hell *is* that? Is that…?"

Then The Heat's grandmother was on her feet and moving. When she reached him, she got her hand above her head, her fist in the front of his heavy coat, and jerked him down. He bent over at the waist, and his grandmother's hand came up and took his chin, turning his face to the side until the earring was in full view.

"Paul!" she yelled out, then jerked his fedora off and cuffed him over the head with it. He struggled up and back from her blow, and now that he was erect and hatless the coach could see him distinctly.

"Is this who I think it is?" he yelled, his voice squeaking in a high register. "This bespangled sissy!"

Then Melchior had him, his hand locked tight on his biceps. I saw him brace and yank the coach back toward him. The coach's arm flung out as he lost balance, and the trophy left his hand and rose in the air. Melchior turned him, and when they were face-to-face, I saw him grab fistfuls of the coach's lapels. Melchior's stance widened, his shoulders bunched, and then the coach was off his feet and against Melchior's chest, his legs dangling in the air a few inches off the platform. His stricken face looked down into Melchior's own, and I could see Melchior's lips moving, his teeth biting off sharp words.

He lowered the coach to his feet after what seemed a long time, and when I glanced to the side of the platform, I saw The Heat in his long coat. He had the trophy in his hands, and Barbara and his grandmother were standing behind him, admiring it. His grandmother's face was still stern, but she had quieted down, and Barbara was smiling. There were a few catcalls from the crowd below them, and The Heat was waving. He had turned his body to the side slightly, so that his earring was visible to all.

Then I saw Melchior come up to them and usher them down the steps. He took his mother's arm, gesturing for her to watch her footing. When I glanced back, the coach was no longer standing. There was another coach in his place now, and when I looked to the chair The Heat's grandmother had vacated, I saw the coach slumped there, his legs slightly spread, his body turned away from the audience.

When we were back in the car and headed uptown, Melchior drove to his mother's apartment on the West Side. He double-parked in front of her building, and helping her out of the seat beside him he took her arm and aided her into the lobby. We watched him leaning toward her, talking, and saw the doorman speak to them as they entered. The Heat began to talk while we were waiting, but Barbara hushed him.

"Wait until your father gets back," she said.

Then we were moving along the West Side Highway, heading up toward the George Washington Bridge and the Palisades on the other side. The sky had cleared completely and the Hudson was lovely and gleaming under a full moon. Though it was dark in the car, I fancied that the lines had faded in Melchior's neck. The column looked smooth and powerful, rising above the collar of his coat. Barbara was again in the front beside him, her hand on the seat back, occasionally touching his shoulder. The Heat had removed his coat and hat and sat relaxed beside me.

"You fixed that fucker," The Heat said, reaching forward and touching his father's head.

"Such language!" Barbara said, but she said it brightly.

"Remember Tijuana?" I said to Melchior, and I could see his head bob vigorously.

Then there was a creak of thin cardboard and a rustle of tissue. Barbara turned in her place, kneeling on the seat cushion, and reached the cake box over to us. The Heat took it, slid over a bit, and put it on the seat between us. It was a simple cake, only three layers, but there was a ring of off-white baseballs around each rim. On the flat surface of the top layer was the word *Pirates* and above it the picture of a pirate, complete with hat, eye patch, and the gleaming dot of a candy earring in his left lobe. Above the pirate's head, and newly sugared in, the words looked brightly up at us: *The Heat.*

2 ❧ Anson

Was there any hint, then, in my relationship with Melchior and the brief regaining of what might have been left of it after fifteen years, a spark of revised recollection in posture and eye contact across the scatter of old photographs on the cushion? Certainly he had reached out for me, enthusiastic and then bewildered and a little desperate when I did not remember. Smokers, a day spent in Balboa Park over pizza and beer, watching summer strollers and the brief vicious argument of a young couple with two small children, desperate in the imagined trap of their marriage. Melchior and I, I and Melchior. The image of our paired aloneness might still be vivid for both of us, but there was no real hint of the reason behind it, or how it might have prefigured Anson.

There was a message on my answering machine when I returned, the vaguely familiar voice of the

Bishop's secretary saying the prelate wanted me the following evening at eight o'clock. It was past midnight, but I knew his machine would be on, and I called and confirmed the appointment. Then I packed my swimming suit in my work bag so that I wouldn't forget it.

I brewed coffee and unwrapped the piece of cake that Barbara had pressed on me as I was leaving. The piece contained a wedge of the pirate's cheek and ear; the one with the earring had been for The Heat, and I remembered the way he had lifted the small glittering dot in front of us all and then popped it into his mouth. Melchior had laughed and then laughed again, smacking me on the shoulder as I was leaving. There had been promises to keep in touch, and because he knew I would be traveling, a small bottle of Dexedrine and another of vitamins pressed into my palms. The small pharmacy was Melchior's own. He was doing well, he said, well enough. I wondered, with a brief pang at the door, if I would ever see him again.

I got the box out on the kitchen table, and eating the cake and drinking coffee and glimpsing the full moon through the small window beside the refrigerator, I examined the contents more carefully than I had before. I remembered the pen and pencil set as something Lorca had given me near the end of our marriage, a gift out of the blue, something that had filled me with suspicion. I emptied the large brown envelope, spreading the school notes and blue books across the table, and tucked between the pages of one of the books I came upon a letter, still in its envelope. It was from Carl and Anne, really from Anne only, college friends I hadn't thought of in years. Lorca and I had socialized with them at L.A. State during the years that we were together there. I remembered their leanness and beauty. Carl was a mountain climber, and Anne, studying physiotherapy as I was, was an outcast from the landed gentry of her heritage. She had a beautiful, angular face, and she and Lorca, who were both tennis players, had hit it off. I remembered evenings of cards and music, of herbal tea and occasional marijuana. The letter was postmarked Reno, Nevada. It mentioned the birth of a child, skiing in the high desert mountains of

Northern California. Anne, evidently, had not known of our breakup; the letter was addressed to both of us, but the date on the postmark was well after Lorca had gone.

Among the scatter of unused postcards, I found one with writing on it. It was from Melchior, a picture and a message I had no recollection of at all. I could see that I had kept it for a long time though. It was addressed to me in Corpus Christi, while I was still in the Navy. The note was brief, smeared and indecipherable. Something about schooling in Kansas. The picture on the face of the card had nothing to do with the Great Plains. It was a photograph of a gravestone, a very large and ornate one. I could see carvings and filigree, but the image had faded and I could not read the inscription. On the back of the card, above the address Melchior had written in, was a printed notation: *Congregational Cemetery, Truro, Massachusetts.* I turned the card over again and looked at the large stone. I thought of Anson, in another state entirely.

Lorca left me. We had been living in the little house behind her parents' house in Hollywood. Lorca had a regular job, the best an English major could get those days, working in a dress shop just off of Sunset, and I had found some night-shift work at a few hospitals. One morning I came back and she was gone. There was no note, nor had she left one for her parents, and when I told them what had happened, simply that she was gone, they were kind and sympathetic, but there were hints of accusation in their eyes. I didn't tell them all of it, that I had figured something might be getting ready to happen for a long time, and I stayed on only for a month, enough time to find another place and get my things moved into it. I was hard up for money, and when the job at the Y came along I took it.

I tried to reach Lorca, checking with the dress shop and with her few casual friends, but it was a dead end; nobody knew anything, or else they weren't talking. She had quit the dress shop, leaving no information behind her. I called her mother at times, but she had heard nothing and cut our conversations short.

Then the brief notes came, one for me and one for her parents. They were sent from Phoenix, were very short and enigmatic. And that was the last we heard.

The Y was the worst of places, only a few massages for a percentage, and those were timed, unimaginative, and grooved. The manager wanted a quick turnover and I had no room to test out what I had learned. I spent most of my evenings in my apartment, a small studio in a poor Chicano section in Eagle Rock, studying anatomy and physiology.

One evening in the early fall when there was a slight nip in the air, I quit the books and went to a bar that I'd been frequenting when I felt lonely. The place was called The Chief, and it was in fact owned by a Chief, a retired petty officer from the Navy. It was a small place, long and narrow, with room for only a few tables and the bar that extended the length of it, and the Chief ran the place alone. Patrons all called him the Chief, though not many of them had been Navy, and I liked the friendly atmosphere of the place.

"Hey, David," the Chief said when I entered. "What's the scuttlebutt?" He talked that way, peppering his conversations with Navy lingo.

"Not a thing, Chief," I said as I slid onto a stool. He put a glass of tap beer on the bar in front of me, said "Check ya later," and turned to the small oven in which a couple of burgers were heating up.

There were a dozen or so people at the bar, and a young couple leaning toward each other and talking at a table behind me. Anson was sitting at the far end, just at the turn, and I could see him pretty clearly from where I was. There was something resting in front of him, a large pad of some sort. His hand was moving over it, and he kept looking up and down the bar, then back at the pad again. His face was a little in shadow and I couldn't make out his features, but I could see the wiry thinness of his upper torso, the way he sat erect and bent over mostly from the waist. He had light hair, and something glittered near his temple.

A woman sat beside him, and a man stood at her shoulder. Both were looking over at Anson, watching his hand move across the pad. There were a few people between us, talking quietly and laughing, but the trio that Anson was a part of was still and attentive.

I turned back to my beer, lit a cigarette, and watched the smoke rise in the dim mirror across from me. In a few minutes the Chief came back and gave me a refill.

"What's going on down there?" I said.

He put his hands on the bar and leaned toward me. "Artist," he said. "A pretty good one. He comes here now and then. I think it's good for business."

We heard a sharp ripping sound from the other end of the bar, and the Chief turned and went down there. I looked that way and saw Anson lift the sheet he had torn from the pad and hand it to him. The Chief took it to the mirror and secured it above the bottles with masking tape. There was a moment while those beside me stared at it, then there was light laughter and a little tentative clapping from the woman and man beside Anson and a few others as well. I felt someone beside me. It was the young couple. They'd left their table and come over to see what was up.

The drawing was a rendering of the faces and upper bodies of those sitting along the bar. I was at the end. He had caught me in profile, looking across at the bottles and mirror, my hand to the side of my face, the wispy smoke-trail of my cigarette. The faces of the others were more animated, heads turned and lifted in various ways in conversation and laughter. I could tell that the angle of perspective was a difficult one, parts of bodies and faces blocking others out slightly and size diminishing into the near distance. Proportions seemed perfect, everything accurate, and no tricks.

He had done a strange thing with our clothing and haircuts, had altered them, not into caricature, but had pushed them slightly into the past, no more than a very short time I thought, so that the rendering had a vaguely historical feel to it. It was not right-now; it was the other day or a year ago. We were not exactly who we were, but possible earlier selves. The rest were, that is. I, in my severe and fixed profile, was not changed in any way, and that and the fact that I looked dead ahead, was not participating like the others, separated me profoundly from them, both in time and in good fellowship. I thought I looked very alone there, and lonely.

Soon people were approaching Anson, and soon he was doing quick sketches and longer portraits. I saw the money change hands, and in an hour or so he was sketching me and we were in conversation.

It was the summer after the summer Lorca left me that Anson and I moved in together. When I'd met him at The Chief, he had only been in Los Angeles for a short time and was doing the bar drawings until he could find something more secure. By the time we moved in together, he had taken a job at one of the movie studios, a position in which he executed beginning costume drawings for period films. I had left the Y and was studying under Gulesarian and working at his spa. We found a place in a better neighborhood, a two-bedroom apartment.

Anson could draw beautifully and quickly, and he seemed to be able to enter into the lives of women in history, to sketch their characters and emotions into the folds of their gowns, the cut of their bodices. I would wake to find him in the kitchen early in the morning, sitting at the table naked from the waist up, his thin arm moving with conviction, his pencil covering his sketch pad with ideas. He would have the coffee ready, and we would sit and talk until the sun entered the kitchen window. Then I'd be off to Gulesarian's, and Anson would gather his sketches and head to the studio.

What I knew of Anson was that he was born in Utah, in some orphanage, and that he had been on the move since he was young. We were close to the same age, but there were ways in which he seemed much younger. He was very thin, delicate but for his wiry arms. He had always managed to find clean work, clerical or vaguely artistic. I knew of no firm relationship before our own except for one, and that had been very early on, when he was only a boy. It was good not to be alone, to imagine his slight form at rest in the other bedroom after I had turned out my light.

One evening, when another fall came and Anson and I had been together for close to a year, he came home into the apartment agitated. I was fussing with dinner, busy with a couple of lean steaks, but I could tell by the way he moved through the rooms that something was up. I kept my peace, but when we had opened the wine and were sitting at the table in the kitchen I asked him what the trouble was.

"It's not important," he said.

"Yeah," I said. "But it *is* something."

He let it out all at once. "They want me to move. To the garment district in New York. It's a good job, a *real* good one. "

"Who's they?"

"It's a guy I met, a partner in a place that does designer clothes, limited edition stuff."

"Do you want to go?" I said.

"Oh, well, shit, of course; I *should.*"

I didn't pain him by withholding and asking him more. I could tell what it was and was a little shocked by it. He didn't want us to part, and only in seeing that in him did I see that I didn't want it either. I hadn't really seen that at all before.

"Well, what the hell," I said. "Let's go then."

Anson's face brightened and relaxed immediately.

"Can you?" he said.

"Why not?" I said. "There's plenty of jobs in New York City."

There were times in the evenings in California when I would massage Anson's body, not the whole of it, but isolated parts, and for practice. I would light the candles on the bureau in his bedroom, set up my portable table and cover him with a sheet. Then I would work his feet, lightly at first, and we would talk. I would begin the talking, and doing that and having the light only from the candles and beginning lightly and at the farthest extremity all came from Gulesarian, were a part of what he'd taught me.

I would start with the flavor of the day, the weather and the gossip, but kind gossip only, those things that could harm no one, nor were designed to do so. Then it would be reminiscences, places I had traveled, things seen and done. I would roll each phalange, press the length of his metatarsals, rotate each foot at the ankle. The oil would be heating in its container, and in a while we would begin to smell it, its faint eucalyptus scent coming slowly through the candle wax and the beginnings of light perspiration. By the time I chose a place, his calf or lumbar girdle, or the heavy muscles of his thigh, Anson would be talking too. And then I would gradually leave off what I was saying, move slowly from monologue to lazy conversation to monologue. I would move deeper then, my fingers searching under the skin, and I would begin to isolate fascia, ligament, and avenues of blood. And most of the hour, Anson would be talking.

"It was not so much that my life was acted upon by others and I was therefore a victim of it and not its captain. It was rather knowing of this, on a daily basis, and unlike most children having no anchor to count on. The stakes were very high. I went to a river once, a small trickling stream really, without permission, and it cost me home and hearth. I was jettisoned as a troublesome boy, and troubled, I found myself in yet another foster home, to begin again.

"Am I moaning again? Grieving about the past selfishly? Nostalgia? But for what?"

"It's okay," I said, running the pads of my fingers along a surface vein. "Go on."

"Once, when I was a truant, I found myself on the edge of town, in a vacant lot across from an old house, where I was sitting and sketching. The house had had no paint for years, and I could figure images and objects in the grain and whorl of wood. There was a wide porch, covered by a roof supported by tall, square columns, and above the steps leading up to the porch a single door, flanked by a row of darkened windows.

"It was late June and warm, and I had been sitting, looking and sketching, for a number of hours, and once when I looked up from my pad I saw a motion at the window, a brief pulling back of a curtain. Then, in a while, I saw the door open and saw Maudie standing darkly in the shadow at the frame. She hesitated so long there that I began to sketch her, at least what I could see of her, a thin figure only, almost an apparition, in long gown and slippers. But she went in then and I lost the line, and when she appeared again I could see that she wore shoes. She moved into the light at the front of the porch and gestured. Then I got up and went over to her.

"Afternoons with Maudie then, when I could get away. She served tea; what could one expect? And cookies and mints. There was old cracked china, antimacassars, and a scent of mildew and dust. But that was the end of expectations, though the shape and subject of her talk seemed superficially clichéd. Talk of dead children and dead friends and of the way the town had changed and what it was before, when she was a girl or a child.

"I slept with her, crawled into the bed once when she was ill. I had found that she was not waiting when I arrived, and after I had knocked on the loose frame of the screen door for a while, I went in and found her lying in the bedroom, huddled on her side, the shades drawn. She said it was just a cold, but at her age (she was seventy-four) such things got her down. Her gray and careful hair was on the pillow, her thin, tucked body hardly apparent under the pile of blankets, and after I had taken my clothes off I lifted the cover and slid in beside her and pressed against her. Then in a while she turned to me. I was fifteen years old. She pressed her face against my shoulder, her hand on my back, and when in her warmth I grew hard, she made way for me and I entered her. I did not kiss her, nor did either of us speak. Only our breath quickened, and when it was over we went to sleep.

"And how to break free of such a memory, a wraith only of sexuality. But the idea of it. It happened I think because of our arts, hers and mine, and because she was no romantic. Her age had brought her to a point where there was no more mystery. She saw me as who I was, like she an orphaned child, bereft of any past but in the memory, that deceitful capacity she had discovered was like some failed organ of the body, a cancerous betrayer. She had one child only still alive, an illegitimate daughter she was estranged from. There was a granddaughter by her who was faithful. She came to see her on occasion, but hers was a very different life, in no way linked in Maudie's memory to her own.

"How I'd lingered in those days, falsely constructing some real family, but Maudie woke me from that. Tales of her own childhood, told always ironically and with that studied smile of hers, that offbeat of exclamation and that clear focus in her eyes that told me she wasn't back there, knew it was all triviality and only good for the enjoyment of the telling, the listening that I did; it could as well have been my own past for what it was worth beyond that. And she would break into the telling, hold up a cookie or her teacup, and say, "But isn't *this* good," as if to say, wasn't that day together in *bed* good, or shouldn't we sit out on the porch *now;* the light is perfect, the shadows of the columns.

"Maudie was an artist, a painter of careful miniatures. Her work, in little gilded frames, stood in lines on the mantel and other surfaces. Her subject matter had for years been bees, and she worked always from nature.

"There were flowers along the sides of the house and ones in pots filled every sill. The bees would come right into the house, and she had a strange way with them. I saw her hold her hand out, saw them light on her fingers. She'd carry them to a place she wanted them, on a piece of root or weed stalk on the kitchen table, and they would stay there, as if posing, while she painted them. They gathered in her hair at times, and there were times I saw hundreds of them, droning in clusters in the air, following her from room to room. When I asked her about it she only laughed. It was nothing to her really, no more than anything else. 'Aren't they beautiful?' she'd say. 'Just *look* at them.'

"And I did look at them, and looked at her exquisite paintings of them as well. She looked carefully at my drawings and showed me things about seeing. I was seeing pretty well already, but not nearly as well as she, and I learned just about everything I value from her. Things developed between us and became a pact. We made it official, but insisted on no responsibility in any way.

"She had been the wife of an alderman, a man of position and visibility in the town. He was a farmer, a stern and sexless husband and a brutal father. But she had had relatives—brothers, sisters, and cousins—and when her children died, all but the illegitimate daughter, and her husband soon after, she had gone back among her own family.

And that's where the photographs came from, those family picnics and outings, holiday celebrations, births and confirmations. But the people in the pictures were all dead now or had moved elsewhere, children who now had their own families, their own photographs and mementos. Once we cut some larger pictures up, glued little stands to the feet of the figures that had been in them, and formed new gatherings and families on the dining room table. Some were done by putting the most unlikely people together, young girls married to old men, matronly women in lesbian relationships, sisters married to brothers. And others were an attempt to get to the perfect family, the people Maudie thought were the best of the lot, living together. We had to span whole generations, put people together who had no common memory, in order to do this.

"I had been experimenting with boys then, those who lived in foster homes with me. Our sex was furtive, guilt-ridden and exciting. I told Maudie about it, and she simply laughed, not derisively but pleasantly, understanding that I liked doing it. I remember that her acceptance of it is what drained the wish for it out of me.

"And then one day she was gone. I showed up at her house, and the door was locked and bolted, the shades drawn, and that was the end of it. She'd told me she might be going, but I hadn't listened, hadn't wanted to hear it. I went back twice that week, but she wasn't there. The closing of the house looked permanent, and all I could do was sit in the vacant lot across the street, sketching the house, doing perspective studies, charcoals and inks. The following week I took off. I was seventeen by then and finished with high school, and it was time to get on with things. Maybe she had only gone on a trip of some kind. I don't know.

"It was the emptiness of my own past that Maudie saved me from, saved me from fruitless dreaming and a nostalgia that had no object. After Maudie's help, even in my first days with her, the drawing became serious. I won school awards; my pictures hung in public places in the town, and I was moved to a better foster home. My pictures, as they do now, had an edge of history to them, an aura devoid of sentiment. They had a way of looking authentic because of that, something to do with freedom from the past and imagination without memory."

The little windup clock I'd set would ring the time then, that it was up, and Anson would stop gradually in his talking. I'd take the white towel and rub the surface I'd been working on briskly. Then I'd sprinkle the cool alcohol and wipe the oil away, until his flesh was shining.

We moved from Los Angeles to New York City a week after Anson took the job offer. I was deep into things with Gulesarian at the time and really did not want to move. Still, I could not make a choice against it. There was no guilt or broken promises involved. It was just that I knew I needed to be with Anson, though I had no clear idea of why. And besides, since Lorca what I did seemed truly portable. Los Angeles meant nothing to me, nor did any other place.

It was two years after we arrived in New York, three of the nine that I would spend with him, that I discovered Anson was sleeping with men, and while the discovery really changed nothing that was between us, it did explain things, mostly the way people had come to treat me, especially women.

It was a rainy evening. I had left Anson alone with his sketches, large life-sized drawings of evening gowns that he was working on against a deadline. He had taped numerous beginnings to the walls of his bedroom, and the bed and floor were covered with the ones he was refining. I had two appointments, both with priests, but when I got to the first rectory the old woman who answered the door told me something had come up and that the father would have to cancel out. She had a note from the other priest as well; he had to cancel also. I caught a bus back downtown, and before going home I stopped for a sandwich at a restaurant near our building. By the time I got back, I had been gone for only two hours.

I found them in the bed in Anson's room, huddled together under the blanket, the bed and floors still covered with Anson's renderings, and the figures taped to the walls looking down on them benignly. They were not moving, had probably been sleeping, though the lights were on. I caught Anson's eye before I closed the door. I left and walked the streets for a while, then took in a movie. When I returned the man was gone and Anson was sleeping. The next morning, over coffee, he spoke of it.

"I don't really understand it myself," he said. "It's only that there's nothing for me now with women. Very little with men, to tell the truth. At least not sexually. There's petting, and a certain warmth, and a certain something that feels historical to me. As if I had done it before, in some other life that I might have wished to have. Maybe it's a failing; I can't seem to care one way or another. Maybe it isn't."

And the women at the parties we went to seemed drawn to me. Fashion parties at elegant apartments, full of beautiful women, young, but wiser than their ages and professions, picture book women, models and sure designers, with lives of another kind entirely under their perfect skins.

I came to see they thought I was living a life

private with Anson, that though I might desire things from them, there was one thing I did not desire, and their mistaken knowledge in this regard seemed to free them into an intimacy withheld from others. I did not disabuse them, because I *did* desire them in that certain way, and yet I feared to reveal this, thinking I would lose them if I did so. I was indeed closeted and private, but not in the way they thought. They touched me when they talked, fingers on my sleeve and sometimes brushing my cheek. They pressed their bodies against me. And they looked into my eyes with the purest of innocence, but also with a sense of fellowship that was thrilling. In their company I was closer than I had ever been with anyone, certainly closer than with Anson, painfully closer than with Lorca.

This is part of why, I think, the years went by gracefully. The secrets of beautiful women and the feel of their completely yielding bodies under my hands as I massaged them. Anson rose to a certain gay level of fame among designers. He was hard to get to, and remained even afterward mysterious. I would see men in rooms gazing at him, but this was no preoccupation for me. I was gazing too, in my privilege, into the faces and secret minds of desirable women.

3 ❧ *The Bishop*

I told the Bishop about the box, the oddness of receiving it and some of the things that it contained, and said that now that Anson was gone I thought I'd be heading out, going back and over a few things.

"Ah yes, the artist," the Bishop said.

"How did you know about that?" I said. "I don't think I mentioned that."

"You did," he said. "Or I learned it elsewhere; that's possible. But that's dangerous."

"What is?"

"You're close to forty now," he said. "The road descends. Disillusionment. The crumbling of whatever pictures you might have. I wouldn't do it if I were you. I did it once myself."

"We'll see," I said.

I'd gotten to the Bishop's house a little early. He lived in a brownstone in the West Eighties. There was a side door that led into a narrow passage. A young priest answered and ushered me in, took me down the passage to a small library and asked me to wait. I had my leather bag, my swimming suit, oils, and alcohol.

The library was lined from floor to ceiling with heavy wooden bookcases, all the books in large matching sets. I saw Dickens, Balzac, and Freud, no Aquinas or Augustine. Those were in the larger library, along with the legal texts and parish accounts. There were dark orientals on the floor, a few comfortable easy chairs, and convenient floor lamps.

In a few minutes, a narrow door opened and the Bishop entered.

"David!" he said.

He was wearing his black cassock, buttoned from the knee to collar. Below his black cummerbund, the tails of which hung to his side, his skirt flared slightly, hiding the bulge of his hips. I could see the edge of the lace of his undergarment. His black shoes had a bright shine.

"David, my son! It's so good to see you! It's been a while."

He crossed the small room, touched me on the knee, and sat in the chair beside me. I saw his foot reach for a button on the floor, and in a few moments the young priest who had let me in entered the room. He carried a tray. On it were two snifters and a bottle of Martell.

"There," the Bishop said, rather vaguely. And the young priest put the tray down on a table, poured brandy in the snifters, and handed one to each of us. Then he padded to the door. I saw he was wearing slippers. "Less intrusive," the Bishop said, seeing me watching the young priest's feet.

I had gotten the Bishop a year earlier. Anson was still alive then, though his weight loss had begun. He was extremely thin, but he still looked healthy, and his wraithlike quality was drawing even more men to him.

At a spring party celebrating a new line of clothing, I noticed a man in the circle of men surrounding Anson who looked somehow odd to me. When I asked the woman I was talking to about him, a blond model in her late twenties, she said, "He's a priest. They usually dress a little too neatly in the beginning, when they're just out of habit. He'll get the hang of it after a while."

Later that evening, I spoke to him. When I asked him what he was doing at the party, he avoided answering, asking me what I did and why I was there. I told him, and as we talked I found out he was new to the city, from the West, and that he had been assigned a legal position in the Church's ombudsmen's office. He was working with the city administration.

He was my first cleric. He had problems with his legs, the beginnings of varicose veins, though he was no more than fifty. I visited him in his small apartment, and the massages seemed to have some effect. Soon he had put me on to other priests, and a very old one who was close to retirement put me in touch with the Bishop. I had been coming to him weekly, but it had been over a month since my last visit.

"You've been well, David? I've been *beshitted* with work! I've meant to have you called numerous times." He raised his glass, toasting me, and drained it. "Well," he said, tapping his hands on his knees, "let's go to the game room."

We passed through many narrow rooms and

hallways, all of them leading down, and when we had reached the bottom of the flight of carpeted stairs and were standing in front of a large oak door, the Bishop turned to me and winked. Then he opened the door and stepped ahead of me into the game room. I had been there before, but the light in the hallway was brighter than that in the room, and it took me a few moments to see clearly and get my bearings.

The room was very large, the ceiling higher than I had remembered, and the floor was carpeted in a thick, wine fabric. There must have been fifty men in the room, some standing at game tables, others sitting on couches with drinks in their hands. I recognized a few faces, city officials and newsmen. I could smell the sawdust from the shuffleboard, chalk from the pool table. A croupier, a young priest dressed in the same garments that the Bishop wore, stood behind the roulette table, smiling and speaking his patter softly. Ice cubes clicked in glasses, and two heavy and redfaced men laughed and gestured with large black cigars.

"Come with me, David," the Bishop said, and

we passed among tables and groups of men. I could see the strained and dour faces looking down at us from the row of large paintings lining the walls, a history of bishops, in elegant clerical garb. I heard the sound of water, and noticed the stone fountain, freestanding, near the end of the room.

"Where are the girls, Father?" one of the two men standing beside the fountain said as we came up to them.

"Now you know better than that, Mike," the Bishop laughed. "Let gaming and drink be enough this night. And the good company of men."

"He'll take men," the other man said dryly, a smile at the corner of his mouth.

The two were thick and heavy, and both wore threepiece suits and loops of gold chain across their vests. The one who had last spoken was a good ten years older than the other, gray above the ears. The younger man looked over at him, his body stiffening slightly, feigning quiet outrage.

"How dare you, you snipe!" he said, raising his hand in a limp gesture.

"Now, now," the Bishop said. "If this continues, I'll have to open the confessional."

The two men laughed, and I forced a chuckle of my own.

"This is David," the Bishop said, introducing me. "He's the one I told you about, the masseur."

"Ah!" the younger man said. "We've heard many good things. Do you have a card?"

I took two cards from my wallet and handed each of them one. They both read them and then put them in their pockets. I figured they would call, and told them about my answering machine. I didn't mention that I would be leaving and that things would probably not work out. The Bishop joked with the men for a few moments, then took my arm and excused us. He took me to the bar that was set up at the side of the room.

"Things will be going quite late here, I'm afraid. I have to make an appearance, you know, say a few words here and there. Can you make your way for half a hour? Then we can go to the pool."

"I left my bag in the library," I said.

"I'll have my boy get it."

"I'll be all right," I said.

I moved among the men in the room, exchanging what small talk I could manage, and tried a spin or two of roulette and nursed a drink. The gathering was clublike, and I was not privileged to a background of information that made even small talk comfortable. Conversations that I overheard were mostly political, and those involved in them were doing kinds of business, making various connections. The Bishop moved from group to group, searched out loners, and spoke intently to a few people. In ten minutes he caught my eye and came back over to me.

"Okay, why don't you go ahead. Your bag is there."

I nodded and went to the doorway that I knew led to the pool. When I closed the door behind me, all the sound of talking and laughter was shut out immediately. I was in another narrow passage, this one also leading down.

What the Bishop called the pool was more like a deep rock grotto than the hot-tub bath it actually was. Entering the heavy door, I felt the weight of the large brownstone somewhere above me. In the past I had tried to figure how deep down the place was. It seemed to me that the game room was in the basement of the house, and if that were true the pool was far deeper even than that. There was a long, twisting passageway to get there, and as I went down it I counted four flights of steep steps descending. As the passage went deeper, the wood lining it gave way to rock, and the rock walls leaned inward, rounding into an archway at the top. There were candles lighting the way, set into small niches, in holders above the small stone figures of saints, illuminating them as well as the way down.

The grotto itself was a large domed room, lighted dimly from sources that were not apparent. The rock walls of the room simply glowed, and the pool in the center of it shone dimly red on its surface. Around the rock walls of the room were more niches, these also with candles and saints in them, and on the smooth marble surface of the floor surrounding the pool there were three leather easy chairs and two metal and glass tables. Beside one of the chairs was a freestanding stone bar, quite large, with an assortment of bottles and glasses on it. A pile of white towels and sheets rested on a low stool at the pool's edge. In the wall at the back of the pool, behind the gold controls, was a massive chair that was cut from the stone of the wall itself. Its back was friezelike, figures of gargoyles and small angel heads, and its arms, cut with handholds and wings at their ends, jutted out two feet or more into the room. Its stone seat was smooth and worn, and handy beside it was a thick stone pedestal on which rested a small leather-bound book.

I went to the gold controls, turned a thick knob to raise the temperature, and then stripped, piling my clothing on a stone ledge at the wall. By the time I had my swimming suit on, a smoky steam was beginning to rise from the pool's surface, faintly rose-colored in the air. I slipped into the pool, the heat of the water perfect now, and moved to a ledge seat, one that was low enough so that the water came up to my neck, and waited.

In ten minutes the Bishop appeared in the doorway, carrying a bucket of ice and smiling down at me in the water.

"Is it comfy?" he said.

"Yes," I said, and he turned and went to the back of the room and disappeared into a cut in the rock. I could hear him humming, hear the rustling of fabric as he disrobed. Then he was back again, wearing only a towel wrapped around his waist. He had his swimming suit in his hand. He moved to the pool's edge, tested the water with his foot, and then lowered himself in, modestly removing his towel, a sodden rope now, only after he was submerged to the waist.

"Ah!" he said, and I saw his knees rise out of the water as he shifted his body and got his swimming suit on. Then he moved to a stone ledge across from me, easing his body onto it, and put his arms back, resting them on the stone edge of the pool.

"How about a drink first?" he said.

"Fine," I said. "I'll get it."

We sat across from each other, then, sipping Wild Turkey on the rocks, enjoying the warmth of the water. In ten minutes we were finished, and it was time to get to work. We left our glasses on the pool's edge and moved toward each other, the

Bishop extending his left arm as he drifted across the water to me.

I took his arm and levered it, holding his wrist in one hand, his triceps in the other. Then I put my fist in his armpit, feeling and rotating the ball in the socket. I did the same with his other arm. Then I drifted back to the pool's side, holding both his hands, and braced myself against it, getting a stiff leg up, a foot planted over his sternum, and pulled the Bishop's arms out straight and taut above the pool's surface. I got behind him, pulling his arms up from the rear, and when he had taken his deep breath and put his face under the water, I pressed my foot against his thoracic vertebra and pulled tight again.

The water bubbled in the pool now, and the rising steam thickened as the temperature rose. We were in a drifting cloud of vapor as I turned and handled him. He squatted until his shoulders were at the water's surface. I stood behind him and locked his head in my arms and twisted it until his neck snapped, the sound sharp against my chest but lost immediately in the muffling smoke. The movements of his legs, slightly arthritic at the joints, pained him, and he yelled out. He held his arms across his chest, and I pressed my own chest against them, locking my grip against his spine, my head against his ear. I pulled up and in, and there was a ripple of cracking, and his breath forced out against my neck. At some point he removed his swimming suit, so I could get at him better.

I worked him for a half hour, our bodies moving and rolling in the pool, and near the end of the time it was a rough massage only. I gripped his flesh, searching deep for bone articulation, muscle insertion and that of ligament and tendon. He was moaning softly by that time, the sharp outcries of pain had ended. In my final move, I worked his fingers and then his toes.

He moved out of the pool ahead of me, the white bowl of his sagging buttocks relaxed now, vacant of the bunching of musculature at his sacrum. Moving modestly, keeping his genitals out of my sight, he went to a pile of towels and lifted one and wrapped it around his hips. Then he went, still wet, to one of the leather chairs and dropped down into it. He pressed his head back against the leather, his chin elevated, and looked up into the thinning mist.

"That was *good,* David," he said.

I had told him about Melchior, about the awkwardness of the time we'd spent together and that strange trip to the Lower East Side for The Heat's trophy.

The day kept coming back to me: Barbara, Melchior's mother, even the coach, his brazenness and then his quick deflation under Melchior's assault. And The Heat too; he'd had a way of handling it all that I now felt as a slight intimidation. We had all traveled into a circumstance that I hadn't known quite how to feel about. I couldn't place what had happened in any way that I felt comfortable with.

It might have been, I thought, the scope of generations involved, that sweet sense of a family saga that I could play no real part in. I'd been an observer only, and yet I'd been drawn into their shared past through my own with Melchior. There was a story there for me as well as for them, but a very different one, and I found I couldn't be sure of it, couldn't think for certain that I was seeing its significance properly.

My entrance into their life and the shape it took so quickly on that trophy day had been oblique, and it came to me that the same might well have been true of my life with Lorca. I'd stood apart there also, looking in from a certain distance, always a step or two behind things, following, never taking hold.

At any rate, the day remained a curiosity, a journey with consequences that did not really touch me, though I felt I wished for that.

I had spoken to the Bishop a little too about Anson, trying to get clear briefly what the years had been like and how when the box had arrived some vague directions seemed right and immanent. I mentioned Lorca but didn't tell him the whole story.

"Well, you surely got some taste of the danger, of what could be in store for you, from this man Melchior."

"I wouldn't call it danger," I said. "Maybe some disappointment, a slight disorientation."

"*That* could be the taste I'm speaking of. Your little trip had some humor at its end, but it could just as well have been otherwise. Not, at least, what you might have expected."

"You're right about that," I said.

We were in the room he had gone to earlier to disrobe, a small dressing room entered through an oblique passage from the grotto. I had him on the thin pad of the narrow table, a towel draped across his hips, and we were at the stage of conversation where I was slowly withdrawing from talking. Soon he would tell me his story.

I worked the oil into his calves; it had a faint bayberry scent, an aroma that the Bishop liked and had asked for. My strokes were still superficial and soothing, done with the flat of my hands and no pressure yet from the fingers. He had his head to the side, his eyes closed. I was watching the backs of his upper legs and the tendons at the cups of his knees, watching them relax and settle in, losing their bulge. His breath was deepening, his back growing shallow in its rise. The light was soft against the wood paneling of the room, and I was rocking slightly, shifting on my legs, getting my whole body into my arms.

"It may be only those years with Anson that you need to understand. They were celibate years, I gather?"

"They were that."

He sighed, deeply and inexplicably, a slight tremor running through his body. Then I took more oil and moved up to his thighs.

"It was thirteen years ago. I was fifty and in a crisis of faith. The episodic nature of my life and my imaginings during my rise to prominence had kept me in a state of mind where action, purely political and secular, focused my thoughts and behavior. It had been many little steps, circumscribed intrigues, but then I found myself close to arrival, and it was almost like a certain illness, a feeling that there were loose ends I couldn't find, let alone tie them. Christ still moved for me, in the sacristy and in the host, but His presence now felt perfunctory, and I began to wonder if I was imagining it.

"Then a letter came, very much like the box that you received, an invitation to a high school class reunion in Utah. I put it aside, but in a few days went back to it, fingered it, and studied its embossed lettering. It had been thirty-three years, and I did not recognize the names of the secretary or class president. Even the name of the school, Nativity, printed in gold lettering at the top of the creamy linen paper was distant and odd to me, an emblem from a life that seemed so foreign that I wondered if I had possibly made it up or dreamed it.

"I thought it over, really not considering it at all at first, but as I thought of it, thought of college and the seminary, the loose ends I was experiencing at the time began to appear to me, tentative at first, until I began to feel that tying them up might be possible. Nativity, the letters in the stone above the large door, and then the classrooms, the dust of the playground, the smell of incense, the vaguely remembered shape of the goblet that I held carefully in my role as altar boy, the hands of the old priest, Father Ghinty, taking it from me and raising it. And then the boy's bathroom, the stall doors, blue uniform pants in a pile on scuffed shoes, pocked white legs rising out of them. And names—Eddie Condra, Cora Cooper, Burl McGee—faces, and the veiled figures of the nuns, their beads swinging and clacking along their narrow hips.

"And in a while, what I thought was most of it, at least the exact flavor and feel of it, was there for me, and I decided that I would go, and by going I would find and understand those pieces from my past that could right my faith again and make me feel whole. I laid my work off on subordinates and applied for a week's recuperative leave. While deciding on my packing, I came across my old school sweater and cap. I remember I held them to my face and smelled them.

"The school and grounds of Nativity had not changed much. I arrived three days early on a Thursday, and after I had checked in to the old hotel in the town center and changed into civilian clothing, I rented a car and drove out to the school. The distances seemed shorter, and I lost my way a few times, but when I reached the right neighborhood I found my way easily, though there was nothing, no landmark, that was familiar. It was summer; the school was empty and deserted, and I walked among the low rectangular buildings that housed the classrooms, standing on my toes and looking through windows. The old church was open, and when I entered it I was shocked to see that it was no longer a church, but a gymnasium. Only the shape of the window frames was familiar; what had been stained glass was now plate.

"Christ, I should have known better, should have got a hint from the way I let memory flood in selectively, pushing some away, letting my eyes rest only on what warmed me, pausing at the door of the boy's bathroom, but not entering. I roamed the school and grounds for an hour or more, and I found my spirits rising. Before I left, I went to the new church building, lit a candle to the Holy Mother, and knelt and prayed with a seriousness that I had not experienced in years. When I left I felt clean and wholesome.

"The night of the party I dressed carefully, wearing the dark suit of my calling and my stiff linen collar. I brushed my hair, smiling at the beginnings of gray at my temples. My stomach was flat then, and in the carefully tailored suit I was wearing I looked fit and healthy. I was right in my soul, I thought, and in my body. I had indulged in just a hint of vanity, having my nails manicured the afternoon before. There had been only women in the beauty parlor, some muffled laughing that a man, a priest, would go there and do such a thing.

"In the failing light of the evening and the bright and colored artificial lighting that flooded out of the old church windows, Nativity was transformed and hardly recognizable. I parked my car close to a row of classrooms, and as I passed the drinking fountains and numbered doors I heard the sound of recorded music, popular songs from years ago, and noted the loops of colored streamers that had been hung from the low outdoor ceiling of the passage. There were forty or so people standing in groups and alone on the gymnasium floor of the old church when I entered it. Long portable tables, covered with various molds, dips, and platters of food, lined the walls, and there were four couples dancing, stiff and slow in the middle of the floor.

Streamers hung from rafters, and there were various class objects, sweaters, banners, and sports uniforms, hanging from nails on the walls. A woman of my own age greeted me, standing at a table at the door when I entered. I did not recognize her.

"'Father. Johnny? Is that you?' she said, and came up to me fluttering, holding a white nametag in her hand. She smiled, somewhat conspiratorially.

"'*Well*, look at you now!' And she pinned the tag to my lapel.

"'Hello, Jan,' I said, reading the name on her tag.

"She steered me into the gym, and after I had gone to a table and gotten a drink, I stood awkwardly to the side, feigning interest in the dancing couples.

"The room was filled gradually as the party progressed. People came up to me briefly, winking and introducing spouses. I recognized some of them vaguely, but had no memory of time spent with them. Then, standing at a table of food beside a man in a bright-colored sports jacket, I saw Cora, recognized her and remembered her instantly. In a moment her head turned my way, her face brightened, and I saw her mouth form my name. She pulled the sleeve of the man beside her, bent to him and spoke briefly, and then the pair turned from the table and approached me. As they were coming, I looked over their shoulders, and on the far side of the room, alone beside a makeshift case of trophies, I saw and recognized Burl; he seemed as thin and delicate as he had been over thirty years before.

" 'I was illegitimate. The one you thought my mother was my aunt,' Cora said. She had gotten free of the man she was with, and we were standing alone to the side of the gym floor. The man was not her husband, just an acquaintance. She had never married.

"Cora's illegitimacy was only the first revelation of the evening, a shocking one indeed, but a minor one at that. She had been my very closest friend. I'd visited her house, spent most of my free time with her, and to learn now that the life she had lived was false, her mother not her mother, did an odd thing to me, strangely falsifying my own past, something I had put away and only now thought I was regaining.

"'Did you know it then?' I said.

"'Of course I did. I think most everybody did. We were both outsiders, you and I. Isn't that why we stuck together?'

"I didn't know what she meant.

"'Why didn't you tell me?' I said.

"'I thought you knew!' she said. 'Most everybody did. Don't you remember how they shunned me, shunned *us*? They thought we were both dirty, foreign and odd.'

"I was stunned by Cora's revelation, and after we had spoken of it and got beyond it, I was saddened that there seemed no more to say. We could have spoken of our years together, of things we'd done. They were coming back to me, in their detail, in her presence. But I felt they were nothing for us to speak of. They would be hurtful in light of this new knowledge, a learning that would make them somehow inauthentic. In any story there would be the line, that I had not known, and this would make the story itself libelous, tainted and unwholesome. Just as I had reached her, had reached some centering in my past, all had begun to dissolve.

"We freed each other, when we could do so with grace. It was clear that Cora didn't want that, but it was clear too that she understood. I saw pain in her eyes as she turned away, and when I caught her looking at me from across the room later, I tried hard not to look back.

"I spent some time looking for other involvements then, but all I found were strained. People would survey my garments as they spoke with me, and in most I saw a look in faces and eyes that was troublesome, off-putting and vaguely disapproving. For an hour I could not find Burl in the gathering, but then he appeared again, alone as before, standing near the entrance to the gym. His eyes fell when I caught them, but in a moment his head rose and he looked at me, his eyes large and glistening.

"'I have to talk to you, Johnny...Father,' he said.

"I had crossed the room to him. He had not watched me as I approached, but I could tell he knew I was coming.

" 'Talk,' I said. 'I'm listening.'

"He glanced around us, a little furtive. There was a couple across the room who seemed to be watching us, their heads close together, talking. I saw another who seemed to be doing the same.

" 'Not here,' he said. He was shaking slightly, his arms hanging awkwardly at his sides. He leaned a little toward the doorway, glancing quickly over at it.

" 'They're watching,' he said. 'Can we go outside?' There was a plea in his voice, a slight elevation in his tone.

" 'Of course,' I said, and followed his thin body out of the room.

"In the passageway there were people coming and going, couples laughing lightly and talking with animation. Burl glanced at them. 'This is no good either,' he said, and he quit my side and went to the classroom door closest to us and rattled the knob. The room was locked, and I watched him go to another door, try that also, then drop his hands in frustration.

" 'Burl,' I said. 'Over there. The boys' room.'

"He glanced sharply at me, a stricken look in his face. I saw his Adam's apple bob as he swallowed. Then he took his lower lip in his teeth, turned from me and crossed to the sign marked *Boys*. I saw him open the door, enter, and disappear in the darkness. I looked around me, found that the passage was now empty, and went to the boys' room and entered also.

"'Burl,' I whispered when I got inside. There was only a dim, yellow night-light glowing in the ceiling. The porcelain on the low sinks and urinals showed in the yellow wash; the stalls were no more than vague outlines in the dark. The light made the place seem dirty, and I felt grit under my feet as I shifted them, getting my bearings.

"'Here.' I heard Burl's muffled voice in the darkness, the sound coming from a stall to the back of the room. I put my hand out, feeling along the doors, and when I got to the stall beside the one from which his voice had come, I pushed the door on its silent hinges. What light there was entered, and I could see the dirty yellow porcelain of the bowl, the low black seat. Once inside, I turned and lowered myself down onto the seat. It was so low my knees almost reached my chin.

" 'Burl?' I said. 'What is it?' and felt the breath of a foot shuffling under the side of the stall separating us.

" 'Johnny, it's been hell,' he said. 'This is a small town. All these years. You were smart to get out of it.'

"I remembered Burl, thin as he was now, almost the same size it seemed. He was always apart, a loner, more left alone than desiring it, I thought. Never even the butt of jokes or tricks, there had been a sadness about him that could not be lifted, even in part, by the high quality of his schoolwork. Even the nuns shunned him, grudgingly acknowledging his intelligence, the cool, conventional exactness of his answers and papers. And as his disembodied voice drifted under the edge of the stall wall, I remembered something else, a day after school and the two of us in one stall, our awkward groping and the touch of small, rigid flesh, the lights dim as they were now, a sliver of late afternoon sun slicing in at a high window.

" 'Burl,' I said. 'I don't understand.' But I think I

was beginning to understand, something at least, at least that the thing that concerned him had to do with that day, a day buried and forgotten, childish and insignificant, and only rising up as the hint of a smile crossed a face, at times, over the years; nothing really, a raw, ignorant experimentation of two schoolboys, a moment of guilt, snubbed and forgotten and never even spoken of in the confessional.

" 'They knew,' Burl whispered, a choke in his voice. 'They all knew!'

" 'Knew what?' I said, the question only a suggestion that he continue.

" 'They seen us. Over the edge,' he said. 'Some kids; I don't know who.'

"And I imagined their crowded bodies, their toes planted precariously on the black ring, their dirty hands, and their eyes looking down at us, so close, from above. *They seen us,* to use Burl's words. He had lapsed into the poor grammar of childhood, and now he was talking again.

" 'And they told everybody! And they haven't let me forget it yet.'

"There was a silence; I was about to speak. What

difference could it make? It was years ago. I was a priest now, almost a bishop.

"'Bless me, Father,' he said, 'for I have sinned. My last confession was ten years ago. I…'

"'Stop it!' I said, sharply.

"'I disobeyed my mother seven times, and in those years I have been with men. I had bad thoughts against associates…'

"'Burl,' I said more gently, but with insistence. 'That's enough now. You must stop. It's all right.'

"'It is *not* all right!' he said, and then he stopped abruptly, and I could hear his choking breath, the scrape of his shoe against the gritty floor.

"We sat there. And there was finally no good solace that I could give him. He spoke somewhat abstractly, about the way people had treated him, muffled laughter and whispers in public places. He said that he had gone out of town, but that it had followed him, possibly not the particulars of the thing, but some advanced sense of who he was, what he was, so that he was not quite taken seriously.

"I thought of the women in the beauty parlor,

their laughter as my nails were manicured. And as he spoke, I thought he had become the thing he feared, had taken on some permanent guilt or self-fulfilling expectation, and that maybe the cause was forgotten, by everyone but him. I wasn't sure though, and I could not find a way to soothe him.

"He left in a while, making his way quickly out of the boys' room ahead of me, and when I reached the passageway he was gone. I went and looked for Cora, but she was gone too. The party was over, only a few stragglers standing in corners of the gymnasium talking.

"Even now, as I tell the story, I feel the overblown nature of the thing, the burgeoning of insignificant details that lead to an arrival in a childhood bathroom and an event that stands, in every world but my own, as no more than a cipher. For how many did a thing like this occur? Who has not been furtive and experimental in this way? The whole thing rings hollow in any significant scheme of things. All I know is that when I got back to the hotel, had removed my neat and careful vestments and had turned the light out and gotten into bed, the thing began to flood in on me, all those years that had formed a ground of origins and become fixed were now like a diorama, rotating slightly on some platform, until ego's center among familiar figures had shifted irretrievably.

"I had seen myself as a loner then, but one who had come to that state out of some fate or choice. I was to be a priest. I knew this by the time I was twelve years old, and that resolution is what had set me apart, a celebrated oddity, good at studies, adequate at sports, invited to parties, vaguely respected by nuns and priests, aside, but also above the crowd. But now the remembered looks and glances of fellow students took on a new significance. 'They seen us,' he had said. 'They all knew.' And it was possible that had I *not* stood alone, had not flaunted my calling, I would not have become that odd spectacle, a boy who plays with other boys who would soon become a priest who would eventually listen to the sins of others in confessional. The looks and glances in my memory now became derisive, cheapening, and I saw myself as a ludicrous figure, a pompus fool among the normal. I had not know of Cora's illegitimacy, of Burl's slow crushing under the weight of lurid accusation, so how could I have known the half of it when it came to my own place in things? Each remembered event was changing now, and I began even to question my time in seminary, a place only a few miles from Nativity. I had been a loner there as well, a student whose concern was with Church politics rather than theology. And I thought now that it was possible that what I took as a certain austerity in my figure was yet again a ludicrousness. 'They seen us.' Had that seeing traveled to the seminary as well?

"And so the platform of the past, the figured matrix I only realized as I regained it was what I stood upon, twisted and warped even as I called it up from memory. And that changed me. I had a lapse of faith that was permanent. I saw the novitiate of my past as little more than a joke for others, and in seeing that I saw my position, almost a bishop, as a joke as well. I was an inauthentic figure, an image of a lie, all the more profound because it was a public one. When I took my vows of office, a year later, I ignored the words. Now I am successful as a politician. I say my daily Mass with charts and appointments in my head. That evening at Nativity could have been avoided. That's a romantic and nostalgic regret. What it brought me to is so large that I try not to think of it at all. It would be a constant despair. If I were you, I wouldn't go back."

When I returned from the Bishop's place, it was close to midnight and I was tired. But before I went to bed I got the box out again and shuffled through its contents. I put Melchior's card aside, together with the letter from Anne and Carl, those messages from the past, and while I was puzzling at the ticket stubs and looking at Lorca's two line drawings again, I thought of the one letter that she had sent me, two weeks after her leaving. It had been a note really, a few hasty sentences, and her parents had received one of their own at around the same time. *Dear David,* the note had said. *Maybe you'll never forgive this. I don't know. I had to leave. I can't really know what to say to make it easier. Take whatever you want. I'll not write again. Lorca.* The envelope was postmarked Phoenix, Arizona.

I never did hear from her again. She left most of her clothes; some boxes, heavy and taped shut; and a variety of folders and never-used wedding gifts. The folders contained pictures of flowers mostly, ones she had cut out of magazines for her drawings. The one she kept gardenias in went with her. I took very little when I left, just enough to set up house.

I set Lorca's note aside in my mind and took up the brighter, actual one from Anne and Carl, their letter about a child and the good life in Northern California. I read it through, and then got paper and envelope and wrote a brief note to them, putting in *please forward* below the address. Then I dropped the letter in the chute in the dark hallway outside my apartment door.

The next few weeks were spent getting the last details of my affairs in order. I wrote a letter to the Bishop and cards to a few other customers, those that I had some firm relationship with. Anson's money, which he had transferred into my name in the weeks before his death, was safe in bank certificates. I cashed one in, for five thousand, and deposited the money in my checking account. Then I arranged for a car lease and notified my landlord and the movers. There was really very little to move, and I decided on storage in New Jersey. I finished quicker than I had anticipated, and spent my last week free of tasks. I walked the streets of this city that I had grown to love. I strolled in the knowledge that I was leaving, and each thing I saw again took on the history of my years in New York, already touched with the beginnings of nostalgia. The day before I left, I received a letter from Anne. I was just going to try to call them that evening. I could almost hear Anne's voice in the mute words on the page, slightly formal as it had been, but fruity and welcoming. She hoped I could stay for a while, we could talk about the old days. Carl had some part-time work at the college, but he was not all that busy and could find time. There were three children now. I wrote a quick postcard in answer. It said I could make it in about a week. I'd call from the road. After I'd dropped the card in the chute in the hallway, I fixed a drink. The living room was bare of everything now, so I sat at the kitchen table. I wondered what the town would be like, Sharonville, in the high desert country of Northern California. I wondered what *they* would be like now, if they would be in any way like I remembered them.

Lorca was sitting in a chair in her white shorts and halter, her hair gathered above her neck in a loose bun held up with numerous bobby pins, a few wet strands stuck against her cheek and ear. Her legs were wet and shining with perspiration. The faint red clay dust from the court had soiled her white socks and her calves above them. She was leaning back in the chair, white wicker and cushioned, and her legs were spread, her thighs resting against the poles of the chair arms. Her nose glistened, and there were droplets of perspiration on her dark eyebrows. She was smiling, her eyes focused above my head. I heard Carl moving in another room and felt Anne's fingers digging into my shoulders, searching along the muscles.

"That's good," I said, lifting my chin up, seeing her forehead as she leaned over me. She was standing behind my chair, facing Lorca, moving her fingers up to my neck.

"This is possibly one of the best days," Lorca said. She turned her head to the window, through which the sun streamed, then back a little as Carl entered the room carrying a tray with glasses of iced tea.

"It would be better if the tennis had been a little better," he said. The four of us laughed, and he handed a glass to Lorca and one to me, glancing over my head a little sharply at Anne. The women were much better players than we were. It was tennis that had gotten them together in the first place, and they suffered our participation with them in it. Most of the good rallies were between them. They didn't much like doubles at all, but would let us in on it occasionally.

Anne let go of my neck and went to a chair. We talked of the day, particular rallies, the poor shape of the college courts, the emptiness of buildings and quad this Saturday before exam week.

"I was just checking musculature, his spinal alignment, you know," Anne said. Lorca laughed, but a little awkwardly, and Carl lifted his hands in mock frustration. He had a way of gesturing that was odd, as if each time he was just learning to do it.

"Nevertheless," I said, "it sure felt good."

The afternoon wore on. We talked of examinations, and Anne and Carl talked of their move. He had landed a job working the ski slopes up north, repairing them in summers, ski patrol during the season. Maybe he could pick up a little part-time teaching, intro to philosophy or something, at the junior college. Anne would try to find something in physiotherapy when they got set up there. Carl had plans for a few weeks of climbing in Yosemite.

I still had a few courses to finish during the summer. Lorca was done, but she had no job at all yet and wasn't looking. Her drawing was a struggle for her at that time. A year before, she had gotten a few pieces, some flower drawings, into a traveling show sponsored by a bank, one of those with branches throughout the West. But nothing had followed that, and now she was working with paints as well as pen and ink. She had only studied in a formal way in a few elective courses at the university. What she had to learn was made harder through a lot of trial and error. She was tenacious about the painting, though, and it had begun to absorb her. There was still some student loan money left, though not much. The free rent of the little house behind her parents' helped, but I'd have to get something soon, before summer's end.

"I'm going to miss them," Lorca said.

We were back at the little house. She had showered, washing the sweat and red dust away, and now she sat in a chair in her robe, the strands of her long, black hair drying where they fell, curled at the tips over her shoulders. Her look was slightly abstracted, her eyes unfocused where they rested, a little to the left of my face as she spoke. I wanted to shake her, to bring her back from the edge of her reverie that had its object in Carl and Anne but was I knew larger than that and really unknown to me. For a while now she had been slipping, secretive and reticent. I would catch her at times in a posture of reading, finding she was not reading but looking a little above the page, her thoughts elsewhere.

"I'll miss Anne at least," she said.

"We can visit them."

"Yeah, we can do that," but there was no conviction in her voice at all.

"There's something bothering you. Something else."

"No," she said. "No, there's nothing."

"Do you want something?" I asked.

She shifted in her seat, as if the robe were binding her, as if there were something in its folds that bothered her. Her chin tipped in a lovely way of hers, and her eyes moved back to my own, the hint of a smile touching the corners of her mouth.

"I want a rub," she said. "Something to fix my bones." And she uncurled her legs and got up from the chair and opened her robe and let it fall at her feet, stood naked before me for a moment, then turned and walked to the bed and stretched out on her stomach on the cover. I turned the light down to the lowest bulb then and moved over to her and began to work her.

Her body was lean, but her buttocks and breasts were soft and full. I could see the bulge of her flattened breasts below her armpits, as she stretched her arms up above her head. I pooled oil in my palm, then ran my hands from the back of her knees up her thighs, cupping the lobes of her buttocks from below, pushing and elevating them, then letting them flow back as I slid to her thin waist, pressing my thumbs along the structure of her sacrum. She moaned deeply, and when I looked down I saw her toes curling.

I worked her back and shoulders, digging in slightly where the muscles were tight and bunched, and when I reached her neck, I slid my fingertips around her head to the temples, rotating the skin in small circles. Then I saw that she was covered and glistening with oil and that a small sweat had risen from her pores, and I moved back to her feet and began to massage her in earnest.

She had her face buried in the cover, her shoulders pushed up a little, and in the dim light the curve of her back looked like the body of a dolphin, almost as dark as that, her relaxing muscles elongating under the sheath of her dark skin. There was, through her muffled breathing, some sense of articulation, as if she were talking in some deeply gutteral language, words mixed with moans, neither of which I could understand.

I ran my fingers between her toes, pressed into the pads, cupped her arches in my palms, held her ankles and pulled her legs back. Then I worked beyond her ankles, holding and moving her muscular calves. I was thinking about what I was doing, watching her body as it relaxed, but I had no idea what she was thinking about at all. She brought her head up for air once, stretching her neck out, and then returned her face to the blanket. I saw her buttocks tighten as she moved, then relax again, the dark place where her thighs entered the cup of her pelvis opening.

And in a while I had my pants off and was on my knees behind her, entering her, holding her oiled waist in my hands. She was up on her extended arms, her head elevated again. I could see the cowl of her hanging hair, but not a bit of her face. She seemed to be looking into the wall in front of her. She moved back to me and I slid my hands from her waist to her spine, digging in again, massaging, and when I held her buttocks I was reaching into the muscles there also. Finally she shuddered and collapsed, and I was stretched out upon her, my hands still moving, rubbing her as she had wished.

Lorca. I remember a sunny disposition, a lilting laugh, and a lean body moving with certain grace over the court. I remember a hand touching a small spit curl, and a brow empty of all care. In the summers we went into the mountains, and she was inquisitive and open. She was committed to her studies as well as her drawing and painting, and her glasses slid to a perch near the end of her nose while she was reading. She liked music, though she admitted to knowing nothing much about it. She seemed to have no secret life at all, happy to live in the little house behind the one in which she was born. I remember how well it had all seemed to be going.

The next morning, when I awoke in the oily sheets, I found a note from her saying that she was at the library. It was Sunday, but exam week was beginning and the university was open. In the early afternoon, I went to meet her, to surprise her, but she was not there. She was at home when I returned, cooking dinner, cheerful, but slightly abstracted. She had taken a shower and was in her robe again. Her hair was wet, and she looked very much the way she had the night before. She was turned away from me, working at a chopping board and talking.

She said she had met someone, had found a job at a dress shop in Hollywood.

"That's great!" I said. "At the library?"

"Oh, yes!" she said, and when she turned to me I was startled by her flush.

5 ❧ *Peking Duck*

There were two goats, a pair of swans, four cats, a German shepherd, a tall Afghan, a pony the size of a small heifer, and yet the yard behind the house seemed in a strange way orderly. It was large and hilly and bordered by a hedge of tended plantings and indigenous growth—cactus, clipped-back yucca, privet, and some desert flowers twined in among them. There was a small pond in a lower tier of the yard, a small oval set under the limbs of a young redwood, and here the swans drifted against each other in small circles. The last border of the yard was the house itself, a large ranch-style structure, and a door from the kitchen led into the yard, into a profusion of potted and hanging plants, birdbaths and feeders.

Abbey was up on the pony, her legs hanging free of the stirrups of the tooled western saddle, her hands cupped over the horn, and leaning forward. She wore a long, colorful caftan, hitched up to her thighs; she was barefoot and her toes almost touched the ground at the pony's sides. She had rushed ahead of me, and when I came out the kitchen door she was already mounted.

"Do you like Oozo?" she said, arching her back and smiling. "That's his name, Oozo."

I entered the yard and moved toward them, the Afghan watching me; she was poised beside a birdbath, the small pond at her right shoulder. When I got between the two goats, the male moved into my knee, butting hard against it.

"He does that all the time," Abbey said. "He doesn't want you between them."

I pulled up, and the male skipped around in front of me, banging into the side of the female, pushing her off toward the house.

"It's a nice pony," I said, and she lifted the reins, heeled him lightly in the flanks and turned him in a tight circle. She was ten years old, but dressed and acting like an adolescent girl a few years older. Her ears were pierced. Long hoops hung from them, and she had combs in her hair.

"Here's the kids!" she said. There was a ruckus

at the door behind me, and when I turned I saw a girl and boy, about seven and nine, I thought, rush into the yard and come up to me. The boy grabbed me around the waist, hugging me, his grip tight and his head pressed into my side.

"Hi, David," he said. "You're David." He held me, pushing into me, making no move at all to let me go. I saw the girl reach out and pull at his shoulder.

"He does that all the time," Anne said. She was standing in the doorway, as lovely and young looking as I remembered her in my past, though I thought I noticed some lines of care at the corners of her eyes.

"Let him go now, Coppie; that's enough."

I had gotten to Sharonville late the night before. The drive cross-country had been very much like a dream, at least in the sense that its time had already slipped away from me.

At a turnpike rest stop a little to the east of Cleveland, I picked up a young man who was hitchhiking at the onramp. He was a boy really, no more than sixteen, and he sat stiff in the seat beside me and was awkward and reticent in our brief snatches of conversation. I took him to the other side of Omaha and on into the plains, where he left me at a help wanted sign at a gas station a little off the highway. He was thin and fair and looked weak to me, and once in a room we shared, him sleeping on the smaller bed beside my own as Anson had in his last days, I awakened in the middle of the night to see him standing at the window. He was hunched over, leaning against the glass. It was raining, and I could see his thin shoulders shake as he wept, quietly and privately, looking out into the parking lot.

I remembered the look of Omaha, near where I had left the young hitchhiker off, but west of that city it had gotten hot, and I had been driving during the nights, sleeping in small motels in the daytime. It seemed no more than a trip through diminishing lights, those coming up in the windshield and those set back in mountains and desert. Faint country music on the radio, breakfast at two AM. Still, time had passed, a week almost, and though the passage had been dim, I had recognition of a great distance between where I now was and New York City. And the distance was more than one of space. I felt out of my recent past completely, not forward into some future but in some kind of suspension, not yet in a distant past, not anywhere yet, though I felt the sight of Carl and Anne could push me in that direction.

The town was small, and though it was only ten o'clock when I entered it, it was fast asleep. On the way in from the highway, I passed what I thought must be the college where Carl did his part-time teaching, a ramble of low adobe-like buildings, copies of that in a modern style, on a piece of barren land with blacktop drives running from building to building. In the town center the only lights were those in the windows of a bar, a few cars parked in front of it. There was a bright moon, and beyond the center I could see the low foothills, and in the distance the shadows of the larger mountains that ran all the way to the Pacific coast. I had seen no place to stay on the way in, and there was nothing apparent in the town center, really an intersection of two streets with a dozen or so stores near their joining, so I decided to call Carl. There was a brightly lit phone booth to the side of the door of the bar. I had called once from the road, two days before. A child had answered and taken a message.

When Carl picked me up, he was wearing the same dark winter coat I had remembered him in on those few chilly days in Los Angeles. It was not that cold here in Sharonville. We embraced briefly by the side of his car. He pulled away quickly and took my hand and shook it, and when he stepped further back I noticed the coat and mentioned it. He looked the same, still lean and straight, and only the faint strands of gray in his dark hair suggested that he had aged. We spoke briefly, and I followed him in my car.

It was only eleven when we got to his house, but everyone was asleep, and there was only a dim night-light illuminating the glass-walled living room where I was to bed down. He had inflated a large, thick air mattress, placing it close to the curve of a grand piano that stood in a corner. We spoke briefly again when he brought blankets and pillow. He suggested a brandy, in a whisper, but I said, "Let's not wake them up; we can talk in the morning." He showed me the bathroom, beyond the door of his own bedroom; then he nodded, and we said good night.

I awoke in the morning with a slight pain in my shoulder, and when I shifted my body against it I found that the mattress had lost air during the night and that I was resting in the middle of two large billows of air, the side of my body on the floor itself. As I rolled over in the waves, I caught a glimpse of the naked back and buttocks of a woman, and knew even before I was completely oriented that it was Anne. She was standing beside her bed, holding a garment in front of her, and her image was reflected in a mirror in the hall outside her open door. She was not moving; I thought she might be thinking, planning something. She had the body of a young girl, dark and perfect skin, her buttocks firm and elevated. I could see a good portion of the small single bed beside her legs, and I wondered about it vaguely. Watching her, I caught the smell of coffee from another room and turned to it, and when I looked back the mirror was empty.

The room I was in was large and rectangular.

There was a massive stone fireplace, freestanding, two thirds of the way down the rectangle in the middle of the room, to the side of which I could see a dining room table. I guessed that the kitchen was beyond the other side. The long wall to my left was sliding glass doors, and beyond them lay a redwood deck. Drapes were pulled over the glass doors at my end of the room, keeping the morning sun out. The furniture was heavy and Spanish, couches and coffee tables well out from the walls in various groupings. Along the wall behind the piano at my head was a stereo setup and shelves of records and books. The other long wall of the room was hung with paintings and prints, neoprimitive Indian works mostly, and there were wooden shelves bolted to the wall below them on which rested various pots and urns. A glass door near the dining table was open, and when I got to my feet and headed stiffly to the bathroom, I could feel a pleasant breeze against my legs under my robe.

There were familiar things in the bathroom, an open white wicker shelf unit containing them. Oils and lotions I remembered from college, colognes and perfumes that Carl and Anne had worn even then. In a clear crystal jar on the rack was the green, organic look of marijuana. I lifted the jar's top and confirmed it. I remembered a brush and comb, a specific brand of bobby pin, the smell of herbal soap. I dressed myself among these familiar scents and some unfamiliar ones, talcum and kid's toothpaste. There was a small window in the bathroom, and I could see the yard beyond it. The swans sat in a morning mist in the small pool, and the pony stood half asleep among hanging planters. I could see movement in the short wing of the house that was the children's quarters, lights brightening as curtains were pulled aside.

When I reached the table, Carl was sitting between his oldest child, Abbey, and the smaller girl, Dana, who lifted her head brightly from her cereal bowl as I approached. The boy was not there yet, but I could hear him talking in the kitchen beyond the wall. Just as I was sitting down, I heard Anne call my name, then felt her hand on my shoulder, her hair and then her lips as she kissed my cheek. After she had brought out juice in a stone pitcher, and eggs and sausage, she joined us and made careful introduction of her two daughters.

"Where's the boy?" I said.

The girls laughed, Carl looked straight ahead, and Anne shifted a little in her chair.

"He doesn't eat breakfast," Dana said. "He'll gulp something down in the kitchen."

The girls giggled and poked each other, and after breakfast and the first tentative beginnings of the small talk that would get us to the larger things, we went out to the animals in the yard.

The driving force of that vague intention that had brought me West was temporarily attenuated and lost in the muddle of events and reacquaintances during my few days with Carl and Anne. The intention itself, though it drove me, was nothing I clearly understood. There had been the arrival of the box, then the first tentative steps with Melchior. I knew it was all traceable to Anson and the painful yet liberating release from my ten years with him. The final year had been a kind of bondage of caring and tending, of trying to somehow right previous years, of setting a life that was passing into some order in which it could be understood. Not Anson's life, I realized after his death, but my own. Perhaps it was the Bishop, finally, his story that had perversely moved me. I knew my resolve had focused in the days after I left him for the last time. I would go back, that much was sure. But what I would go back to, what I expected and wanted, had no clarity to it at all.

"Lorca said something, I think, about Utah a few days before Carl and I left. Something about a woman at that dress shop, as I remember."

We were sitting in the living room after lunch that first day. Carl had put a quiet chamber music tape on the recorder, and large photographs of Yosemite were scattered on the glass coffee table around which we sat. It was Saturday, and the two girls were out, playing at the house of some friend. Coppie sat on the couch beside me, his head against my side, his thin arms around my waist, holding tight. I shifted a little at the discomfort of his squeeze, patted his head, and looked at Anne.

"It'll be enough for him in a while," she said, smiling faintly and without pleasure.

"Coppie, it's almost time to feed the animals," Carl said somewhat sharply, but the boy just pressed his head into me, snuggling closer. He was tucked under my right arm, and it was difficult for me to find a place to rest my hand; to touch him would be to encourage him, so I lay my arm along the back of the sofa, straining a bit at the shoulder. Carl stared at the boy, unblinking, but I couldn't read the emotion in his look, didn't know if he was angry or curious.

"I've never been there," I said. "There's Salt Lake City, I guess, but I have no picture of it."

"I don't think it was there, anyway," Anne said. "It was the clothes Lorca said she was buying, too casual and outdoorsy for that."

For lunch we had a salad. I had seen a gathering of large ripe avocados and artichokes drying on a cart near the kitchen door, but we had not eaten them. Coppie had eaten with us this time, using his fingers, munching at the lettuce and onions like a small animal at my shoulder. He reminded me of what I thought Anson might have been like as a child, a little wild and without the guidance of parents.

Anne had her legs pulled up under her on the couch across from me, and when she shifted and her legs parted I could see into the darkness between her knees. Carl shuffled through the photographs, looking for the one he had told me about, a day a year or so ago when he and others had made a continuous assault on El Capitan, a sheer and rocky ascent in Yosemite. The photos were full of the shapes of huge rock pillars, cottony clouds, and slate sky. They were scattered over the glass coffee table and on the couch.

"Here's the one," he said, and reached a floppy glossy across to me. His voice was slightly portentous, almost pompous, as he pointed out dots that were figures, like fly specks on the sheer rock face. I could make out hairs that were ropes, possible arms and legs.

"Which one are you?" I said, and he took the photograph back and studied it.

"I'm not sure. I think this one."

"Who are the other two?"

"Kip and Banyon, I bet," Coppie said softly into my shoulder, and then released me and got up from the couch and headed for the kitchen.

"Anyway," Anne said, moving her hands—I noticed they had been gripped tight in her lap as she moved them—and running them along her legs, "the woman was buying many things, all of them bright and colorful, things that could be worn in layers, winter or summer. She told Lorca the colors were against the environment, to bring some variety and brightness with her into the place. Or maybe that was just Lorca's idea of it. I'm not sure."

"Utah?" I said.

"Right. Red rock, and dust, I guess. Lorca was taken with the idea. Or something. There was something about art involved in it, I think." She fell silent then, glancing at Carl's hands among the photographs, then looking out the glass windows of the room.

"And that's it?" I said.

"No. Not all of it. It's that she talked about it, was somewhat insistent about the woman, their talking, and the clothing. She was a very old woman, as I remember. I thought she talked more about it than the situation warranted." She shook her head and her long straight hair, not unlike what I remembered of Lorca's, rustled on each of her shoulders.

That evening we ate fresh Washington salmon, salad full of chunks of avocado, and cold artichoke. The children joined us, Coppie again sitting close to my side. Dana told me the names of all the animals, and Abbey asked me if I would watch her ride the pony again after dinner.

"But to bed early," Anne said.

The girls scowled a little, but were soon bright and cheerful again.

"This is like when Banyon was here," Coppie said softly, leaning against my arm.

"Who's Banyon?" I said.

"Just somebody who was here for a while," Carl said.

"Or Kip," Coppie whispered again.

"That's enough now," Anne said gently. "Eat your fish."

Coppie nuzzled against me, then picked up his fork again. I wanted to ask who Kip was, learn something about Banyon, but before I could ask anything Carl spoke.

"Kip was just another guy who was here for a while. This is different, Coppie."

"Will Karla be here tomorrow?" the boy asked plaintively.

"Yes, tomorrow," Anne said.

"I'll be here too," I said, and the children laughed.

Later that evening, when the children were in bed, Carl started a fire and we sat in the living room, drinking tequila from low stone mugs. Earlier, I had watched Abbey ride, steering the pony in various tight turns and mincing steps. Dana and Coppie had stood in the yard with me, laughing at the way Abbey's toes touched the ground as the pony moved. The two goats had sidled up to us, as if they too were watching, and the dogs had lain close to each other as the twilight came on. At one point Coppie looked up at me.

"This *is* like Banyon and Kip," he said.

"So it's possible she went to Utah," I said. Carl had put a tape on the machine, this time quiet jazz. There were lights in the room, but they were dim, and the wall of glass that opened onto the deck was opaque, the night only a blackness beyond it. I had been to the end of the deck, to the side of what I found was Carl's bedroom. I could see a partition through the window, separating the room where Anne slept from his. There was a single bed in each. At the end of these odd sleeping quarters, a small deck cantilevered out from the large one, reaching into a stand of thin aspens.

"Is the tub hot?" Anne said.

"Right. I gave it a push this morning," Carl said.

"Her mother didn't say anything about that in the note, just that she had heard nothing from her," I said.

We hadn't as yet gotten to our past in the way that Melchior and I had tried to get there; there had been enough with the children and animals, seeing the place, and learning about their current lives. Anne seemed to feel the weight of the children a little. Carl had his work on the ski slopes and those few philosophy courses at the college, but she had all she could do to stay connected to her therapy at the prison that stood at the foot of the higher mountains a few miles from the town.

"What's it like there?" I said.

"At the prison? Oh, mostly old down-and-outers, arthritic. The doctor is a real hack. Not much that's interesting," she said, glancing quickly at Carl as she spoke.

"I'd think it would be good," he said. "You know, the underlife in some way." He was speaking to me, but it was Anne who answered.

"It isn't," she said.

I could tell she wanted to get back to Lorca. She spoke of a woman she had found there, a good player. But the courts were poor, she said, even worse than those at the college in L.A. She meant the ones we had gone to together, and she was beginning to get back there, mentioning things that had happened, some of which I could recall, others that I had no memory of at all.

"Remember the way our hands used to ache? When they had us doing three-hour stints at the table? You'd do my hands for me, while Lorca and Carl were studying."

I remembered something of the sort, but only once. And yet she spoke of it as if it had been a common enough occurrence. We had been mostly in different classes, though in the same program.

"It's getting late," Carl said.

"It's early yet," she said.

"We have to get ready for Karla," he said, "and the ducks."

"Is that much to do?" she said.

There was a certain quiet civility between them. They looked directly at each other when they spoke, but there was too much formality, and I couldn't tell if my discomfort came from that or from my not knowing what they were talking about.

"What ducks?" I said. "Who's Karla?"

"Oh Karla!" Anna said, stretching her body up a little and laughing. "She's a photographer. Takes pictures of children. You'll see tomorrow night. The ducks are for a dinner."

The time in the tub was pure California, or at least I saw it that way, a California that had started well after I left the place. We were old friends, had known each other close to fifteen years, but until that morning when I had glimpsed Anne naked in the mirror I had seen neither of them without clothing. And fifteen years wasn't really accurate at all, though there was something about that span of time that brought me at least comfort. I had known them actually for only four or so years, the ones when we had been together in college. For ten they had only come up a little in memory. But we were in middle age now, or close to it, and it was as if our friendship had grown and deepened in that time that we had no real contact at all. It was like a family friendship, one in which the early cementing carried one through as a matter of time only. I knew them really very little at all, but I felt I knew them as well as I had known anyone, better than I had known Lorca, possibly even Anson. Had I not found them again, it would have been otherwise, imaginings of what had happened to them and how they might have changed. But their behavior, their hand movements and the sound of their voices, had enough in it of what I remembered to make me feel that the changes were unimportant. It was as if we had all been transported here, placed in this steaming tub, from a time in which we felt we knew each other.

These were at least my feelings; I had no real idea at all of theirs. They were familiar enough with me, but the gestures and idiosyncrasies that I saw and remembered as terms of familiarity had a way now of effecting a kind of closing off of the present, a turning only back into the gone past. It was difficult to place our naked bodies together, there in the hot tub facing one another, in any way that I could find appropriate. They acted about it as if it were a common thing. I felt that whatever it was, it could not be that. I remembered the Bishop and his figure of the turning platform; we sat in the tub as if in a diorama. Anne's breasts floated on the steamy surface of the water. Through the steam that rose into the cool night, I could see Carl's face only a few feet away from me, but I could not place his presence behind the familiar mask of it.

"Ah," Carl said, and stretched his arms on the flat of the deck at the edge of the tub. The wet hair down the middle of his flat chest looked pubic. I could see the shape of Anne's hips below the water's surface. When her foot touched mine, I shifted and moved away. I attributed the whole event to a new California, to that stream of larger life in which they had swum for many years.

"Oh," Anne said, sinking her nipples below the surface, the dark hair in her armpits touching into the steam at the surface of hot water. She had her arms up on the edge like Carl. Perspiration streaked her cheeks and neck. I believed that I was grinning foolishly, and I dipped my chin down into the rising steam. Carl lit a thin marijuana cigarette, drew at it, and passed it across the pool to me. I sucked deep at the smoke, welcoming it. There were drinks and ashtrays on the wood at the lip of the pool.

"Mn," Carl said, after he had exhaled, lifting the joint that I had returned to him and reaching it across to Anne. She shook her head slowly, refusing it, and he moved it back, drew at it again, then passed it over to me. We sat in the hot water and smoked; the glasses and ashtrays at the pool's edge became vibrant, and the steam rose up into an even blacker night. Carl mumbled something about pleasure. In a while I saw Anne's arms stiffen, and then she lifted herself up into the thinning steam above us.

"Enough for me," she said, and I saw her breasts dip away from her as she climbed from the pool, then saw her belly and the wet black hair at her crotch.

"A little longer for me," Carl said, watching her as she lifted her robe up from the deck and slipped into it. When he turned his head from her, it was as if he were canceling her presence out entirely. He smiled at me through the mist. It was a strange smile, one without any quality at all that I could determine.

"Okay?" he said.

"Okay," I said, and watched the swing of Anne's hips, the water dampening the robe over her buttocks as she walked away, down the deck and into the darkness at the door.

Karla arrived in the late afternoon the following day. She brought two children with her, two little girls, and a box of slides and a projector. Coppie had stayed close to me most of the day, looking up into my face and speaking with quiet anticipation. Karla would bring the pictures and the girls; they could all play in the yard with the animals. But the pictures seemed the important thing. When they did arrive, he stayed even closer to me, almost walking on the sides of my shoes as I passed from room to room, watching Anne in the kitchen, going out to see Abbey feed the swans. Carl had gone into town to get the ducks before the three showed up, and Coppie and I found ourselves alone in a house full of women. This seemed to unnerve him a little. I felt his head brush my elbow, his hand always insistent along my hip and leg.

And from the time we all arose in the early morning, Anne had been touching me too. It would be her hand on my shoulder as she pointed things out, her hip striking against me as she passed by, and while I was sitting and eating or drinking coffee, or sitting in a chair on the deck in the crisp air, I would feel her fingers at my neck and shoulders, her searching massage as she directed the children, telling Coppie to give me some room, Dana to wash the dishes, or spoke to Carl. Carl did not seem to like it that she was touching me, but he didn't speak of it. I caught his look though and the way his jaw tightened. If the touching bothered Coppie, I was unaware of it. He only moved closer to my side, pressing and running his cheek against my shirt.

When the time came for Carl to go for the ducks, he asked me if I wanted to go with him, and for some reason, though Coppie's insistence was beginning to get to me and I could have used the freedom from him, I decided to stay behind. Carl simply nodded and then left, and I think from then on some small place hardened between us. It was not that he didn't continue to reach out in conversation in that passive way of his, but that he absented himself from most talk of the past, wanting only to speak of what he was doing now or what he had done in the past that was separate from our shared experience then, separate I thought too from his experience with Anne and his children. He spoke of climbing and skiing, his music collection, a little about his teaching.

I was in the living room. I could hear the children in the yard beyond the kitchen. Coppie had left my side when he heard loud laughter coming from the girls. Anne and Karla were somewhere else in the house. It was good to be alone, briefly at least, and I looked at the primitive prints on the long living room wall and lifted and turned some of the pots and urns on the shelf below them. One of the pots had a hunchbacked flute player on its side. It seemed very old but was almost completely intact, just a few chips at the base and rim and the once-vivid paint almost all still there, though faded. When I lifted it, I heard a sharp click and froze with it in my hands, thinking for a moment that I had broken it. But then I shook it carefully and found that the sound was that of a stone, a piece of flint or something, in the long curved handle, something loose in the hollow, placed there intentionally by its maker.

The flute player sat on a large brown rock, hunched over, his hump like a bag with something alive in it carried high on his back, pushing against his neck. The flute was long but only half visible, remnants of fingers on the stops; the player's elbows stuck out and his head tilted a little as if he were listening to his own music. There were other figures that his playing seemed to send around the pot. They were vague now, but they looked like children or old men, or animals. They were dancing to the music, their movements animated and in a kind of slow frenzy. They were close together and some were touching or holding on to one another, but they didn't seem in any way geared to touchdancing. Each was in his or her own world, that world possessed and structured by the tooting. And the flute player seemed above it all; he *was* above it all on the pot's surface. There were a few markings that looked like clouds and birds, and his head was up at a level with them. This made him a kind of god, a figure half in heaven. But his feet were on the ground to the rock's side, his toes gnarled and clearly gripping at the earth. His loins were indistinct now, the paint worn away, and yet they could be guessed at as massive, muscular, and made for travel. He was naked, but the dancers wore garments, even the ones that might have been animals.

The pebble or flint in the handle seemed a kind of joke or at least a surprise to make you laugh, it was so bright and sharp sounding, and it broke the concentrated yearning to hear the music of the flute itself, turning the pot to see the player and the dancers. The bottom of the handle was affixed close to the flute player's head, the other end in the birds and clouds at the rim. Holding the pot upright and shaking it, the pebble would rattle and ascend, a music without clear rhyme or melody climbing from the flute player's mouth up and into the vaguer air of another world.

"He's Kokopelli." Her voice was soft, but it startled me; I had been so concentrated in my study of the pot. Then Karla was at my elbow, looking down at the hunchbacked figure in my hands.

"It's an Anasazi piece," she said. "Carl got it on one of his summer trips. He said around Yosemite, but I wouldn't count on that."

"All of these?" I said, looking along the shelf. There must have been ten pieces at least that looked like the one I held, various shapes, but the same color to the clay, similar-looking figures.

"I'd have to think so. They're seven hundred years old at least. The sites are mostly in Utah." We heard the children's voices rise up a little from the yard, not laughter this time but yelling. And Karla raised her hand, interrupting our conversation, and turned and headed for the kitchen.

She was tall and rather striking. In her worn and tightfitting jeans, her black satin shirt and paisley sash, she looked like one of the models I had spent time with when I was with Anson, and noting this I missed Anson for a reason that gave me discomfort, a slight pang of guilt. If she thought I had no interest in women in that certain way, I could get close to her, and I was missing Anson as a tool.

She had beautiful dark hair, like Anne's, but hers was fuller and had a wave to it. Her face was bold, with heavy features that I found out later came from a bit of Indian blood of a tribe I have forgotten. She moved like a model, had that slight slump, loose in the hips, and had a way of gesturing boldly with her hands and arms. Her daughters, one Coppie's age and the other just a little younger, seemed to imitate her walk and gestures, and they were also dressed beyond their ages. Both wore tight pants, had their hair done in womanly ways, and wore the kinds of slightly baggy shirts that hinted that there might be the shapes of breasts beneath them. Once in the yard with the other children, they acted their ages, but in the house with their mother and Anne and I they slipped around objects and sat in chairs with the kind of careful conviction of adults.

"And what do you do?" Karla said. She was seated beside me on the couch, her legs crossed, a thin gold strap of her heeled sandal cutting across a thin ankle. Anne was in a chair across from us on the other side of the glass coffee table. We were drinking herbal tea.

"I told you before, on the phone, remember? Physiotherapy, like me," Anne said.

"Mostly massages now," I said.

"I could always use one of those," she said, shaking her hair out over her shoulders and smiling. She was acting provocatively, but in a friendly and formal way. Still, her comment seemed inappropriate, too familiar, and I felt I was blushing slightly. If she saw this she didn't acknowledge it, but moved gracefully into her next question.

"Where's Carl?"

"Out for the ducks," Anne answered.

"And you're a photographer?" I said.

"Yes," she said. "I take pictures of children." She looked over at Anne. "Have you decided about it yet?"

"Not yet," Anne said. "I'm not really sure if the girls want to."

"Abbey is almost too old already."

"For what?" I said.

"For the kinds of pictures I'm taking."

I looked up at a slight sound and saw Coppie standing to the side of the fireplace. He was grinning, leaning forward a little, arms to his sides, and his slight body was almost vibrating with excitement.

"David, Daddy's back," he said. "He's got the ducks!" Then he turned and rushed out of sight, and in a moment we heard a door slam in the distance.

"Better go see, I guess," Anne said, and the three of us rose and went to the small section of deck that ran along the kitchen end of the house.

Carl had the ducks lined up beside each other on a redwood table, and all five of the children were gathered around so close that Carl had to elbow between them in order to make his preparations. The children were smiling and touching each other, but they were quiet, slightly intense in their interest in what was going to happen. There were six ducks, all plucked, and it was clear from the parchment color and texture of their skins and the slightly elongated shapes of their bodies that they had been hanging and drying somewhere for quite a while. Their webbed feet were still brightly yellow and white, and their eyes were closed, their smooth bills no longer glossy but looking as if they had been lightly brushed with steel wool. On the deck beside the table was a tall cylindrical tank, painted bright red, with a complex system of valves and gauges at its top. Coppie was standing close to it, glancing at it occasionally, being careful not to touch it. The tank stood in a braced structure, a kind of miniature dolly with small rubber wheels at its four corners. On the deck beside the tank was a large pile of coiled tubing, plastic and rubber, in various bright colors. Beside the bodies of the ducks on the tabletop was a small kit of some sort, a heavy plastic container the size of a cigar box.

There was not enough room around the table for all of us, and Anne and I stood back a little, looking over the heads of the children. As Anne leaned forward, standing on her toes, she put her hand on my shoulder.

"This is *some* business," Karla said, her hand on the shoulders of Abbey and Dana as she leaned over them, and all the children laughed. Carl looked up, aware of their interest in the things that he was doing and was about to do. His expression was blank, but I noted what I thought was a certain intensity in the lines at the edges of his eyes. We were close around him and attentive, but he gave no sign at all that this pleased him.

He stepped to the end of the table and rolled the tank a few feet away from it. Then he reached toward Coppie, not touching him, and urged him back and to the side. I realized that I had not seen him touch Coppie even once since my arrival. The tank turned slightly as it came to rest on its wheels, but I could see no marking of any kind to indicate what it might contain. Then Carl opened the small kit that sat beside the ducks and reached in and withdrew a ball of what looked like thin nylon twine and six long and blunt needles, each with a small shut-off valve attached to it.

"Scissors, Coppie," he said, and Coppie looked up at him, startled, and then rushed into the kitchen. We could hear a clatter as a door slid open and then another.

While we waited, Carl took the end of the twine from the ball and gathered the feet of the nearest duck in his hands; then he looped the twine around the sticklike ankles and knotted it. When Coppie came back with the scissors, he cut the twine string, leaving a length of ten feet or so gathered in a loose circle on the table at the duck's bound feet. He proceeded then to tie the legs of each of the ducks, leaving the same length of twine for each.

While he fussed with the dead birds, I noticed that Abbey and Dana were getting restless. He was taking a long time, moving his hands in slow and methodical ways, and they were shifting from foot to foot, each glancing away from the table at times, watching birds and the slight wave of the trees. Only Coppie was tensed and intently watching every move that Carl made. Karla's girls might have been restless too, but they did not show it in a way that children usually did. The small one, Beth, stood with her hip slung out a little, her hand resting on it. She watched the table, but she seemed to be posing in some way. She would turn her head slightly, move her hand to adjust her hair or touch away some invisible speck from her cheek. She, like her sister Nina, had a smile on her face, but the smile was somehow inappropriate to the circumstances, not a smile of delight or interest but one of boredom, or bored seductiveness, or wistful memory of something intimate and private. They both seemed perfectly at ease where they were, as if they were not really there at all.

When I looked down from their faces, I saw that

Carl was finished with the tying and was beginning to insert the needles under their parchmentlike skins somewhere near their groins. Coppie flinched at each insertion, moving his body back a little, his hands gripping the edge of the table as he watched.

After he had taped the needles in place, Carl went to the piles of colored tubing on the deck and brought six lengths of it back with him. Then, as he attached an end of a tube to each of the valves protruding from the ducks, he began to talk. His voice was soft but unhesitant. It was almost as if he were delivering a lecture of some sort.

"Freeing the skin from the fatty layer beneath it can be done in various ways. The skin can be cut away with a knife, the fat then scraped free with some instrument. Or one can cook the duck using copious amounts of pepper to dissolve the fatty layer. Neither of these ways is the best way; with both of them the skin can be damaged, making for an unattractive presentation at mealtime. The best way is with air, inflating the skin slightly, causing it to pull away from the fatty layer gradually and without any serious trauma. Doing this is not uncommon. A bicycle pump is a good bet. I, however, like to use helium; it's lighter and makes for a cleaner job."

I glanced at Anne, whose smile was broad and fixed and slightly panicked, then at Karla, who I thought had not really been listening at all. She was watching her girls at the table across from us, measuring and judging their poses.

"Daddy!" Dana said in a frightened and slightly whining voice, and Carl looked up at her and smiled broadly in a vacant way.

"Almost finished, dear," he said. I would have thought he was speaking to Anne, his voice was so formal and adult, but he was looking a little to the side of Dana's face.

When each duck had its tube attached to it, Carl afffixed the other ends of the tubes to the complex of valves and dials at the top of the cylinder. Then he asked each of us to take a duck, being careful as we carried it, and follow him as he pushed the cylinder down and around the deck to its longer section that ran outside the glass wall of the living room. He gave these instructions very slowly, but with no falter in his voice at all, as if he had memorized them.

There were eight of us, and only six ducks, and Anne and I stepped back from the table, letting the others lift them. The deck was broad, but there were a lot of us and the lengths of tubing and twine dripped and looped over most of the surface of the deck and up from it to the tank and ducks, and the going had to be very slow and careful.

Carl was slightly ahead, pushing the tank, but he glanced back every few feet, checking for twists and warning us when he saw pending diffficulties. The children stayed in front, Karla behind them, and Anne and I stayed as far to the side as possible, pressing against the outer railing of the deck as we moved along. Those carrying ducks had to stay close to one another, and the slowness of the progress was unnatural enough so that they bumped into one another from time to time, shifting the ducks up or down in their hands as tubes and twine brushed against each other or against those on ducks carried beside them. There were brief outcries of exclamation, quick words of warning, and these were mixed with Carl's measured instructions and guidance. Karla and Carl seemed equally uncomfortable with the slowness of the pace, and the slight jostling of the children had a way of forcing them to walk like children too, their steps abbreviated, their torsos tight, and their arms moving almost in adolescent gesture. Even their faces looked a little childlike, their lips pursed and their eyes bright and moist. Karla's children no longer moved like models, and even Anne and I, though to the side and slightly disengaged from the progress, stepped awkwardly, our fingers running along the railing's surface.

In a very long time we reached the turn of the deck and made our way down the living room length of it, and when we got to the middle of that length Carl instructed Karla and the children to spread out at equal intervals and place the ducks on the railing of the deck. This too had to be done with care, making sure that tubes were not tangled.

When the ducks were in place, the duck carriers stepped back from them, lifting their feet from the coils of tubes and the hanging twine, until they had made their way to the glass wall of the living room. Then as we watched him Carl set to work with the final steps in the process.

The bodies of the ducks rested on the railing, a good five feet between them, their heads hanging from their limp necks visible on the far side and on ours their yellow, webbed feet. There was about the same distance between us as well, where we stood in a row with our backs to the sliding glass doors that formed the long wall of the living room. Only Coppie was out of order. He stood tight against me, his right hand tucked under my belt, holding on to it like a handle, his head cocked to the side, pressing into my hip. When I looked down into his hair, I saw he was watching Carl. He was shivering slightly; I could feel his body vibrate along my leg. When I looked to each side and down the line, I saw that the rest, except for Anne, were watching Carl as well. Anne was watching me and Coppie, and I thought I saw something slightly desperate in her look. Then I heard the hammer, and when I looked back I saw Carl raising it and bringing it down.

He was tacking the terminal ends of the twine attached to the duck's ankles into the top of the railing. The tacks were small, and after he had started them he wound the ends of the twine around them under their heads, then drove them in. When he had finished with this he moved back to the cylinder in its dolly and adjusted it, tracing each tube that ran from it to the needles in the ducks' groins, making sure that each tube was free of the others. Then he turned to each duck and opened the shut-off valves attached to the needles. When he had checked the last duck in the line, he turned toward us and smiled.

"This is it," he said, and then he returned to the cylinder, his back to us.

I saw him bend down over the system of cylinder, tubes and gauges, then saw in the way his back tightened and shifted that he was making adjustments. When he was finished he rose up a little to the side of the cylinder and stood erect, his left hand resting on the metal knob at its top. Then he slowly turned the knob, and I could hear the beginning rush of the gas as it flowed into the tubing.

In the first moments the ducks remained the same, limp and flattened and hanging over the sides of the railing, though the tubes began to writhe and stiffen along the deck's surface. Then I could see some swelling in the ducks' bodies, and one by one their heads began to come to the horizontal in the air, their necks thickening. One at the far end began to rock then and roll slightly from side to side as its body swelled to an oval. In a moment, all the ducks were rocking. I felt Coppie press tight into my hip and watched the ducks come up, their limp ankles dragging along the railing until they seemed to be standing, their yellow, webbed feet doing an awkward tap on the wood. Then they were in the air, their dangling feet inches above the railing. They rose up, not quite in unison, until each reached the end of its tether, the thin nylon line tacked into the wood, and as they reached that terminus and the line snapped taut they bounced a little and drifted to either side, their feet kicking, their heads rotating on their stiff, inflated necks.

They moved toward each other in their drifts, but they did not reach each other. Their heads turned at times, as if to make note of impending contact, and then rotated back to look at a place above us over the roof and into the sky. Then they began to settle in their bobbing. They looked like nothing but inflated ducks, plucked oval animals, as the late-afternoon breeze pushed them against their lines, their beaks lifting and scenting, their webbed feet bound and touching where they hung, standing in the air, against the sky and clouds.

"Kip and Banyon?"

Her voice came muffled out of the blanket and the edge of the pillow against which she had pushed her face. It was dark now, only the light of a candle illuminating her body and the white towel that crossed over her hips, covering her buttocks, where she lay on her stomach under my hands. I could see a duck bobbing through the high window of Anne's bedroom. The deck was illuminated with spots, and the ducks had been drifting there in clear view throughout the late afternoon and evening. I knew that the backyard had lights as well, and that the children were out there now with the animals.

We had sat with them, watching them eat their early dinner, and I could hear the faint sounds of Anne in the kitchen, the clack of dishes and silver. I wasn't sure where Carl was.

I worked her lower back and the backs of her thighs; that's what she had asked for. The oil I used was a mix of clarified animal fats, scented with a perfume that smelled vaguely oriental, very subtle, but tart as it heated in the friction and came through. Her words were mixed with moans as I held her waist in my hands, then pressed my thumbs in toward her spine. We would see her slides in a while, and then the children would go to bed and we would eat our dinner on our laps in the living room, cold leftover salmon with mayonnaise, and would drink tequila.

In the beginning she thought I had more in mind than the rubbing, and when I came into the room to find her already undressed with the towel over her, I could see that her body was tense, the muscles in her shoulders and legs visibly bunched. She had shaken her hair out to cover all of her head, and I could see nothing of her face and features. But now she had swept her hair back. Her ear and cheek were visible, and I knew where her mouth was and could see the edge of her brow. I had touched the creases below her buttocks, had run my fingers close to the cleft, and when I had done nothing but that, had pressed her only for her deep comfort there, she had relaxed and spread her legs slightly and given in with trust.

Now she was talking. "Kip and Banyon?" She seemed reluctant to start at first, as if her embarkation would take her to places she would rather not arrive at, to things of unpleasant memory. I kept pressing into her, and before long her faltering ceased and she was telling me details.

"Kip and Banyon were here earlier, at different times, and I'm sure they didn't know each other then. I think they were each here for a year or so. It was before I came. Maybe I was here at the end of Kip's stay; I'm not sure. There's talk among some in the town still, I know, but because of what I do with my pictures nobody talks to me about it, or about most anything, for that matter. I'm sure I'm talked about as well. This is a small town, very tight and conservative. A woman without a husband, doing what I do, well, it's no wonder.

"Banyon was the first of the two. And I think he had known them vaguely from somewhere, had known Carl at least, and he came for a brief visit and stayed a whole year. Then, when he left, it was Kip, I guess in the same circumstances. Both were about the same age as Carl and Anne. In the town they thought it was a *ménage* both times, but I think I know better than that. Kip was a carpenter or handyman of some kind. I believe I recall seeing him in the town once when I first got here. He looked like a drifter, was silent and guarded, a little frail and wild-looking."

I thought of Anson as she described her recollection of Kip, and pressed, almost involuntarily, close to her crotch, sexually close to it. But she only grunted softly and moaned and opened her legs a little more. I had her trust and I did not further abuse it.

"Not a *ménage* because I came across them, together with Carl, in Yosemite about three summers ago. That was a strange coincidence. I was there taking pictures for a travel mag. I hardly knew Carl and Anne at all then, had only met and talked to them briefly at some art opening here in the town. I recognized him at a distance though. He was with the other two, outside, somewhere in the park itself, and he was touching both of them. When he saw me, he stopped. The other two had been swishing a little, but they stopped that when he saw me and talked to them. It came to me very quick that they were sleeping together and that they had probably been doing that when the two were here in Sharonville. I knew right away that the one was Kip, and guessed that the other was Banyon. They had a girl with them.

"Luna was her name. She was about seven years old, very thin, and a little awkward, I thought— serious and formal when they introduced us. They all seemed to be keeping an eye on her. One of them always went with her when she moved away, went to look at a tree or rock or some tourists moving along the paths. Carl didn't have much to say, but the other two were effusive. He told me that he came here most every summer. The three of them climbed those large rock pillars in the park. Anne wasn't along this trip. I found out later that she never was, nor were his children.

"I had a hat and scarf, some sunglasses and some other things in my bag, the kinds of things I always carried when I was out shooting, in case I ran across a kid I wanted to shoot. I'd been doing kids for a while already then, and I asked if I could shoot Luna.

"I don't think Carl liked the idea at all. But things were touchy, tentative I thought among the four of them, as if they were out together for the first time in this grouping, and Kip and Banyon seemed to get a kick out of the idea, and Carl stopped after a few beginning objections. I got a couple shots of the girl sitting on a rock, pretty good ones as it turned out. I think I've got them with me.

"And that's about all of it, I guess. I took the pictures of the girl, we all had a Coke together, and then we said good bye. I'm sure those three were together sexually. I've never spoken of it to Anne. Really, we're just casual friends. The kids go to the same school. She's shown some interest in my photographs. We don't socialize much at all, just when the kids get together. Carl acknowledged our meeting only once, in front of Anne. He didn't mention the other two or the girl, and I got it that he wanted to close the subject off once and for all by noting it."

"What about those pots in the living room?" I said softly. I was moving my hands over her left scapula, feeling the edges of her trapezius, working in toward her upper thorax. I had leaned down over her, and my mouth was close to her ear. I felt her breath against my lips when she answered, smelled something fruity.

"Nothing about that," she whispered. "But they don't come from Yosemite. You can bet on that for sure. And they're not legal."

The change in Carl materialized for me in the way I imagined a character developing and then becoming fixed for an author writing a novel. He too now seemed to be who he was, and not that memory of him that I had held vaguely for many years. And what he now was made me question my memory of him in the past entirely. Perhaps there had been some inkling of the base of his character for me then, but search my thoughts of him as I might I could not find it. And I did not think, either, that he had changed, that he was fundamentally different from the Carl I had known then. I could only think that I had not really known him at all.

We had sat with the children while they ate, and I had seen him watch their mouths move, their fingers tear the flesh of the chicken from the bone. Not one of them alone would have appeared ravenous at the trough, but together, and in the fact that there was no clatter of utensils on our part, no grind of mastication or flavor to divert us, the sounds and sights of their feeding was almost frightening in its energetic, desperate insistence. Even Karla's girls, Beth and Nina, had abandoned their veneer of sophistication. Wisps of their hair hung, disheveled, from their pins and combs, they had milk mustaches, and their silk shirts were stained with grease.

Karla and Anne were talking across the table as

the children ate, but Carl was watching them, and I watched Carl. He had a faint smile on his face, and I took it that he was finding some satisfaction in what he saw as their gluttonous pleasure. But I didn't think it was that. It was more desperate, more needful, as if eating were their only sure place of satisfaction, temporary and fleeting. Even Coppie was drawn into the feeding. His eyes closed as he swallowed, forcing the half-chewed gobbets down his throat. I don't think he was hungry, but was only reaching for the momentary safety that the others seemed to be finding.

At times their heads would come up from their plates, pieces of flesh in their teeth, their cheeks smeared with fat, and they would look at the ducks bobbing in the air through the glass wall. It was twilight, and the ducks were aglow in the wash of the low sun. The light had tricked their eyes into opening; they were small glittering stones now above their burnished bills. But Carl never looked at the ducks. He had his chair slightly back from the table. He was no longer the center of attention he had been while stringing the ducks up. The children ate and ignored him. The women looked at each other and talked. Anne's eyes went to the children at times, but I could see no surprise or outrage in them, rather a deep, sad resignation, as if she recognized this as their only real solace and bore it because of that in silence.

I watched Carl, but he did not know this. His mouth was moving, and at first I thought he was imitating, with no awareness of it, the children's chewing. But then I saw that the timing was all wrong and that he was talking, rehearsing something, silently shaping words. When he paused and nodded and pursed his lips and then moved his mouth again, I saw it was a conversation. When I saw his eyes focus, I realized that he was talking to someone no more than a foot from his face.

When the children's meal was finished, Karla began to set up her projector and arrange her slides in the carousel on the now-cleared dining table. Rather than turn the lights on the deck off, Carl pulled the thick drapes across the wall of windows, closing off our vision of the floating ducks. The children were left to play while Karla was getting ready, and Anne took down the print that hung on the wall at the end of the dining room, providing a screen.

I had no idea of what to expect from the slides, but I did know that it involved pictures of children and that there was some hint that in the future Anne's two girls might be involved in it. Beth and Nina had acted blase about the showing, but Dana and Abbey had brought the subject of the pictures up from time to time. Coppie would step aside when the pictures were mentioned, look away, or interrupt, urging another subject entirely. He would pull at my sleeve or lean against me, as if he wanted to keep me away from the slides as well. This all seemed odd because of his excited anticipation of Karla's coming earlier on. I didn't know what to make of it.

When the white square on the wall was adjusted to a proper height and focus, Carl went to the yard and called the children in. The girls gathered around the table and found seats. Anne sat down as well, and so did I. Coppie stood at the side of my chair, his head brushing from time to time at my shoulder, and Carl moved to the light switch on the wall. The room went dark, and Karla clicked the first slide in.

It was a picture of a woman sitting in a white wicker chair in a yard, under a large flowering tree. She was at a distance, and her features were not clear. She was dressed in a billowing flowered dress that fell to her feet; she had a large feathered hat on her head, and over her shoulder a small parasol. Her left arm was raised, holding what looked like a long cigarette up to her mouth. Her legs were crossed, and her black patent leather shoes were visible at the hem of her dress. There was a massive car parked beyond the fence of the yard, a good distance on the other side of the tree.

"That's Beth!" Dana said.

"Of course it is! You've seen this before, silly," Abbey said in the darkness.

It was indeed Beth. When I knew it, the size of the car gave it away. It was not gigantic at all. It was the tree, the chair, and the figure that were out of scale. They were child size and the car was normal.

"It was something with distance and scale I was trying," Karla said from above us where she stood at the projector. "I thought the car was interesting."

There was a click, and another slide appeared. This and the next few were of Beth and Nina together. They were photographs of the children in dress up clothing: dresses that trailed behind them; women's high-heeled shoes, in which their feet were swallowed up; hats sliding down to their ears; even fur pieces draped to their waists. And strings of artificial pearls and long, looping earrings. In each they wore makeup, too much of it, applied in a childlike way. They were standing in bedrooms, on porches, and out in yards. They were not posing, but seemed to have been caught candidly in their play. Still, there was a slight hint of staginess in the pictures, and it was clear that they were dressed for the occasion of them.

Karla commented upon the slides, talking again of scale and speaking somewhat vaguely of the girls becoming women by putting on their garments. Coppie grew restless as she spoke, and I felt his hand running very lightly over my shoulder and along my arm. He was making little sounds in his throat, something between swallows and breaths.

Then the clothing in the photographs became tailored to the children's size, the dresses and shoes began to fit, and pieces of lingerie replaced blouses and skirts. They began to appear in bedrooms exclusively, lounging in beds or in armoires, half dressed and strangely provocative, the bright, clear eyes of their childhood betrayed by postures and what I took to be instruction in looks, head tilts and makeup. They gazed out from under carefully arranged hair. Their eyes lowered to reveal light rose and blue on their lids. Their wet lips were moistened now with lipstick rather than the animal fat that I had seen on them at the table earlier. They would have been women but for the fact that in every picture there was an object or piece of a gesture designed to betray the fact that they were children.

"It is all intentional," Karla said, softly and seriously.

"Yes, I can see that," Anne said without expression.

Nobody laughed or pointed. Beth and Nina

spoke somewhat archly, in the way the models had spoken to me when I was with Anson, about poses and lighting. Karla hummed her approval.

"Do you want to do that?" Anne said in the darkness.

"I don't know," Dana said, and Coppie said "No" at the same time.

Abbey laughed at that, but her laugh was tentative and quickly cut off. I heard Carl shift his weight and grunt quietly in the distance behind us.

"Look at this one," Karla said, and clicked another slide into view.

It was a photograph of a large bathroom with a large lounging chair in the middle of it on a wine-colored carpet. The chair was tan and covered in cut velvet. To the left in the background, the hard porcelain of the toilet was visible and beyond it a dressing table covered with bottles of perfume, ointments and powders in various crystal containers. They were reflected in the mirror above the table, appearing in such abundance that they suggested a kind of surfeit. Both Beth and Nina were in the chair, and on the floor beside them there was a green teddy bear, with green, sparkling eyes, sitting with his legs spread and his arms gathered across his chest. The two girls were dressed only in silk teddies, one black and one red, with matching highheeled shoes. They both wore earrings and each had strings of fake pearls and other beads, long rows hanging to their hips. Their legs were pulled up in the chair, and Nina had her arm around Beth's shoulder. She was leaning into her, her arm across her body, her hand resting on Beth's knee. They both had their hair pulled tightly up and piled on their heads, affixed there with bone combs and jeweled stickpins. Their makeup matched their garments, red and black, and Nina held something between her teeth, a ball of red bubble gum, I thought. They were both smiling innocently. On Beth's shoulder, to the side of the strap of her teddy, there was a black speck on her alabaster skin, a large fly, its wings slightly elevated, luminous and translucent, even the wires of its legs, pressing small indentations in the soft white turn of her shoulder, clearly visible.

Karla went on with the slides, and I began to feel my eyes begin to ache from the sight of them.

The girls remained quiet, intensely interested in what they were seeing. I would forget that Coppie was at my shoulder, but then I would feel his touch again and remember him.

Near the end, a slide came up that was different from the others, less polished in technique, hastier in setting. I heard Carl shift in his chair behind me when it appeared.

"Who's that?" Coppie said, his voice dry and raspy at my shoulder.

"Somebody I shot a few years ago, down south of here."

The girl sat on a large rock in an open place. There were trees in the distance behind her, but none close enough to give shade. She had a large floppy hat on, and she held a pair of what looked like fancy rhinestone-studded sunglasses in her fist across her chest. The hand that held the glasses and the whole arm were slightly hazy in focus, and I guessed she had snatched the glasses off a fraction before the shutter closed. The hat was tilted back on her head, not as it should have been worn, and the whole of her thin face and forehead were visible in the frame. The palm of her other hand rested flat on the rock to the side of her worn jeans. She wore sad little blue strapped sandals, cheap and frayed, and her toenails were torn down to the quick. Her shirt was a drab check, and strands of her bone-white hair stuck out from under the hat, brushing her shoulders. She was about seven years old. "Luna," I thought.

There were human shadows falling across the ground in front of her, more than one, but I could tell that she was not looking at the source of them. Her eyes went directly into the lens, into the dining room where we were sitting, into our eyes, and the look was powerful in its focused vacancy. She was not looking at us, but through us, not into us in a visionary way, but through to a world of total inaction and mistrust, a world in which there was no single thing to be measured against another for value. I thought it must be a gray world, one that could offer nothing.

Worse was the resignation. Her look and posture, the empty defiance of the snatched-off sunglasses, her mutilated nails, her palm on the rock without function, her hair that seemed drained of color, and those blasted and washed-out hazel eyes, all gathered into an image that was beyond despair. There was nothing any more of the past in her. I could not believe in a single memory, nostalgia, or plan.

The ducks floated, straight in the air from their tethers now. There was no breeze, and though they rotated to face each other and look in on us, they were no longer drifting to the side at all. Some were higher than others. It was a staggered line, and as I looked out the glass wall at them, I saw that the lower ones had deflated slightly, and that the twine tacked to the deck railing below each of them was no longer taut in the air, but was hanging in limp loops. Carl saw it too.

"The skin's leaking a bit. That's good," he said. "The pores are opening," and he pushed himself to his feet and went out one of the sliding doors to the deck.

I saw him go to the cylinder and reach for the valve at the top. Then the ducks slowly rose again, until the lines were taut and each floated at the same level, bobbing slightly when they reached it, then coming to rest, the wiggles in their webbed feet settling, only the black sky now behind them, the trees invisible on this moonless night.

I watched them, and even after Carl had come back in and seated himself again, I kept watching them. I was avoiding Karla's look, which I felt was on me. Anne was sitting next to her on the couch, and I was in a chair across from them, low mugs of tequila over ice on the glass coffee table between us. Carl sat in another chair, faced so that he could look at all of us and see the ducks from the corner of his eye at the same time. The children were in bed now. It was close to ten. The cold salmon sat in a dish with plates and silver beside it on the tea caddy that Anne had rolled in. I could smell the hot bread in the straw basket beside the platter.

"You know, it's really Coppie I'd like to photograph," Karla said. It was Carl who spoke before Anne could respond.

"Fat chance," he said.

"I didn't think so," Karla said. "It would be interesting though."

Anne got up and began serving the salmon.

"They'll be ready by tomorrow morning," Carl said, looking out at the ducks. Their bodies were fully oval again, smooth in their inflation.

"Did you know that Lorca stole clothing from the store?" Anne said.

"Who's Lorca?" Karla said.

"His first wife."

Calling her that rung hollow. There was no second, at least not yet. I had no idea what she was trying to get at.

"I knew that," I said.

"She took colorful things, after that woman had been there, the old one, casual western wear, bright knits and paisleys." Anne shifted in her chair, handing the basket of hot bread across to me. Her eyes were bright with the information, but the shape of her mouth was enigmatic. I searched my mind to remember something, wondering where she might have hidden them.

"How much?" I said.

"Oh, a lot!" she said. "I guess a whole wardrobe, you could say. It was just before we left L.A. though, and I never saw them. I'm not sure about it all. You know, it was shocking, and we were leaving. She sent me one letter after that, but she didn't mention them. It was an odd letter."

I knew about two dresses only.

"What was odd about it?" I said.

"Well, I don't know; it was very vague. There were no details in it at all. Not a bit like Lorca."

"What was she like?" Karla said.

Her question hurt my eyes in its quick inappropriateness, all the more since she addressed it to Anne. I thought I had then a hint of the flavor of what I found wrong about her photography.

"She was beautiful," Anne said, saving a bit of the situation.

"Hair the color of that wine rug in your pictures," Carl said.

I looked sharply at him, but he was looking at the wall across the room, his eyes unfocused. Her hair had not been that color. It was black, like Anne's, but I thought he was sure about what he said, though he was wrong.

I had the mug of tequila at my lips, and over it

I could see Carl rolling a marijuana cigarette on a sheet of yellow paper on the coffee table. I hesitated to drink. Dinner had been quick and perfunctory. Carl lit the joint and drew deeply at it, then handed it to me. I put the mug down, took it and drew at it, then reached it across to Karla, letting the smoke stream out of my lungs. We were through with talk about Lorca and the stolen clothing now. There was some brief talk about Karla's pictures, talk in which I tried to participate a little and Carl kept silent.

Carl turned in his chair and checked the ducks. I could see that two of them were lowering again.

"I'll give them a few minutes," he said, speaking to himself.

"Too much with the ducks!" Karla said, and she and I laughed, Anne joining in, leaning back in her chair and looking over at my shoulders and at my neck. She licked her lips, her tongue like a bright pink arrow.

"Ooo, this is powerful!" she said.

"It is that," Carl said.

I saw Anne was drifting in her high. She was looking along my shoulders and arms, studying my clavicle, my chest. Her lips were moist and her eyes wide and swimming a little.

"The ducks," Carl said. I heard the words completely formed in my head, audible, before they entered the space between us. They bounced a little when he spoke them, and I turned my head past Karla and Anne and looked out through the glass wall at the deck. Two in the middle were no more than a foot from the railing now, and the slight movement of their feet suggested that they were reaching down, like parachutists, searching for a foothold in landing. I watched the loops in the twine and had to pull my head away with the muscles in the side of my neck to avoid getting fixed in gazing. Anne was already talking, gesturing, and I came back to her in midsentence.

"... what she did. And it was preparatory for some change or leaving. She backed off from our friendship. Something about painting."

"Lorca again?" I said, and Anne looked at me. Then her eyes lost focus and she grinned, losing the train. I felt Carl rise to his feet, and when I turned I saw he was heading to the glass wall, a little stiff-legged. He went out a sliding door and moved to the tank. The ducks shot up in the air, their tethers quivering, and bobbed violently for a few moments.

"Christ! He'll send them to outer space!" Karla said. Then Carl came back in, took the bottle of tequila from the glass table, and filled all our mugs.

"How about a tub?" he said, his words a little too loud in the temporary silence in the room. Anne was on her feet and heading for my chair, and when I looked across at Karla I saw she was slumped, her head on the back of the couch, her eyes gazing up into the beams of the ceiling. No one responded to what Carl had said, and he sat down carefully in his chair and crossed his arms.

Anne circled behind my chair. I saw her hand touch the back of it at my head, then felt the tips of her fingers at my shirt collar, then at my neck, a drag of nail below my ear.

"Sure," she said. "In a few minutes."

"Sure," Karla said, her voice rising above all of us in the air.

I felt Anne's thumbs press into the muscles at

the base of my neck, smelled a perfume from the distant past, and heard something deep, moist, and despairing in her throat.

The steam rose in a thick, perfect cylinder from the hole in the far end of the deck, thinning and then dissipating into the black night well above our heads. It was cool, and when I removed my pants I felt the pleasant bite of it high on the backs of my thighs. My groin dampened immediately as I faced the tub. I could see the two women, ghostly, through the steam, and then the curves of their naked bodies, neuter and unformed, as they stretched and moved and lowered themselves into the hot water.

Carl was already in up to his neck, his head bobbing in the mist at my feet. I stepped down and in then, the water like a hot wire wound around each leg and ascending as I went in. The tub was small, and as I moved to make ready for the shock as my groin entered, my legs struck against other legs, which shifted away or pressed into my own as I sat. Then I was in up to my chest, and settled.

I was still high, but the shock of the air and then of the water had brought me back a little, and I wanted to talk. I felt there was more to say, more to find out and get clear between us. But the mist, though I could see through it slightly now, could see the three heads beside and beyond me, swallowed up the words that were spoken, each sentence seeming to end in a slight moan, and conversation was impossible.

I picked out the words *Lorca* and *ducks* and thought I heard *Kip* once, but I couldn't be sure if it was a name or a click in somebody's throat or a slap of small waves against the wood. I slipped deeper into the water, feeling the ripples against my chin, and thought of my head like a duck's body, suspended, as the others beside and across from me were.

Karla said something I could not make out at all, but it sounded like an invitation. It had a warble in it and a serious laugh. I think Carl spoke, but the steam confused direction and timbre. I know Anne laughed in that strangely despairing way that I had come to hear from her often since my arrival. I recognized her hand on my own on the tub side.

And then all movement and talk ceased. I felt a knee hit against my own, but it moved away. I put my head back and gazed up into the steam. I thought I could see the hard blackness above me. I had no idea whose leg had touched me. The heat of the water had deadened my senses. But my arms were alive. I could feel the wood along the decking beside the pool. I took what I thought was Anne's hand and held it. My head was free of my body, and I was glad for the dark, starless void above me.

As Coppie clung to me in my staying and leaving, so it was that Anson had finally reached out to me in his final weeks.

"You're leaving," Coppie said. "You'll miss the ducks." And before I could answer he was on his feet and beyond the room, something of Anson's tone and weakness left in the air behind him.

"He always does that," Abbey said, "leaves before you can talk."

In the tub we had drifted into a kind of somnolence. My part had been to make no move, and the leg that touched my own had soon enough moved away. It grew too hot in a while, and one by one, like dreamers, we had lifted our bodies up in the rising steam, then shivered against the cold on the decking above the tub.

Before I rose in the morning, Karla and her children had departed, and when I moved to the breakfast table I saw through the wall of windows that the ducks were gone.

Carl was gone too. He was committed to a morning's work, preparing the ski slopes beyond the town in anticipation of the winter snow and activity there, though it was more than six months away. Anne said he would be back by afternoon, but I told her I found I couldn't wait, that I would have to be heading south.

I embraced her at the door and asked her to say my good-byes to Carl. The girls had hugged me and then gone somewhere in the house, but over Anne's shoulder as I held her, I could see Coppie standing beside the fireplace. He was watching intently.

"You don't approve of the pictures, do you?" Anne said into my neck.

"No," I said. "I'd keep the girls away from her."

I felt her head move against my cheek. And then she said that she had not said all there was about Lorca. There was more at least of the flavor of it, maybe some hints about what had happened. She had no more important facts, but she thought we could have gotten closer to the mystery, things about the way she was in those last days before they left.

"Maybe so," I said. "What about Kip and Banyon?"

"That's no mystery at all. You can see it in Coppie. And the girls too. But we don't speak of it. I can't yet."

"And the girl in the photograph?" I said. "What about her?"

"I never saw that one before, but I think that ripped it for me. I won't let the girls get involved with her. I don't think they really want to anyway."

I didn't persist. She seemed to know nothing of what Karla had told me about Yosemite, and when she released me and I could see her face again, I saw that her eyes and lips were moist and that she wanted something else before I left. I'd given her Melchior's New York address, telling her she could reach me care of him. There was no other place that was home for me just then, but I'd felt a need to keep in touch, have a place that she could reach me at least. I'd given it to her privately, while Carl was out of the house. I hadn't checked it with Melchior before leaving. I'd kept a box number in the city, but I didn't figure to be checking it for a long time.

"What is it?" I said.

"I don't know. I've been moving around it for years, I think. Carl and I. It's mostly the kids. You saw the way they ate? Mostly it's Coppie, that nervousness. None of this is good for them. It's not good for me either."

"I'm sorry," I said. "What will you do?"

"Oh, I don't know. I don't know what to do."

"Would money make any difference?" I said. "I could help that way."

"No. Nothing like that. You see this place. Carl gets whatever's needed. I don't know how."

"Maybe it's those pots?"

"Maybe it is," she said. "He tells me nothing."

As if he could hear our interchange, Coppie moved from the fireplace and came out to the door. We were standing apart when he got to us, holding each other's hands. He didn't say anything, but I felt his arms gather around my waist, his head press into my hip. He held fast, but only protested slightly with his grip when, after a few long moments, Anne reached down and pulled his arms away from where he held me. He just stood back then and looked up at me, and there was something in his face or posture or in the still mechanics of his hips and shoulders that reminded me of Anson.

It was well after the winter, the early morning after a late and startling April ice storm in the city, and when I woke the windows were glazed over. Anson slept in the cot beside my bed now, and when I rose to the narrow space between us, I felt his hand at my thigh, his fingers tugging weakly at my pajamas. I looked down at him, his sunken face and the slight protruding of his nose. He was so thin that it was hard to find the configurations of his body among the crumpled sheet folds and tucks of blanket. But his eyes were still clear and bright.

"Get in here with me, will you?" His voice was raspy and without verve.

And then I had him in my arms in the narrow cot. It groaned as he did as I lowered my weight down beside him. His knees touched my knee and his thin chest was like a fragile bird's nest against my own. We said nothing, and he did not weep for anything in his life. I gave him what I could, which was holding him. I could not really protect him, and though we both acknowledged this in some way silently, when he sighed and pressed his face into my shoulder I knew that it was not for nothing. This was the first time, I think, that I had ever touched him. Oh, beyond massage, a handshake, or a brief embrace of greeting. It was too late, I knew, for what it might have been, and I knew too that the might have been was never really a possibility. Knew then, I think, that it had probably never been possible with Lorca either. And then it was I who wept a little, a thing Anson mistook and about which I did not disabuse him; it gave him some comfort.

In the beginnings of that last year, Anson's illness was not apparent to others. The social gatherings and the work went on, and though his weight began to slip and his clothing loosened, most took it as a change in style, and I think I noted that there were other young men, those fresh from art school or new in the city, who mimicked it. I would see them at parties, lingering at respectful distances, their collars resting away from their necks, their pants a little baggy at the knees. The women, I think, sensed it; their looks grew curious and unsettled, and they came to both of us when we were standing alone, came in pairs and stood closer to us than they had before. Their health seemed more robust when they gathered around Anson, and his wit and energy seemed stirred by this, so that their grouping was always animated, the women leaning close to Anson, touching him on arm, shoulder and cheek, as he spoke and made them laugh.

The other men, his business acquaintances and friends, noticed nothing. Anson was doing new and marvelous things with his designs, drawing dresses that were thought of as something on the brink of the new in the industry, and the men seemed hungry for his secret, exhilarated to be in his company.

Anson drew in the mornings, napped in the afternoons, slept very late and deeply on the days following social events. I took him to doctors, but all they could speak about was infection. They gave him antibiotics, but he had reactions. They said massages wouldn't hurt, but they began to pain him a little when I pressed too hard, and after them he was exhausted, and so I limited myself to few and only those in which I used my palms superficially. Anson ceased to talk under them. He would fall asleep halfway through. I persisted beyond the point at which I should have stopped, beginning to realize too late, and desperately, that there were things he might have told me earlier on had I pressed him. I had no idea what these things might be, but as I felt the coming closure of our time together, I recognized the ten years of it as something that I really did not understand. We had been young in our joining, young men sharing a bachelor pad, two youths in a period of moratorium, and that was fine. But we were no longer young, and there was now no conventional device left to justify our bonding. We had moved in view of middle age together, almost there, and I felt that not to understand the years between us was to in some way have wasted them.

And so I tried to push the words from him, going on too long, until sadly he had to tell me. And when he told me, his face and voice muffled by the towel, I knew from the half-despairing tone in his voice that the rubbing had been some kind of surrogate, for him at least, and that he knew that I did not understand this but might when he spoke of its ending. And I did understand it, but I think now that our use of it was different, mine more complex than his, deeper and having more to do with fundamental things, a mire below the physical. But I am not absolutely sure of this, of Anson's feel in the feeling of being massaged.

One morning, Anson asked me to remove his earring. It was only a thin post with a small pearl at the end of it.

"It presses into my lobe when I sleep; I think it wakes me."

"Where did you get it?" I said. "I think you said it was California? "

He was sitting on the edge of his cot, swallowed in his pajamas, his arms resting on his knees, his thinning hair sticking up in twisted spikes.

"No," he said. "It was Utah."

I got some alcohol and a cotton swab and sat on the cot beside him. When I lifted his lobe, I could see a crusty substance in the loop of the fastener. I twisted it carefully on the post, and the crust broke and fell in tiny bits to his leg.

"It was no place to get an earring in those days. I mean you couldn't go into some jewelry store and get it done, a boy couldn't. But there was a place outside of town, a woman's house, where bikers went to get them; I think there were stories too about abortions being done there. It was no hangout, just a house, and a middle-aged woman. She did it with a needle she held under a match. I remember I thought her clothes were strange, leather and a lot of emblems and chains and such. It didn't hurt much, and I bought the earring from her. But this isn't the one. I got this one from Maudie."

The fastener came away easily, but when I pulled the post out it was moist with a clear liquid. Then I swabbed both sides of his lobe with alcohol.

"Utah," he said. "Maybe I should have stayed there."

202

"Not a chance," I said, and touched his shoulder and shook him lightly. He lifted his head then and smiled wanly up at me.

The bitter winter faded and the first tight buds of spring began to push their delicate colors from their encapsulated husks. And with the slowly rising temperature and gradual unpeeling of the many layers that women wore in those days, the fall lines passed from Anson's renderings into first cuttings and pinnings, crude and primitive joinings of fabric that were like premature births, featureless but with promise, like the first growth of spring.

Anson removed little of what he had worn in winter, and I remembered him standing in his open overcoat watching a model who had her side to him. Only that one side of her was draped in heavy patches that when sewn together would be a fall cape. Her other shoulder was dressed in cotton, bright colors, vertical stripes falling in many pleats to her knee; she wore sneakers and her legs were bare. It was too warm in the room, and there was perspiration on her brow. Anson, however, was shivering, and he pulled his heavy coat closed, gripping it in his fist in front of him, as he moved around her, making suggestions. She was clearly uncomfortable in the weight of the heavy fabric, but I saw her watching him and knew that it was concern and not the heat that knitted her brow.

Summer came, and the men who came to parties in that season wore appropriate and gay clothing that was no term of sexual preference in those days but a matter only of style. Barney, a bright and measured model who had a taste for his female counterparts, stood awkwardly in flowing shirts and pocketless pants. He told me he preferred the winter tweeds, cordovans, and flannel. He had a chiseled face, and though he might have been a friend I couldn't bring myself to press the truth about Anson and me. Most of the other men, designers and models, wore those feminine clothes called unisex with a certain flair and comfort. Only Anson and I were different, I in the casual and nondescript clothing that still hinted of California, Anson only slowly unpeeling, still in sleeveless sweaters that had grown baggy, heavy cotton shirts, and wool socks.

Along with the sap of the new season there was

fluid coming from Anson in places other than his ear, small wounds that would not heal completely, a constant moisture at the corners of his eyes. He had little vanity, but he kept a small mirror on the table beside his cot, and in the mornings he would carefully clean his face with cream and tissue, and I would help him swab the small eruptions on his neck and chest. He took to wearing makeup, a light blush, and once he asked me to buy him smaller clothes, a few shirts and trousers. I did that, but in a week he had receded even further, shrinking beneath them.

And then the last weeks came, and in them I began to feel as if I were his husband, an incompetent and bewildered man with a dying wife, one who pulls himself together each morning and manages. I would rise into sounds of his stertorous breathing, see the night's drainings near his carotid pulse and clavical. I would move to the kitchen carefully and with my head hanging. Not to wake him. Slow with the coffee and the click of metal. And when the sun entered the bedroom windows, I would hear his stirring, note the groan of bed and body, measure his sighs and movements against the previous day's. I would look at the stacks of plates, saucers and cups, the shapes of shakers and colanders, implements hung on hooks. Everything began to look different, poignant with history. Then I would go into the bedroom and tend him.

Early on, we went for brief walks as the weather warmed. There was a park a block away, and Anson would lean lightly on my arm. We crossed only when the street was empty of cars, and we would sit for a few minutes on a park bench, listening to the birds and watching the traffic. On the way back home, I'd stop for brioche and yogurt, and we would eat it in the kitchen, with a cup of fresh coffee. Then Anson, when he was up to it, would work a while on his drawings. In the late morning and early afternoon he'd nap, and he would be in bed early, usually before nine.

But for the time I had found Anson in bed with a man, I had never seen a hint of physical affection between him and another beyond the warm casual, and when the visitors began to come to our apartment, this aspect of his behavior continued. The men only held his fingers in gentle handshake or put their cheeks against his briefly in formal greeting.

He had called a friend and asked him to pass the word, to say that Anson felt he probably would not be going out any more now and that he would welcome visitors. I brought flowers and arranged them, had a woman come in to clean the place, stocked coffee, wine, cheese, some fruit and cookies. I organized the kitchen and living room, putting things in their proper place and order.

Anson asked me to hang some of his most recent drawings in the living room, and when the visitors began to come I saw the point of this; the drawings gave them something to talk about in the face of Anson's appearance, the painful clarity of his condition. It was easy to see that he would not be coming back from it.

Though the drawings were of women and men in clothing, they were not really fashion renderings. There were buildings and other structures in the background, and it was these that the eye went to.

Anson's old way with history, that unsentimental past that I had seen in The Chief bar so long ago was there in them, refined over the years into an exquisite fixing. I looked at them when I felt the need to fight against my own beginning nostalgia, that which was coming on as the fact of Anson's leaving became increasingly apparent.

The men who came brought things, drawing pads and pencils, small boxes of fine candy, potted plants, art catalogues. Anson received them in the living room, fully clothed and carefully groomed. The men would sit in a tight circle around his chair, laughing lightly and talking with animation, denying everything they knew. They would touch each other to make a point, touch Anson lightly on the knee, look at the drawings on the wall, and never stay for very long. They were mostly lean and delicate men, but beside Anson they looked robust. I would see the moisture in their eyes when I took them to the door. Some would touch me on the arm familiarly in their leaving, look at me knowingly and try to smile.

In those final days, Anson received many cards

and some long letters. Most of the cards were ones with no printed messages inside of them, museum cards with fine historical illustrations and handwritten notes inside. The letters mostly said that the writer found it impossible to come visit, business and distance, but I think we both knew that the real reasons were otherwise, fear of contagion, fear of contact with the dying. None of the letters came from women.

All of the women we knew came in person, and unlike the men they were not guarded in their behavior. Some wept openly when they saw Anson, smiling through their tears, dabbing at their makeup and squeezing his arm and embracing him gently. There were those who even spoke with him about his illness, asking questions, drawing Anson into animated talk about doctors and medicine. They stayed longer than the men did, and the gifts they brought were mostly useful things, seldom things to eat or look at, handkerchiefs, soft pillows and towels. They came mostly in groups of two or three, models in gay summer clothing who knew each other both professionally and socially, and most in their stay spent some private time with me in the kitchen over coffee.

Being in our home seemed to relax them with me even further than before. They seemed to feel even safer, and many poured out their hearts to me, speaking of wishes for major changes in their lives while there was still time. They spoke of sex intimately, of their dissatisfactions with men and what they wanted that the men they knew could not give them. I listened to them, watching them, fascinated and in a passion that was so deep I could feel it in the roots of my hair, in the tendons at the backs of my knees.

And in the ways they sat facing me, the ways their knees opened slightly and their breasts hung forward against the fabric of their blouses, the way their hands shaped the holding and touching they longed for and described, I felt that sad, false intimacy, but a sensuality beyond what I had ever experienced. They pressed the whole lengths of their bodies against me at the door in parting, but I knew they only felt free to do this because they thought they knew I would not rise up against them. And I didn't rise up. Something in me, though I wanted what their talk had brought me desperately, checked me. The fabric of our clothing was like a real wall between us. They really didn't know me any better than I knew myself, any better than I knew Anson or he me.

I would have hoped, in those last days, for more talking, for something, any little thing that could have brought me closer to an understanding. But there was really nothing, or at least very little. Anson did say, laughing at the absurdity of it, that he would miss me. And he talked also, in reminiscence, about things we had done together, places and events. Still, there was nothing really that came close to the root of it, and I began to wonder if there was a root. Maybe it was just the years themselves, us and our comings and goings. Maybe it was only habit and trite dependency. I said these things to myself, but I did not believe them. I thought of Lorca and knew there was no real difference. Anson talked of Maudie some, and that seemed to be a blessing. His eyes would brighten in the memory. He spoke in detail of her bees, her miniatures, what she had done for his art. There seemed nothing of nostalgia in his talking, just a pure pleasure in reminiscence.

Then Anson died. I knew it by the silence in the cot beside me when I woke in the morning. The night before had been no different from other nights near the end. There had been few visitors, and by nine o'clock Anson was ready for bed. We talked a little, lying beside each other, when the lights were off. But though I searched that talk later for significance, there was none that I could discover. It had been about the visitors, medicine that I would pick up for him, a gift of a thirties fashion book that he had enjoyed receiving. I couldn't remember how the talking had finished, whether it was Anson or I who had fallen asleep first within it. There were no last words that have stayed with me.

The woman came and took Anson to Utah. The cot remained in place for a few days, and I left the drawings hanging in the living room where I had affixed them temporarily to the walls. I ordered Anson's clothing in the closet and in his drawers, but for a while I did not pack it. And there were cups and saucers with the dregs of coffee still in them that I left as they were on the kitchen table and resting on the edges of open shelves. There were smears of lipstick on the rims of some of the cups, and I used them for my own coffee in the first few mornings, placing my lips over the red smears as I drank. It was only after a week that I cleaned the place thoroughly, longer still before I had any sense that I'd be leaving. Then it was that Anson faded, ever so slightly, and images of Lorca rose up, opaque shadows at first, but growing stronger as the days and weeks passed.

We had lived in that small house behind her parents' house, it seemed to me as I began to think of it as a way against our possible commitment to one another, our taking on of a real and separate life together.

We had not started out wrongly. From the very beginning there was a certain passion between us, acquisitive and for details. Mine was for anatomy, names of body mechanics that had soon enough spilled out its attention and focus to the world at large. I began to know flowers, the exotic ones in that city, and the names of trees lining the freeways. Then I turned it to anything: small pinwheels at a carnival; automobiles, the workings of which had frustrated me as an adolescent; the way fabrics were woven; variety in the chemistry of herbs. Lorca's passion was for literature, the details of its spectacle, and the ways objects and events in it could echo in her life. I would speak of the way something worked, name all its parts, and she would place it in a context in which its workings could have significance, and had in a novel or in a poem, and how that significance was related to our own, to her own at least, and mostly in the past. The world, in our beginning, was rich; I gave it voice and name and Lorca gave it context. And while that context was not always in the present, it was enough for both of us. It generated a certain closeness that there seemed no reason to question, because we had it. I knew nothing of her real past within its own prosaic frame, but I did not know this. She was drawing all along, even beginning to paint, but she seemed to hold this secondary, relatively unimportant, and I saw no passion in it.

And there was that other passion too, limpid, though we were unaware of that. It seemed fired in ways we did not think about by our proximity to her parents' house, the flicker of lights there and the shadow movements of her mother and father as I entered her. They were no more than fifty feet away from us, and while they might have thought vaguely about what we might be doing, the lights off, the flicker of candles that they could see, they wouldn't have had the images, the vision of their daughter who remained young because she still lived there, and of a young man, their son-in-law, who was not their child, the two playing the adult game, no more than fifty feet away. That, at least, was our unspoken feeling of it, was why I think we sometimes laughed like little children playing with matches. Lorca may have had some passage in mind at such times, some similar dance of characters to place us. I watched the way her muscles moved, gauging the distance to the house over and over. It was sexuality in a story, and what we did not find at all within it we found around it. We did not know that it was mostly vacant, not until the end at least, but it was too late then.

Lorca stole some dresses. Our marriage had been no accident of time or proximity; we courted methodically. But there had quickly come that time when we felt that we knew each other deeply. The evidence was quick thought and a kind of common perception. We laughed at the same unfunny things, we articulated structures that others seemed to miss, we felt we were attuned in the same ways to the world's flow. We lived behind her parents' house for economic reasons. We had started out late together, and I was raw in my profession. Then the stolen dresses came, heavier than the clear air we felt we lived in. They were a missed opportunity, maybe, for a better closeness. At least I saw things this way. I'm not sure about Lorca.

It was winter, a time for fall clothes in California, but the two dresses were for summer, cottons and paisleys, and not from the shop Lorca worked in.

They had her in a cage in a too public room in the women's section of the county jail. It was a lesson, something possibly good for adolescents, but she was too old for it. Her father had some influence. He had paid the shop immediately and made some phone calls. They detained her only until we came to get her, then let her go with a warning. She was in the cage in her own clothing, and before they let her out they gave her father the dresses he had paid for. He held them in his arms, and watching her he went to a metal trash can in a corner and stuffed them into it. I was at the bars, and though I saw her eyes as she watched her father I could see no real expression in them.

"Nice dresses," I said. "But you goofed the season."

She looked at me, but there was no intimacy or sharing in her eyes.

"It was because I wanted something," she said.

"Who from?"

"You wouldn't understand," she said, and though I touched her hand at the bar I could feel nothing in it. It was cool and relaxed. I stroked it and she didn't move it. Much later I was to remember the feel of it and to think that it was like the feel of

Anson's hand when I held it in his last days. It wasn't until after Anson died that I thought of it again, thinking that it might not be the same at all and that I might better look to what was common, my own hand, the real constant in the two events.

The stolen dresses brought the beginning of the end, or at least marked it. But it was a slow ending. It was no drawing apart, but a growing recognition that what we thought was closeness was other than that. It was many good things, but it was not that. And what that was, our frustrated search for it, or at least mine, is what kept us together, the search moving away from the personal entirely, becoming almost philosophical, then returning at the end, for me at least, as an abasement of knowledge, not about us, but about myself.

We did things with Carl and Anne. I thought about Melchior on occasion, moody and nostalgic in that sense that with him things had been right I thought. Anne spent private times with Lorca. Carl and I acted like friends together. There was the dress shop and my massages. And there were long evenings spent in quiet conversation, playing cards, drinking and smoking. There was the subtle season's turning in California, the longing even in that undramatic, western fall. Then Lorca left suddenly, but not before the end. We had been lingering, and when she left I knew it, knew we'd been fixed in inertia and that there would have been no marking of the ending otherwise. There was some time afterward that I don't really remember vividly, the move from the little house, a settling of affairs. Then, after a while, I met Anson and that other thing began.

Lorca and Anson. Each was afterward like a puppet standing knee-deep in the folded contours of my troubled brain. And after both of them left they were figures on strings, hitting against each other lightly, the strings twisting, then spinning out away from each other, but never far enough for me to lose them. I always found a way to tug them closer, considering, not knowing. They were on the shifting platform of the Bishop's diorama, the light changing its focus as the platform turned, Anson in enigmatic profile, then Lorca, her dark hair obscuring her features. Each was in the middle of a gesture, a hand uplifted, a hip slung, or a chin pointing, and each seemed ready and on the brink of speech. But there was thick glass between us, and even had they changed to animation and language I wouldn't have heard them. At least I saw it all this way, and in seeing it was shocked at my imagination, my fancy. It was something about my life I was after, nothing to be gained or gotten at through metaphor. I acted as if I were in literature, one of Lorca's analogues, or in Anson's past which, also like literature, was only a story for the mind to work as it saw fit.

And now I was heading south, down to the roots of my own past, at least that part of it that had been moving me since Anson's death. So far, with Melchior and Carl and Anne, I was not sure I had gained anything, though I might have begun to see my own posture a little more clearly and for what it was, a little cool, as Anson had once joked of it, a little distant and without connection. Still, that may have been a part only of awkward reconnection. So far the kind of world the Bishop had warned me about, its powers to change me should I enter it, had not been there, or at least I had not noticed it if it was. I felt I wanted that. Unlike the Bishop, I saw my life, my years with Lorca and Anson, as a kind of uncentered drifting, and anything that would correct that seeming I'd welcome. At least, that's the way I saw it, recognizing that I might be totally naive, a middle-aged Pollyanna, and in for more than I wished.

Lorca. I remember the titillation of the little lights, diffused through our curtains, from the main house. Our own candles, dim and at a distance on counter and bookshelf. Lorca faces the wall. She is on her knees, her back arched and her head elevated, and I am behind her, holding her at the waist and entering her. I see her hands make fists, gripping the coverlet, feel her knees walk open a little. I cannot see her face at all. Her long, hanging hair cowls it completely. Though in her and moving and holding her, I feel I am trying to somehow keep up with her, to get to where her indistinguishable sounds tell me she is going. It is as if she will soon ram her face into the wall, will go through the wall, that I will drop out of her as she heads away from me. Her hips will slip from my oily hands. I will be left in the posture of one who has dropped a large urn, his hands still shaping it in the air, his head down, looking at the shards. And when I look up, past my distended sex, I will see the final closure of the wall her body has broken through. My hands will reach out, pressing against the intractable wood where she has passed. I will feel my sex falling, my muscles and head sag, imagining what a sad and comic sight I would be for anyone standing beside me who cared to look.

I was haunted by glimpses of things I half remembered as I passed them: a street on the left, ending in a blind glow of afternoon sunlight but beginning in familiar roofs and facades, stores and parking lots. I had spent two nights on the road, one in Yosemite and one in San Francisco, and had made the last long leg to Hollywood in a single day. In my hours in Yosemite I had seen El Capitan, that huge rock obelisk that Carl, Banyon, and Kip had ascended, and I had walked through open places among rocks and trees where the picture of the girl might have been taken, though it might have been miles from where I was. The park was beautiful, but for me a moody feel hung over it; the girl's white hair, that dead look in her eyes, and what had been furtive for Carl there added a mystery, not a titilating but a strangely frightening one. I realized that fear could well have played its part in Anne's decision to remain with him for so long, even after she knew it was time to be leaving. I hoped I had precipitated something while with her, but I found I feared that possibility at the same time. I found a shop that handled Indian artifacts, but there was nothing there that looked like the ones in Sharonville.

Reaching the street we had lived on and turning into it, I saw that the white paint on the curbs was chipped and that the numbers in front of many of the houses were worn away. At the end of the block the hedge lining the sixth fairway of the golf course was ragged and untended, and when I got closer I could see that the fairway itself was brown and burned out. I parked in front of the house, the third from the end, and moved up the cracked cement

223

walkway to the door. The white lintel was flaking, as were the windowsills, and the door was scarred and cracked at the hinges. The sun was behind her, coming through from the back of the house, when she opened the door, and I could not see her clearly.

"David?" she said, no real surprise in her voice at all, and stood aside so I could enter.

The house hadn't changed much, the same heavy furniture and the same lamps and carpeting. When I got past the glare, I could see clear through to the other end, to windows in the dining room through which the little house was visible.

Lorca's mother was much the same as well. She still had bits of her sporty carriage, though by then she must have been in her midsixties. She moved a little stiffly, but I suspected that was a simple awkwardness in my presence.

"Sit down," she said, opening both her hands, indicating I should choose my place. I took a chair, the one Lorca's father had used in the evenings, and she sat on the couch across from me. I saw the lines at the sides of her eyes then and the way the flesh hung a little at her neck. There was a pot and cups on the coffee table between us, and after she had poured she held up the cream pitcher, looking at me, and I nodded.

I leaned forward and took the cup from her hand. "I'm sorry about Jack," I said. Her eyes blinked and she looked away.

"Oh, that was three years ago. Almost." Her eyes returned from the window. "But why did you come west?" she said. "I sent you everything I could dig out." I saw the cardboard boxes piled in the room beyond us, a carpet rolled in a corner.

"I don't know," I said. "Ready for a change, I guess. Something. You said in your letter that you were moving, to Riverside?"

"To my sister's place. That's right. Since Jack died the neighborhood has gone down. It's time to get out."

I could tell it was more than that. There had been a sureness in her in the past, a way of speaking and acting, that was now gone. I knew I had things to ask her, but I despaired of answers even before I spoke.

"You wrote that you'd heard nothing at all from

Lorca. Have you ever heard where she might have gone?"

"You know as well as I do," she said, her shoulders rising a little in a halfhearted shrug. "Only those letters we got in the beginning. The one you got and the one we got. Jack and I. Didn't they come from Phoenix?"

"Do you think that's where she went?" I was only going through the paces now. She knew no more than I did, and that was clear to me. Still, I had to get it said. To say something.

"Well, who in the world can know? There was nothing I found in the little house after you left. She could have done. But there was nothing said about that at the dress shop, as I remember."

I caught a brief remnant of concern in her eyes and the British locution, a holdover from fake language at the tennis club. Her hands were fidgeting with her cup and saucer; a little of the coffee had spilled to her fingers. I looked down at my own hands and saw they were not too steady either. I was bringing things up unfairly.

"Do you want to see the little house?" she said,

and she rose to her feet, settling the matter before I could answer. She left me at the back door, handing me the key that hung on a hook beside it.

The little house was dark, the shades drawn and the curtains pulled across them, and only after I had bared a couple of windows could I see that the place was almost empty. The bed and furniture were gone, only a couple of end tables remained, pushed into a corner, and there were a dozen or so cardboard boxes resting, helter-skelter, on the floor. I opened a few of them, finding only Lorca's things: books, some old clothing and school notes. Then I saw my name on the side of one of the boxes and went to it, opening it and spreading its contents around me where I squatted.

The box contained remnants and tag ends of my life with Lorca, things she had saved that dealt with both of us. There were ticket stubs and programs, notes I had left for her, pieces of clothing that I had bought her as presents. There was even a worn deck of cards that we had used in games with Carl and Anne, and there were two sticks of incense, wrapped carefully in tissue, which I opened and sniffed, the faint remaining smell bringing her back to me briefly.

Her mother had packed this box. At least I guessed she had. Packed up what remained of that broken life of ours. It's a shame I thought, but I wasn't sure at all that I believed that. It was at least a shame for her mother. I'd had no right to come here, to bother her in this way, not even a good reason for it. I'd really expected nothing. It was just a necessary stop. To see the little house again, to return before I went further.

When I got back to the house, Lorca's mother was in the living room, sitting as she had before, looking down at her cold cup of coffee. She glanced up at me as I entered the room.

"Did you find anything?" she said.

"No," I said. "There's nothing."

She nodded, touching the edge of her saucer, then moved her hand to the side of her nose and absently rubbed it. "Well, I'll be leaving," she said. "Pretty soon now. What will you be doing?"

"I'm going," I said. "Is there anything at all? Before I leave? "

"I wish there were. For my own sake, but there's nothing. I don't know any more than you do."

I felt her last words as a little accusative, saw her eyes sharpen as she looked over at me. But that didn't last. She sighed and her eyes unfocused again. She lifted her cup, looked into it and put it down.

I left her at the door, and when I got to the car and looked back she was still standing there, the last of the sunlight at her back obscuring her features. I lifted my arm in a wave before I got in, and I saw her hand reach her chest for a moment and then fall back to her side. I made a u-turn at the end of the block, and when I passed the house again I saw that she was still standing where I had left her.

Book 2

UTAH

7 ❧ Entrance

If in the passage of time there were a place of pausing and reversal, if in some instant I could turn
and return into my own past again, could find them
there, each in the clarity of all that specific detail,
what would the quality of that be like, recognizable,
a dream come true that was never the way it was ?
Nostalgia: the Bishop had warned me against it,
and still I had places to go. Utah this time, down
into *his* past, possibly that of Anson, the wished
for of Lorca's, that was at least in link with my own,
those undiscovered reasons for her leaving and my
return. I wanted all friends and lovers to be together,
in some hive of activity, of answers to which I had
no questions. But of my ways with men and
women, that was an understanding that I could
not fear to search for, that possible changing, as for
the Bishop, of my whole life. Brief little wedges so
far, moments of quick revelation, with Melchior,
with Carl and Anne, but nothing much lighter than

air, but for the weird Peking ducks, an earring, unclothed bodies in a circular pool: nothing final, no real turning of the diorama.

I lingered. There was so much change along the coast and in L.A. and San Diego that it was hard for me to keep my bearings. New buildings everywhere; low, gentle ridges of hills along Route 1 ripped away and replaced with condominiums; fresh, major arteries in the freeway system. Gulesarian's was now a parking lot, and when I found the place where Anson and I had lived, there was new aluminum facing on the old brick and the street was under repair. I parked a block away and walked in front of the place a few times. The ground floor was now a fast-food joint, and the windows that had faced the street from our apartment had been ripped out and replaced with awkward bays.

I found The Chief, on a relatively unchanged street, but there was a different name over the door, and when I went inside I found myself under the gun of video machines. The mirror was still there, and I lifted a beer to Anson, looking at the place where the Chief had taped his drawing up. The Chief was no longer there. It was a young woman in knit stockings and a short, little skirt who waited on me, perfunctorily, not meeting my eyes or smiling. I searched for the place where Carl and Anne had lived, near the university, but I couldn't find it. Lorca's dress shop was now a record store.

I lingered for a week in that sprawling city, a place that I had known intimately but now hardly recognized. I shopped for rougher gear, camping equipment I thought I might need, and had the car serviced. I took in a few movies, watched television in bleak motels, went to the restaurants I remembered that remained. Food was awkward in my mouth, like childhood dishes that are too sweet or bland when tasted again. Then I headed for San Diego.

The Naval Hospital was very much the same, but though I stood on the unchanged wards where Melchior and I had worked, even managed to find my way into the corpsmen's barracks where our cubicles had been, finding the same paint, the same layout and furniture, I could not call nostalgia up, and stood blankly in spaces I could not feel I had ever really been in. I even went to Tijuana, but that was no good either.

Then I found myself, on a sunny day, sitting on a bench in Balboa Park. There was a strong, soft breeze blowing, carrying a faint scent of the zoo with it, a pleasant smell, and I was eating something from a vending wagon, drinking a Coke. It had been two weeks since I'd left Lorca's mother at her door, and though I knew I'd been lingering, holding back, I had not really articulated that to myself. The park was full of people. It was Saturday, and as I watched the strollers and sightseers, I caught a glimpse of Anson. He was standing at the brink of a small cactus garden, beside large eucalyptus trees, and I felt myself tensing and rising from the bench as he turned. He even looked like Anson when I saw his face, but when he walked from the eucalyptus shadow, I saw he was a younger man by far, hardly more than a teenager. I went back to my hotel then and packed up. I had lingered long enough.

I spent the night in a barren little town the other side of Needles, in a small motel. There was nothing odd about the town itself, just one of those places with no visible industry, no reason other than a few remnants of long-gone tourist trade for its existence—dusty streets, haphazard boarding of shops, weeds growing in the baselines of an abandoned ball field. Few people were in the streets or in cars when I entered the place at five, too early for lights in the windows of houses.

At the end of the short main street I saw a sign, a broken wooden arrow pointing the way: *Motel ¼ mile.* I was well out of the town itself when I came to the place, a brief, boxy rectangle, six identical doors with identical windows beside them. In front of each room, on a cracked concrete slab, was a metal chair with a garbage can beside it. The hacked-off trunk of a dead tree stood at roof level in front of one of the rooms. There were no cars at all, only a dusty pickup, and that in front of a room at the far end of the building, marked *Office* above the door. The doors of the rooms had been painted a deep red once, the window frames, matching the metal chairs, an olive green. The paint had oxidized, and was now a worn pastel. It was as if the whole place had once been colorless, like a black and white photograph that was then tinted. The sky over the roof was still black and white, low storm clouds holding dry desert dust.

"Is anybody here?" I said. The screen door below the *Office* sign was opaque, but some stirring of air told me the door beyond it was open. I heard a shuffling, like paper, and the scrape of a chair, then a cough or a word spoken.

When I opened the door, she was on her feet, putting something away in a metal box at the desk; the lid of the box kept me from seeing what it was. Her body seemed young, short, economical, and wiry, but when her face came up I could see she was over sixty. She just looked at me.

"I'm just in from Needles," I said, though that was a little misleading, and I wondered why I had said it.

"Needles?" she said.

"Yes," I said. "Do you have a room?"

She came from behind the desk, a small metal

office desk; the room was no real office but just another motel room with the furniture removed. There was an old refrigerator in the corner, two metal chairs like the ones outside, and a hot plate on a card table. She kept her hand on the metal box.

"Oh, sure. Plenty of them," she said. "Do you want a waterbed? "

"Oh, no," I said. "Just a room."

"That's good. There certainly aren't any of those here." It was a joke, but she did not laugh or smile.

She took me to the room, the one with the dead tree trunk in front of it, and handed me the key. I gave her the twenty dollars; there had been nothing to fill out.

"Is there a restaurant, a place to eat?"

"Oh, no," she said. "There's nothing like that here."

"How about Needles?" I said.

"Needles? I wouldn't know about that. I'd guess so."

"Okay, thanks," I said, and she turned and walked back toward the office. I was only in the room for a moment when I heard the pickup truck. I went back to the car to unload what I needed and saw the back of her head through the small rear window as the truck pulled out to the roadway. I had to turn against the dust that rose up, and when I looked back she was gone. I went down to the office and opened the screen door. The inside door was still open, but there was no one there.

After I had unpacked the trunk and taken my things into the room, I laid what I had on the bed and chair and took inventory. If I needed other things, I felt I'd better get them soon. I had no idea what was ahead of me. I had my leather work bag, one small suitcase, and a small duffle. I'd brought a suit, a few white shirts, socks and underwear. The rest of the clothing was the rough wear that I'd purchased on the way: jeans, sweatshirts and work-shirts, a pair of outdoor boots, tennis shoes. In the duffle I had the camping gear, figuring it might be nice to sleep out when I got into the right country for it. The sheaf of Anson's drawings lay on the bed, as did the box Lorca's mother had sent me.

I took my ditty into the small bathroom, stripped to the waist, and washed up. Then I got the one smudged glass I could find, poured out a shot of bourbon, and went and sat in the metal chair in front of the room and sipped it.

The sky looked angrier now, the clouds had darkened, and though I could see the low roofs of the small town in the distance, beyond them the air was dust- or rain-filled, opaque. In a while I got up and walked clear around the building, but there was nothing to see. The ground was empty all the way to the horizon on all sides; only the small-town buildings rose up from it, and they were low, and the sky seemed to be pressing them down into the earth. A gust of windblown sand came up, and I could feel it stinging against my arms. I went inside then and got my wallet and jacket, figuring I'd better find someplace to eat.

When I got to the main street again, it seemed to me that there were more buildings boarded up than I had noticed before. There were no cars at all on the road now, and though the dark sky had faded in the last remaining sunlight before dusk, there were no lights in the windows of houses down side streets that I passed.

When I reached the town's far side, I found the

highway turnoff and accelerated in the direction of Needles, which was no more I judged than a few miles away. Soon it was raining, only large and well-spaced drops, but enough to smear my windshield, and I had to slow down. In twenty minutes I realized I must have taken the wrong road out. Real dusk was beginning now, and though the road was straight and flat I could see no lights or buildings in the distance. I drove on for another mile, found nothing, and took a narrower road that wound off into the desert on my left. In five minutes I saw the lights of a gas station, slowed down, and pulled in at the pumps. The pumps were lit, dim coronas of light reflected off my hood. I reached over and rolled the passenger window down and saw lights and movement in the office beyond the pumps. After what seemed a long time, the door opened and a figure in coveralls came out.

At first I was startled, thinking it was the woman from the motel, but as she approached I saw that this one was a little younger, taller, and smiling in a way the other had not done. I leaned over toward the window. Halfway to the car, the woman stopped and looked up. There was a sharp crack of thunder, and the sky opened, the rain coming down immediately in heavy sheets. She turned in it, judging the distance back, then shrugged and bent into it and trotted to the car.

"Needles!" I called out in the roar the rain made. Her face and hair were flooding with water when she reached the door; drops bounced from her brow in through the open window and onto the seat.

"What?" she called out.

"Needles!" I yelled.

She shook her head, then lifted her rain-soaked arm and pointed back in the direction from which I had come. Before I could speak again, she turned and ran back toward the office. I looked through the rain, following her, hoping she would come back again or give some other sign. The windows of the office were sheeted with rain, and I could not see in to her once she had entered. Then, in a few moments, I saw the lights go out, then the lights of the pumps themselves. I turned around then and headed slowly back up the road. The rain was already running in shallow rivers at the shoulders, and I could make no more than fifteen miles an hour. When I reached the narrow highway, I drove for another twenty minutes, but came to nothing. When I found my way back to the motel, it was still raining. There were no lights in the building at all, though it was no more than eight o'clock.

The next morning I bummed a cup of coffee from the woman in the office. She gave it freely but without a smile.

"Good dinner?" she said, as I took the cup to the door. "Not really," I said. "I couldn't find Needles."

"It rained hard," she said.

"Right," I said, and left.

Back in the sad little room I bathed, dressed, and prepared to leave. I'd gotten a local map in Needles, and I ran my finger over it, tracing the way northeast, figuring the regional byways against empty spaces on the small atlas that I had brought with me. The atlas showed empty areas of desert, but on the local map there were veins of secondary roads that could take me through. My tank was over half full, and I wouldn't have to stop for an hour or more. When I reached the highway again, I headed northeast, away from Needles or the direction in which I thought it was; I wasn't exactly sure after my trouble the night before. It seemed that Needles was a hard place to get back to, and I felt as if some door or other had closed behind me once I had left it. I was glad I wasn't heading back or trying to. Not yet, at least.

There were no signs at the place where I entered the highway, but I knew from the map that I would pick up the road I wanted in a short time. I drove slowly; the blacktop on the road was rough, the shoulders narrow, and when I found the turn I wanted, I had to drive even slower. I settled on a comfortable forty miles an hour, flipped on the air conditioner, and shifted in the seat until I found a good place for myself.

I had nothing but the name of the town the woman had taken Anson's body to and Anson's sketches of Maudie's house; he'd kept them all those years, and they and just a few other things were all I had kept of Anson's belongings. There were things in storage with my own things, but I hadn't gone through them with any care. The town was small and not on the general maps, but I found it on the local, sectional ones I'd looked over. It was southeast, just over the border in Utah. I figured to get there in the morning. I would camp out under the stars tonight. The air was clear, the clouds gone, and though it was hot, it was dry and there was a light breeze stirring in the few growths poking up out of the desert. And the desert would fall away soon; I could see higher country and green, I thought, in the distance.

Of Lorca, I had absolutely nothing, only the state itself as a possibility. I had the name of the Bishop's school, Nativity, but could figure no help at all from that. I had some resolve, but no real place to put it.

When I left the desert and started up into low hills and pine, I found a road that took me a little south but still east. I would avoid the Grand Canyon, then head due north, up into the bottom of the state. I ate breakfast and lunch in small gas station restaurants, ones without tourists, almost empty, just a few men, an occasional woman, people with lives I had no idea about.

I stopped at a park in a small town, another wasted place like the one near Needles, and spread out maps and Anson's sketches on a picnic table and studied them. No one was in the park, and though I sat there for most of an hour, few cars passed by and not a single figure walked the streets. I heard a few sharp birdcalls, ones I could not identify, and deep rumbling in the sky far to the north. When the sun began to sink, I left the place, driving slowly to the outskirts of the town, and looked for a campground, but I couldn't find one. Finally I settled for a short hike up into fir trees off a winding dirt road, and set up camp in a clearing. The sky was in view above me; there was no moon, and the stars were cold and brilliant. Though I had put the tent up, I slept outside, gazing into the sky, letting the sight soothe and help me to sleep. In the morning I made instant coffee, using the car's lighter socket to heat the small element, and was back on the road by seven. At ten o'clock, I came to the gates of Utah.

The terrain had leveled, the road straightened, and I saw the two white obelisks a good mile before I reached them. Even at a distance I could make out the fashioned structures at their tops. They looked like thick white stalks of asparagus, one standing at each side of the road. As I got closer, I saw the web of grating that was a gate between them and the large iron letters of *Utah* spanning across below the tips.

When I came to a stop at the gates, a man in green fatigues stepped out from behind one of the pillars. He had a rifle slung from his shoulder. He came to the gates, opened them enough to get through, unslung his weapon, and moved carefully off to the side of my left fender, then motioned with his barrel. I could see he was saying something, but my window was closed, and I could not hear him.

When I looked to the gates and pillars, I saw that three more men had appeared, all with weapons. One was dressed like the first man; the other two, their hair pulled back tight and tied in ponytails, were clearly Indians; their dress was less military, and they had fringe and beads at their sleeves and necks. I leaned forward a little and looked up through the windshield. The structures at the tops of the obelisks were stone beehives, extremely stylized, almost abstract in their hard-edged compartments.

"…roof of the car." I heard the end of a sentence as I rolled the window down.

"Get out and put your hands on the roof of the car."

I did what I was told, keeping my hands in view and in front of me as I opened the door and slipped out. The other three were standing well away from each other, and they had their rifle barrels leveled at me. I turned my head from the roof and started to speak when I was in position.

"Not yet," one of the Indians said and then moved over to me and frisked me carefully. I felt my wallet slip from my pants pocket, and for a moment I tightened, suspecting that this might be robbery.

They kept me where I was for a good five minutes. I heard a car door open, the crackling of a radio. One of the men in fatigues stayed off to the side and watched me while the two Indians went through my trunk, glove compartment, and backseat. No one threatened me in any way, but they were all very efficient and serious and I could tell they'd done this many times. It was getting hot. The sun reflected brightly off the roof of the car and into my face, and I could feel sweat bleeding out on my brow. Then I heard the car door slam, my own truck lid close, and the sound of the crackling radio was cut off. After a brief silence, the spokesman, in a softer tone now, told me it was okay, I could move and turn around. When I did so, I saw that the rifles were slung again and that the four had relaxed their postures. I didn't speak, but they must have seen the questions in my face.

"It's pot hunters," one of the Indians said. He was tall and broad, and he spat the words out, leaning on *pot*.

"I don't know what that is," I said. The uniformed men stood a little away from the Indians, but it was clear that they were all committed in this thing together.

"Better to let it be," the spokesman said. "They come up this way is all; we watch for them. You can go through." The two Indians were already working the gates open.

When I was back in the car and driving through, I saw the two Jeeps, both with long aerials, off to the side of the obelisks. They had thick and studded off-road tires, and there were tubes of roll bars spanning over the cabs. I couldn't figure how they could catch anybody, clustered in one place like this, but then I didn't know the terms at all. Pot hunters. I'd never heard that, but I did remember something. There were Carl's pottery pieces on that shelf in Sharonville. Kokopelli, Karla had said, and something about illegality.

On the other side of the gates the terrain changed immediately, from the green and trees of the other side to red rock, sand, and low scrub. Four large soaring birds, buzzards or hawks, I thought, rode currents down the state line, high in the air to the left. They seemed to tip in toward Utah when they got close to crossing. Before I'd gone a hundred feet, I knew I was in another state entirely.

I found the house that Anson had sketched with very little difficulty, and to my surprise I found the place, I was sure, where he had gotten his ear pierced. It was now no more than a rambling shack on the far side of the town, a mile or so out on a back road. There were four motorcycles parked in the dirt in the small yard, one of them with a dark leather jacket draped as an insignia over the saddle. I could read the jacket's inscription as I drove slowly by; *Pot Warriors,* it said, and there was a green beehive under the bold lettering. In the window beside the door, there was a small broken neon sign, *E RS,* with the glass tubes curved in the shape of a crude ear under the letters.

It had taken longer than I had expected to get to the town. The roads were not well marked. At one place, what I thought was the road in ended in a sawhorse barricade, and I had to backtrack for a few miles. Just when I thought I was lost and would have to find someone for directions, the road I was on turned and dipped down a little, and I saw the first buildings, set in no clear order, well back behind overgrown yards.

The town itself was even more wasted than the one I'd stopped in outside of Needles. The difference was that it was not on flat land, but set deep in a canyon, ringed almost totally with huge red rock pillars, dusty-looking, that seemed to suck up whatever sunlight washed over them. I could see large birds soaring among them, sometimes dipping low, their long necks extended, their heads down and searching drifting over the town itself, over the buildings and the tall dead trunks of the numerous oaks and old maples that spiked up in careful rows along the town streets. It was clear that the trees had been planted, in some lost time, had needed care and had not gotten it. Now they had been topped, some at thirty feet or more, and some had what looked like man-made objects set in the stubs of their hacked-off top branches, organic-looking figures, some facelike, others like limbs and viscera. I saw few people, and no children, a few motorcycles and old half-primed cars in the yards before the houses. Windows were broken, peeling paint and cracked shingles. The only open business-places that I saw as I searched for Anson's house were a gas station, a rundown-looking coffee shop, and what I took to be a kind of general store. I did not explore the town, but only took what slow turns I needed to find the house in Anson's sketches.

It hadn't changed much. The vacant lot across from it was still there. The street it was on seemed totally abandoned, vacant places where houses had burned or been demolished, boards on the windows of those remaining. A very short street really, a dead end, with cement fractured into dirt where it petered out at a thick wall of twisted vines and brush. I sat across from the house in the car, at a place where I thought Anson himself might have sat, working on his sketches. The steps, porch and door were the same, though one of the porch pillars was leaning, and the porch itself dipped down a little at its center. There was nothing but a dark vacancy in its windows. I could evoke no presence at all of anyone having ever lived there.

I suppose I had thought something might come to me when I got there, something I could use in some way, but nothing did. The house had no real history for me at all. It was Anson's story and not mine, and though I gazed at it for a long time, trying to imagine Maudie standing at the door, picturing what might be inside, what living room and bedroom might look like, I could not get beyond its real deadness, into his history or hers, and through that back to myself somehow. At least the place was not haunted for me, not in the way it had been in Anson's story of it. It seemed final now, unimportant, and glancing from it to the sketches on the seat beside me, they too began to deaden, losing what had been of the presence of Anson and his past and self in them. I suspected *that* at least was a gain for me, though the loss of it hurt me. Could it be such closure of romance that I was after? To go back in order to get rid of Anson, what I thought I held of him in memory, to eat away that dreaming in the face of hard reality? The house had been old even when he'd sketched it; *she* had been old too. And now it seemed the house was ready to crumble, the pillars to fall and the porch to sink into the earth. I could come back in a few years and find no remnant. Would that be better, be enough for me? I felt disgusted in my now specific frustration. I knew less of what I was after than before I'd begun. Where there were plantings, flowers, along the sides of the porch in the sketches, there was nothing now. No bees moved in the air that I could see. Oh, Maudie, I could sleep my way into death with you. I have no child to begin again, no Anson or Lorca. What I think I want is still beyond my understanding.

I loosened my grip on the steering wheel, my palms coming away sticky, as if some residual of oil had worked its way to the surface. I flexed my hands and looked at them, the muscles still prominent along the fingers. I had touched no one in massage for a long time now, not since Karla's body was under my hands in Sharonville. I needed that again and itched for it, my hands on Lorca's body this time, if I could find her. I started the car up and did not look back at the house as I pulled away.

I found the cemetery on the other side of the town, a little up in the barren foothills beyond a closed up school of some sort. The school was fenced around, barbed wire strands at the top of cyclone webbing. Maybe it was a school that Anson had attended. There were broken and boarded windows there too, and along a high wall below windows I could see a faded complex of once colorful graffiti, what now looked like vague animal shapes, broken words, a progress of some kind, attenuated as it receded to a distance.

There were a few trees in the cemetery, not stumps this time, but young trees, growing wild. The place was untended, the fence of white picket that had once guarded it perfunctorily was full of broken slats, bleached out to a powdery grayness. There was a place to park, under a tree, and I pulled in and got out.

The cemetery was small and bound with the remnants of fence ended by a row of straggly low bushes; there was a portion of it, over a low rise, that I could not see from where I'd parked, the tops of gravestones getting close to the ground in that direction, until they disappeared beyond the rise. Above the ragged young trees, I could see the red rock towers, the birds still floating among them, not too far in the distance. At their tops they thinned into blunt and spikey figures, slabs of cracked and twisted eruptions rising hundreds of feet into the bleak sky. Lower down they were thick and sheer, at places large as the sides of massive buildings. They seemed to lean in a little over the cemetery and the town, and though the sky was clear and cloudless there seemed insufficient light. I could see no shadows on the red rock over which the birds floated, appearing suddenly, then drifting out of sight, entering crevasses, then gliding out again, always returning.

I started with the closest row of stones and worked my way along. The carvings were simple, only a few severe messages and crude angel-shapes. Most often just names and dates, no clear ethnicity in the names that I could determine, short lives mostly; few seemed to have lived beyond seventy. I didn't find Anson, or even Maudie, and I began to wonder if there might be another cemetery and if I should check that possibility. I did find a fresh grave, the earth newly turned and mounded along its length. The gravestone was bright and more modern than the others. I did not recognize the name, Corabina Ramholst, and the dates meant nothing to me. She had died three weeks ago. I looked at the grave site for a while, wishing it read differently, then I proceeded down the row.

I had my head lowered, reading along a group that was a family plot, when I reached the cemetery's ridge and heard the scuffling sound. I looked up, but it took me a moment to find the source of it. The stones were higher on the other side of the ridge, the plots clearly older, and I had to move to the side a bit before I found the kneeling figure. He was on his knees in front of a large stone, one in a tight gathering, an older family plot I guessed, deep in a corner of the cemetery. He had a paper taped over the stone, and he was rubbing it.

I could see the muscles in his broad neck rolling as he worked. He wore a t-shirt and jeans and was hatless. Though there seemed nothing ominous about him at all, the cemetery and the town were unsettling, and I moved quietly toward him, a little anxious and not at all sure of myself. There were stones between us at times as I made my way down to him, and then I was to the side again and had him in view. He was no more than twenty feet away. I relaxed a little then, though I felt a flush rise in my cheeks. I shuffled a foot to get his attention, so as not to startle him. I saw his back stiffen, but it was the ridges in his neck that had relaxed me. I knew, before he turned on his knees, that it was Melchior.

We sat in the small kitchen of Melchior's Airstream trailer, miles from the cemetery and the town, at a place where a dirt road ended and a small river ran. There were shade trees growing along the river's bank, willow and tamarisk, and I could see the gentle waving of a few green leaves outside the little window across from me. Barbara had brought me the letter and was now at the stove working at our dinner. It would be shad and small pieces of shad roe. "But this is a small house," she said, and then she laughed, that laugh that I remembered and liked very much hearing again. Melchior had some rubbings out on the table between us and was shuffling through them, looking for the ones he wanted me to see.

In the letter, postmarked only six days after I had left them in Sharonville, Anne said she had heard from Lorca. "Out of the blue," she wrote. And now that Carl was gone—"not coming back.

That's true. I'm not kidding"— she was taking the kids and heading out to find her. "She sounds okay. She says she has something to tell me. I hope you get this letter sent ahead." She didn't say where Lorca was exactly, but she mentioned a place called Manti.

"That's the other side of Dark Canyon," Barbara said. "To the right of it on the map from where we are now. It's a big national forest or something. I looked it up."

"What's up with The Heat?" I said.

Barbara laughed, glancing over her shoulder.

"Oh, he's okay," Melchior said. "Working the summer at some hotel in the city. He gets to wear a uniform!"

Though it felt odd to me that I was with them here, Melchior and Barbara seemed in a way relieved. They had come in from the south as I had, though by a different route, and the wasted, barren nature of the place had touched them too. They spoke of not seeing many people, of finding their maps inadequate. Melchior commented on the weirdness of the town where I had found him, the motorcycles and the empty roads.

"It doesn't seem like America," he said. "Certainly not like the West Coast, right?"

"It's not my idea of a loose vacation spot," Barbara said, flipping the shad fillets and pressing them down in the pan with a spatula.

"But the cemeteries have been great," Melchior said. "Take a look at this one." He moved the pile of rubbings aside and spread the one he held in his hands until it covered most of the small table.

The part that was taken from the stone itself was hard to separate out at first, but after Melchior had run his finger along the outline of it I could see what it had been before he'd painted it. It was halfway between a child's face and a skull, and the wings that had flanked it on the stone were still in evidence. Melchior had changed them though. They were now wings of hair, feathered back behind the face's head. He had added hair above the wings and brought some wispy strands down to the cheeks, so that the face now seemed the part of a face that was visible behind a wild wig or fashionable teased cut. The hair was not unlike what I had seen on the heads of some of the models I had known when I was with Anson. But the properties of the face that were skull-like made the head of the figure sickly or at least in some way wasted. He had added a neck below the face, a long, white one, and narrow shoulders and breasts, and where the breasts swelled, low and a little aged, he had added a hint of ruffles, the beginning of some gown or other. The whole thing was done in pastels, ones that clashed slightly in clearly intentional ways. One ear lobe was visible, a little bluish, the dot of an earring embedded in it. It was a skillful, beautiful and unsettling thing that Melchior had done. I was surprised at it, and I told him that and how much I liked it.

"From the morgue, I think," he said. "Remember that? I think that started it. I've kept my eyes open since then."

"He's been doing it for a long time," Barbara said. "It's good, huh?"

"As far as I know, it's very good," I said.

And now there was another thing. Had Melchior mentioned this when I had seen him? I couldn't remember, but decided not to ask. Surely he had not been doing it when we were in the Navy. I would have known about that, unless he had a part of a secret life he kept from me then. Not very likely. Still I thought of the Bishop's warning of the past.

"When did you get the time these years?" I said.

"I took it when I could. Barbara and Paul and I took little summer trips, New England and the South. A lot of graveyards in this country." He touched the edge of the pile of rubbings draped on the chair beside him. "This is only two weeks' worth, this time around."

"He was in a show once in New Jersey. He and a few others, mostly women. Pictures of flowers; you know, at a community center."

"Why Utah?" I said.

"The fish is almost ready," Barbara said, and Melchior got up and cleared away the rubbings and took them to the bedroom, only a few feet away, and then returned and began setting the table with plates and silver.

"You mentioned it the day you visited us. We

never thought of the place at all, but then we started to check out maps. It seemed a good place for our summer trip."

"Did I?" I said. I couldn't remember, but I must have mentioned something about Anson, the fact of the woman's taking his body here. Had I mentioned Anson to them at all?

"Did I mention Anson?"

"I don't think so," Melchior said. "Who's that?"

We ate our dinner and talked about what we might do next.

"We're free and easy," Barbara said, and Melchior nodded.

I filled them in a little on the letter, told them who Anne and Carl were and that I'd been married to Lorca. They said I'd mentioned her before. Barbara had the maps out on the table before we were finished eating. I thought I'd have to find a place to leave my car, but Melchior said he had a hitch and that the Jeep could pull it easily.

"I don't know about the roads though."

"We can try it anyway," Barbara said.

"I'd rather ride with you than follow," I said.

When we were finished eating and cleaning up, Melchior and I went down the few feet to the riverbank and had a smoke. It was dusk now, and the night birds were coming out, sitting close to us in the limbs of the young green trees and singing softly. The river was running low, but quickly, and we could see the streambed, lined with smooth rocks, through the clear water. On the other side, beyond the bank, there were older cottonwoods growing, and up the rise beyond them, and fixed against the darkening sky, we could see the barren structures of the huge rock formations of Dark Canyon. They looked like silhouettes, backlit as they were now, but at their jagged tops the last of the sun bled through, rounding the red rock into ominous figures, giant body parts in vague gestures. They seemed poised, ready to move toward us, unseen, when darkness finally came. I could hear the birds twitter just above my head, and it was they who helped me pull my gaze away and back to the running river.

We smoked, and Melchior talked just a little about San Diego again, then talked in some detail, and with quiet enthusiasm, about his rubbings and painting. It was something he would have done full time, had he been able, had he gotten any encouragement. He *had* from Barbara, and he suspected that that was why he'd married her in the first place. He thought too that had she known, early on, how important they were to him, his life might have taken a different course entirely. She would have stayed with him anyway. He might have become an artist. I told him that he probably was one. He laughed and shook his head and flicked his ashes in the river. I told him that I envied him, that doing massages only loosened others, gave *them* something. It came to me that I had been a watcher, a surrogate, and no participant. I didn't mention this, but Melchior seemed to know my thoughts or at least my sad feelings in thinking them. He didn't put aside my praise of him, but touched me in a while on my shoulder.

We set out in the morning, three abreast on the wide front seat of the Jeep, the Airstream and my car hitched to the rear of it behind us. We were a strange caravan, but the Jeep was new and had plenty of power, and Melchior seemed to know the right way to drive it.

For the first hour, the road was blacktop and the trees high enough to prevent our seeing very far ahead. It was a twisting and descending road, but the turns were wide and gradual enough to allow our caravan to pass with ease. At times we could catch glimpses of the tops of rock formations through upper tree limbs. Then in a while the trees began to thin out and shrink in size, and the rock became a constant presence through the windshield.

When we reached the edge of Dark Canyon, the road turned from blacktop to dirt and began to descend quickly, becoming in less than a mile a vague and little used cut. We were down among the rock formations before we had any good sense of their size and scale in the larger scheme of the canyon. We had paused only briefly at the lip, and most of our concentration had been given to the sight of the initial steep descent. There were tire tracks visible in places, deeper ones where occasional spurs cut off from our way as we went down. The going was slow and careful, and Melchior had to keep his eyes in the side-view mirrors to get us through places where the rock came close up against our passage. Then we were down on the canyon floor; the road leveled out, though still descending, and its twists and turns became severe. We hit open stretches, rock and red dirt valleys, and in one of them we saw a huge hawk drop down and lift a running jackrabbit from the stubble of the valley floor. When we stopped to rest and got out, there were hawks and what I was sure now were buzzards, high and drifting at the pinnacles of the rock formations, against the rust-colored sky. It was hot, and twice the Jeep overheated. We had to wait for it to cool, and Melchior had to add water to the radiator. We saw no one the whole day, but once we saw the shape of a low rectangular dust cloud across a valley in the far distance, and were sure that it was the trail of some vehicle moving on a dusty road.

The rock slabs and obelisks that rose around us were various in size and shape. All were massive and barren, but wind and blown sand had shaped them differently into enigmatic figures, some half organic, others like violent dream images of tilted and fractured cathedrals. In the beginning there were smooth white structures, almost marblelike, but these soon gave way and we were left only with massive and dusty red rock.

As the day passed and our way wound and straightened and wound again, we seemed to be going deeper into the endless canyon and constantly descending. But then, around three o'clock, I was sure we had reached the bottom. Here the spaces were tighter; there was red rock all around us, and we had to lean well out of our windows in order to see to where the slab walls tapered into spires, hundreds of feet above us. It was still early in the afternoon, but the red rock blocked the sun and deep shadows bled into the narrow trail.

There were scratches on the sides of the Airstream now, rusty streaks where we had scraped against and crumbled the dusty rock surfaces as we moved slowly between them. In places, the road had no shoulder at all, and our tires crunched through small alluvial fans that spilled into our path from the base of the rock slabs that pressed in against us.

It was as if the rock were some kind of oxidizing metal. Once I had stood against it, to the rear of the Airstream as I guided Melchior through, and where the trailer had scraped it there was a redder rock underneath. I touched it, and a handful of powder and chalky chunks came away. They grew hot in my hand as I held them. My back was burning, and I realized the red dust had come away on my shirt where I had leaned.

"You're a mess," Barbara said, as she dusted off my back with her hand. "This is *hot!*" she said, and went quickly to the trailer to wash up.

We found the canyon bottom in another hour, a small circumscribed *arroyo,* a miniature canyon: slabs of rock all around us, but a rough and flat area, enough room to pull the caravan off what remained of the road. Large boulders, many dead-end cavelike entrances into slabs at ground level and ones vaguely visible in shadows the sun had left high on the rock walls above us. The Jeep, the Airstream, and my car, each were covered with a red dusting. It was so thick on the car's windshield that I couldn't see in at all.

Though it was only four-thirty, we ate a light dinner. Melchior kept shifting in his seat, and Barbara reached to her neck often and rubbed it. It was too hot in the trailer, though now that the sun was sinking there was some relief, purer air and the remnant of a breeze outside.

"I'm stiff all over," Melchior said.

"And my neck's killing me," Barbara groaned.

Melchior worked at his sandwich with little enthusiasm. "Do you think maybe we can sleep outside? It's too close in here."

"We can try it," Barbara said. "Maybe we can get the bed out. It unhitches for cleaning and such."

"The bunk comes out," Melchior said.

"How about a brandy?" I said, and I went to my car and got the bottle.

The three of us sat on a large stone boulder, drinking. Melchior couldn't find a good place for himself and kept getting up and stretching.

"Let's look around," he said finally. "I can't sit still."

We started out along the roadbed, hoping to find its exit and more open space, but when we had gone a few hundred yards we saw that there was no immediate end to the rock enclosure we were in. When we returned, Barbara was out of sight in the Airstream. We could hear the clatter of dishes. Melchior suggested we explore the rock itself a little, and we headed out again, in different directions. I found a spur that I had seen earlier, and decided to check it. In no more than a hundred yards I found the cave.

It was set in the broad face of a slab of sheer rock. To the left of the slab wall the valley opened up and the road widened and trailed away in the distance. The angle where the spur had left the main roadway was too severe, and we would never have been able to get the car and Airstream around it, to get beyond rock that way.

I had to climb over a pile of loose stones and small boulders to get to the cave's mouth, and as I went up I could tell that some of the rocky leavings were freshly turned, probably shoveled from the cave itself to widen the opening or in search of something. Inside the cave the air was still, a little dank, and cooler. I could not see to the end of it, didn't have a light and had no idea how far back the opening went. A few feet in, where there was still enough light coming from outside to see, I found a piece of khaki strapping of some sort, a beer bottle, something that glimmered (a piece of broken glass), and beside it a shell casing. There were fresh shovel cuts in the cave's floor and ones I took to be the same thing up the sides of the walls, vicious-looking cuts, without apparent motive or any care in them. As my eyes became accustomed to the dark I went further in, and in a few feet I found a place where real, serious digging had been done. Here there were deep holes, excavations, but I found nothing but dirt and stone. On my way out, and near the fan of rock rubble that spilled from the cave's mouth, I found a rough circle, darker red than the rock over which it washed. It flaked off at the corners when I touched it with a finger, bits of it getting under my nail. When I got below the spew of rubble, I saw another shell casing, this one still brassy and fresh.

"I found a cave," I said. We were back together again, standing beside the Airstream.

"I found three of them," Melchior said. "Somebody's been fucking around."

"It's the Anasazi," Barbara said.

"Say again?" Melchior said.

"The Anasazi. Seven hundred years ago or more. I read about them in the guidebook."

"The fucking shovel marks and beer bottles weren't," Melchior said.

Barbara laughed. "Did you find any shards and things?"

"I think I found some blood," I said.

It was a double bed, on a platform that was hinged at the center. We worked the mattress around the corners and managed with just a little trouble to get it through the door. The platform was easier, designed for such exit. We found a relatively flat place and set it up; then while Barbara and I made it, tucking the sheets and blankets in, Melchior unhinged the upper bunk and got it out as well. We found a slight rise for it; it had no legs, and we figured to get it as close as possible to a level with theirs. When we had it in place it was ten or so feet away, slightly higher, and at an angle.

"Those are *some* accouterments," I said, and Melchior threw his arms up, laughed, then winced as the gesture caused pain in his tight shoulders.

"That fucking wheel jumps a lot."

"Right," I said. "But what about the pillow cases, sheets and blanket cover?"

Barbara stood behind Melchior, rubbing his neck and shoulders. She was slightly taller than he was and looked even larger, standing on a rock behind him.

"His mother," she said, smiling over Melchior's shoulder at me. "She always wanted a girl."

The sheets and pillow cases matched the blanket cover, bold flower-figures in bright colors, with butterflies and golden bees among them. Some of the bees were sucking at the flowers' cups, and there was a snail or two climbing up green stems. There was plenty of white space between the figures to set them off. There was not a single color on the fabric that was like those dour ones around us, and the bed seemed to glow, catching the remaining sun, reflecting it, and sending bright light out to the shadows that were now lengthening on the dull red rock of the massive slabs around us.

"This is almost like Bambi!" Melchior said.

"Or Flower and Thumper."

"I'd say Dumbo," Barbara said dryly, and we all laughed.

Later, when the sun was almost gone but the bed still glowed, Melchior got a lantern out and placed it on a rock between our beds. Barbara showered in the Airstream and then Melchior and I did the same. They wore matching pajamas, but we were all too tired to joke about that. I wore a pair of loose cotton shorts and a light robe. It was still not completely dark, but it was darkening. There was not a single bug or moth around the lantern light, and just a hint of a breeze. I sat on the bunk bed, my bare feet on the rock beside it, knees almost to my chin, drinking a last brandy and smoking.

"Oh," Melchior groaned as he lifted his arms up behind his head. Both were lying on their backs on top of the blanket cover in their pajamas.

"Would you like massages?" I said. I spoke quietly, but my voice sounded loud to me in the still evening. "It might be good."

"That would be just swell," Melchior whispered, and Barbara sighed. "I told you about that, didn't I, B.? In San Diego?"

"You did," she said. "I could sure go for that."

It was sweeter there and then than it was, this time, in memory. It had been practice in those early days with Melchior, my concentration then on anatomy: muscle groups, ligaments, and tendons. But the memory had its power, because I was learning then, was making the first steps into mastery, was beginning to understand purpose. I could have easily let it slide and been nostalgic. Melchior was really the first man I knew well since I had massaged Anson, and I liked Barbara, felt in a strange way that I could not understand, that I knew her better than any other woman. Part of that, I was sure, was that there was not even a hint of sexuality between us, though with her I didn't wear the mask that Anson had provided me with for others. I think I loved her very purely. I know I wanted the feel of her body under my hands.

I sat on my bed, smoking, drinking my brandy, and began talking. I spoke of The Heat, Melchior's mother, that day of the trophy and the cake. I spoke softly, working to get at humor we could share gently. Just a few light chuckles and smiles. Then I turned to the past, the smokers in San Diego, then forward to Barbara's meeting with Melchior. Somewhere in the talk, I moved over to them, helped them to take their pajamas off and get settled on their backs. I had gotten my bag from the car before I began, and while they shifted and found their places slowly, I got the bottles and towels out and put them on a level stone beside the bed. The sun was almost completely gone now, and the lantern seemed to glow brighter. There was its light, the glow still on the coverlet, late dusk light on the rock, the massive walls of red stone, only shadow figures forming a dark cathedral around us.

Then they were doing the talking, reminiscing,

telling me and each other tales of their time together, long and lazy stories without revelation, though containing bits of new understandings, nothing jarring, brief and minimal discoveries that when added up might come to something.

I started with Barbara, time only for the back of her body; we would need our sleep. And there was no flinching in her at all when I touched her, beginning with her feet and calves, the backs of her knees, the shapely large tendon of her lower thigh. Melchior lay on his back beside her, talking. I was kneeling over her, and could see his face. He did not look at me, but upward into the sky. When I lifted my head I could see that it was full of stars, was a ragged and brilliant circle outlined by the vague presence of the rock high above us.

She groaned when I reached the backs of her upper legs, my finger edges brushing the fatty softness of her buttocks. She was no longer listening to Melchior's story. It droned on softly, and though I picked out bits of it I was well into her and let him talk on for himself only, which seemed right and good. Her lower buttocks were like thick cream, but higher up, at the insertion of muscle at her hip cup and spine, there was a tightness that needed working. She opened her legs slightly, and I could see the strands of black hair in her crevice. When I reached her thin waist, her buttocks tightened, then relaxed as I got beyond her sensitivity. She was ticklish there, but I was deliberate and impersonal, and that soon passed. As I moved her, her legs closed slightly, touching my knee where I knelt between her thighs. The movement relaxed her spine, and that was clearly the reason for it. The wings of her scapulas had already receded when I reached them. Her face was buried in the pillow, and the pillar of her neck was smooth and without tension. My fingers touched her ears with oil as I reached the apex of her spine, where it entered her skull. I touched the skull sutures through her still-damp hair.

"Just for a few years, when I was a child," she said, "we lived north, in Saint Paul, Minnesota, while it was still a manageable city. I had a girlfriend there with a tall, serious father; I think now that she must have been a Swede. She told me a story about when her father was a child, what he used to do then, and why, around Christmas, they ate fish and how it had become a family tradition."

Melchior was under me now, on his stomach, and it was Barbara who was on her back, naked, her brown-tipped breasts evident in the starlight, mottled a little with shadows cast from the lantern. Melchior was silent now, and we were listening to Barbara. Hers was a more formal story, one to be heard and understood. I had Melchior's thick thighs in my oil-slippery hands. The towels I had used to wipe Barbara down shone in the starlight on the low rock beside the bed. The flower and bee figures on the cover were dimmer but still apparent. One bee dipped his feet into the cup of a blue gardenia beside Melchior's elbow. There were no sounds in the night at all, no bird or animal, only a light breeze, the shift of the lantern flame, and Barbara's voice. I dug deeper, moving his muscular flesh, feeling the tributaries of blood flowing through it, his pulse, diastolic, pausing, constant.

"As a child her grandfather had come to Saint Paul from the old country, near the sea, and landlocked as he grew up, he missed it, the flavor of holidays and what his own family did then.

"Her father lived on a farm, far from the city, in his growing up, and the farm was near a small way station where the train that made its slow progress cross-country from east to west stopped briefly to take on water, a steam engine train.

"In the winter, on the day before Christmas every year, as her father remembered it, his father would take him to the siding where the train pulled off for a few minutes. They would stand calf-deep in the snow. The straight rails running out in both directions to the far horizon were no more than a slight rise in the earth, covered as they were by the white blanket, and they could see only the small snowcovered watering shed and a few spiky winter trees when they looked out over the empty expanse of whiteness. It was bitter cold, and their collars would be up, and her father would stand close to her grandfather, downwind from him. It was very silent, only the sharp clack of a few blackbirds in the skeletal branches of the trees.

"Then the train would come. They would see

its approach for a great distance, well before they could hear it. It was a white cloud only to begin with, as it kicked up snow from the drift-covered rails, plowing along. Then they'd see the smoke, gray, rising out of the snow cloud. They'd hear it, a rumble under their feet in the beginning, then the whistle, muted as it sounded in the billows and smoke. The man would come out of the watering shed then and wait with them, looking every so often to make sure the suspended hose was in the right position. Her father would step back a little as the train got closer. It looked much larger than it was, swollen in its snow cloud halo. Her grandfather always stayed put, waiting.

"Then it was there, scraping and pulling up to a stop only a few feet from them, huffing and spewing steam, coughing and blowing, a terrible racket, blackbirds in rolling snow clouds, bare branches shaking, and then a deep sigh as it came to an idle and the water was pumped in.

"They would go to the side of a boxcar, and when the door slid open, her father would see the blocks of ice, steam rising from them as the outside air entered, and the wooden box would be handed down to her grandfather.

"Christmas Eve. Snow falling in heavy flakes out the dining room window. Grog and salted herring. And a large platter of fresh oysters, alive on the half shell, on a farm in the center of Minnesota, turn of the century.

"But her story stayed with me because of another thing, something that happened a few years later, when I was around twelve. We were visiting friends of my parents in Madison, Wisconsin. It was winter, though not Christmastime, and we were snowed in on their friend's farm. I remember there were children my own age there, and they took me out in the evening to smell the wood smoke from the chimney and watch it drift into the icy air. The man had met us in Madison, to guide us out to his place, and had made a stop at the small airport, where I saw him load a large refrigerator box into his car. Halfway out to his farm it had started to snow, and the last few miles it was a blizzard. We arrived around noon, and by six we could hardly see the curves of the cars under the drifts. When we had watched the smoke for a while, we went back into the house. All the adults were gathered around the large kitchen table, smiling and laughing, looking down at the ten small lobsters that were ready on the plates. The man had them flown in from Maine for the occasion of our visit. I remember the way the shells cracked, the smell of the seaweed they had been packed in. Lobsters in a blizzard in Madison, Wisconsin. I remembered the story about Saint Paul.

"Thirteen years later, at a dance in Philadelphia, I met my love Melchior. He was drunk and in some disturbance or other, and I noticed the strange sense of goodwill in his drunkenness. He seemed to be only half in it, wanting to do vibrant and good things, but feeling that all he had to show for himself was his physical, farm-boy strength. He was familiarly violent with objects, pushing people around in his great strength with a smile on his face. Not angry at all, looking as if he wished to have similar feelings in sobriety.

"They threw him out, and since the girl I had come to the dance with had taken up with a young man there, when I left to go home I was alone. And there was Melchior, sitting at the same bus stop bench I arrived at. We got to talking, and we have been talking ever since.

"I think it was not a matter of love with us in the beginning, not that kind of thing in which the beloved is a romantic object to be learned about, rounded out, and tamed. There was never that progress into familiarity in which the one fallen in love with is changed from hero into husband or wife, faintly disappointing by comparison. But there is this story, and it says something about romance, about the past and nostalgia, and maybe it accounts for our good beginning.

"On our first date, Melchior took me to the house of a black family for dinner. He knew the son from the Navy; both of them had worked in the pharmacy, and the young man had asked Melchior over to meet his parents.

"The mother of the young man was from Washington State and she still had family there, and one of them, her father I think, worked as a loader for some commercial airline. What he had loaded and flown out fresh for the family that very morning were giant crabs, right out of the water in Washington. We sat in North Philadelphia, in an Eastern dining room, eating them; they were piled on newspaper. As fat as chickens, better than lobster, huge chunks of crabmeat dipped in butter. Melchior was smiling. He was very impressed with himself. It was a good beginning.

"The last thing in this cycle happened after we were married and on the road one summer looking for graves. We were in Massachusetts, on Cape Cod. We got in late, a small town just below the tip. All the stores were closed, except for a small one, and that had been hit by the rush of weekend tourists and had very little left on the shelves. We settled for frozen pizza. We were staying in a small cottage-colony, a family business, and in the office I got the loan of some packaged hot peppers from the woman who owned the place. She inquired about our dinner, and I told her about the pizza.

"I was just turning the oven on in the little kitchen, when I saw her walking toward our cabin from the office. She was carrying a paper bag. I got to the door before she could knock, and she reached the bag out to me with a smile. There was a pheasant in it. Scalded in a bucket and plucked, roast pheasant instead of frozen pizza our first night in.

"I have no understanding of this story beyond the obvious links between its elements. It's not so much a matter of incongruity as it is one of pleasure in surprise and then the experience, over long moments, of eating and talking. I can't help but think, though, that it's a measure of how I came with my past to Melchior. He loved this story when I first told it to him. He figured that the crabs capped it, that the pheasant in Massachusetts was a kind of sweet coda. I guess I can see it that way too.

"He had entered the stream of accident from my past. With the crabs he had been motivated to please me, somehow knowing in a way he could not really know that he could please me by linking the beginning of our life together to my own separate life before him. He liked to romance it that way at least. The pheasant made him sure of it. Now he had two accidents that were like my two. Together, through my telling him about it, we had the four of them.

"My, what a sweet tale, I think sometimes. Bringing the past this way into the present. Such accidents of the past. Maybe shad roe here in the wilds of Utah is another one. Surely the congruence of events that brought us together here is. Let's say that the roe is too."

By the time I had finished with Melchior's body, Barbara had finished her story and was deep in sleep. I lifted myself from their bed then, and by the time I had returned to my cot I could hear by his breathing, his faint snoring in the quiet night, that Melchior was asleep as well. He had listened to Barbara's talk with a certain satisfied intensity, and at times, when I'd looked over at him, I'd seen him smiling up at the stars.

I took another brandy, another cigarette, and sat at the edge of my cot, my feet on the now cool rock. How I envied them, I thought, realizing as I thought of it that it was an idea and not really a feeling. I had had a chance with Melchior too, with that drunkenness that Barbara had spoken of, but it had been too early for both of us then, or too late, and what it might have come to had it not been early or late was not at all clear to me. I knew that the way I turned and twisted my past was not the way Barbara had addressed hers in the story. I wanted to right something, to alter and correct; her nostalgia was sweet and pure, tough in that she wished nothing from it but its accuracy. But there were analogues for me as well, though larger and vaguer ones: my marriage to Lorca, my time with Anson, relationships with men and with women in various pairings.

Bile rose up in my throat as I realized that once again it was I who had been the agent for mild revelation, agent only and not participant. I flexed my fingers, pressed my feet down on the cool stone. It had been weeks since my last massage; these had been thorough and careful ones, and my wrists and palms ached a little. I took hold of my own naked legs under the folds of my robe, but my hands could not feel formal enough. There was nothing, right then, that I could do for myself. I could only lie down, pull the blanket up over me, and go to sleep.

9 🐝 *Chance*

It was the feel of a light breeze stirring the hair on my leg, the heat on skin over which the hairs tickled, that woke me up in the morning. I must have kicked the covers off in the night, and when I rose to my elbows I saw my naked leg, half of it in shadow, bare to the thigh on the coverlet. Turning, I could see the sun on the red rock slabs around me, and when I glanced at the bed I could see how it shone in the rumple of flowered sheets, lighting the bee figures up. Barbara and Melchior were not in the bed, but just as I rose and put my bare feet on the cool, shaded rock to the side of my pallet, I heard them, laughter and what sounded like splashing. I got to my feet, slipped my shorts on, and followed the sounds.

The pool was no more than fifty yards from our encampment. It was fed by a slow, narrow stream, three thinner tributaries running from it on the down side. We must have missed it in our reconnoitering because it was around a tight corner, through a narrow gap in the rock, and because the stream that fed it was so level and quiet. The way to it led through the same red shale that surrounded our encampment, but the pool itself was formed in granite, very white and smooth. The splashing that I heard was mostly Melchior.

They were both in the pool to their waists, Melchior chunky and pink, Barbara, her small breasts waving above the surface, darker, and just as happy. He was hitting the surface of the pool with his palms, splashing her for her pleasure, watching the water wet and then dry quickly on the white rock surrounding it.

"David, it's wonderful!" Barbara said. "Warm on the surface, and cool, cool down below." Her breasts elevated as she raised her arms in gesture, not a trace of modesty, false or otherwise in her clear eyes.

"Come on in, man, it's fine!" Melchior said, and so I stepped out of my shorts and lowered myself into the warm and then cool water.

"What have you been doing in here?" I said. I had squatted a little, standing on the balls of my feet, lowering myself in up to my neck. I was looking between Barbara's breasts.

"Wouldn't you like to know," she said, and Melchior laughed a little sheepishly behind me.

The pool was big enough for four more people, but we stayed within arm's reach of each other, changing places as we dunked our bodies and shifted to see the rock formations rising close on all sides from different angles. There was a smooth ledge in one place, and we took turns sitting on it while the others splashed each other and threw water up into their own faces. I felt feet and knees brush against my own at times, but there was enough drift on the surface to keep it opaque, and I was never sure who they belonged to. There were small deposits of sand at various places near the lip of the pool, and we used handfuls of it to scrub each other's backs. We must have spent an hour or more there, and when we got out and stood at the side in the air, I could see a faint aura of steam around Melchior and Barbara as the hot sun quickly evaporated the droplets of clear water on their shoulders and arms. I felt my hair bristle and flex everywhere. I don't think I ever felt more ready to begin a day.

When breakfast was ready we decided to eat it outside, on a card table a good distance from the Airstream. Melchior and I had folded up blankets and sheets, dismantled our two beds and worked them back inside, into their places. Then we brought out chairs and covered the table with a bright striped oilcloth. When we had set it with silver, cups, saucers and plates, we helped Barbara carry breakfast out. There was juice in a stone pitcher, fresh ground coffee with milk warmed for *cafe con leche,* scrambled eggs and sausage, toast and bagels, cream cheese, butter, and lox that Barbara had saved, tucked back in the bottom of the small refrigerator, as a surprise for Melchior. We lounged in our chairs, sipping the last of the coffee and talking when we were finished. It was seven-thirty in the morning by this time, and the sun was still soft and low, coming into our enclosed space refracted, entering between the high stone pillars, not yet shining full from above us. Shadows fell, hard-edged and large on the ground and stone, and some cut in across our table. It was an easy matter to move the head or arm a bit, when it grew a little too hot, to get the part into the cooler shadow.

We talked about their son Paul a little, about the Airstream and how much they were enjoying its amenities, the pleasure of the new Jeep. But mostly we spoke of the place we were in, the soundness of our sleep last night and the pool. Melchior wondered about the caves we had found, the source of the tire ruts running off into the distance, and Barbara told us more about the Anasazi. It seemed there were people called "pot hunters," she said, who were running through this state and adjoining ones, ripping these old caves off, taking what they could get of value. "It's a real problem," she said. There weren't enough Interior or local people to guard all the caves. The space was just too big, and there had been violence. "A little like the Old West," she said. "Gold rush. Valuable old pots and shards." I thought of the dark, ragged circle I had found at the cave entrance and remembered what Karla had told me and the vessels along the wall in Sharonville. Melchior seemed ready to get more information about the Anasazi from Barbara, but he quickly let it drop as he looked at the stone rising around us. The way the light now lay on the massive red rock slabs was a better subject, and we picked out figures and faces on the rock's surfaces, noted particular formations, and talked and joked about them.

Once we had cleaned up after ourselves, put the table and chairs back inside and washed up the dishes, Melchior and Barbara got out brochures and maps and began studying them at the small kitchen table. Barbara seemed to be the real navigator, and I went back to my car, checked out the hitch and tire pressure, then sat on a rock for a last cup of coffee before we departed. I had a place in the shade, close to the rise of a broad wall of rock. I could feel the slight sunburn on my arms, how they and my legs under my pants were comfortably cool now that the sun had left them.

I could not really understand yet how things had changed, my mood and the actual progress of events that had started well before I had entered Utah. Coming into Utah had at first seemed the real beginning of some kind of descent into a past of the kind the Bishop had spoken of so long ago, a place where I had literally never been, but one in which things might be revealed to me—Anson and Lorca, an understanding of myself through possible revelations about them.

Now I thought back to Carl and Anne, realizing that the descent had started there and that I had begun to feel an edge of ominous and depressing expectation ever since my arrival in Sharonville. Entering Utah had only exacerbated it—Needles and that town beyond it as a kind of crossing, then the gates of entrance, and then that wasted and somehow frightening town of Anson's origin, its emptiness and decay, motorcycles, dead tree stumps, and the cemetery.

But then I had found Melchior squatting and rubbing the stone, and since then something in my spirits had lifted, a weight that I had not recognized in my arms had gone out of them as I had my hands and fingers in the oil, feeling the give and resilience of tissue as I massaged Barbara and Melchior under the stars.

There were new things to deal with—the absence of Anson's grave, the letter from Anne, the reconnection to Melchior again, his gravestone art. I had been watching him, trying to figure him out, but that had been lost in my quick awareness of his insouciance. I had come to believe that there was nothing that bothered him, not in the way at least that I was bothered; his past, though I remembered little of any of the particulars he might have told me about it, both recently and in our years together in San Diego, seemed a book that was fully open to him. He had nostalgia, but of an appropriate kind, a kind that did not seem to prevent him in any way from going forward. He had Barbara, and I suspected that was the crucial thing. They were perfect together, whatever that might mean.

And as I twisted these thoughts, extending their serpentine maze, then turning them back on each other, fanning and constricting them, forgetting the rock I was sitting on, losing the feel of the cool shade, I recognized that it could be seen as a matter of syntax, at least as a symptom. They were direct about things; she asking, he answering. She reminding, and he executing. Tasks at hand, whether ideas or the practical matters of activity. She was a wonder; it was true. But they were also a wonder to me together. Had there been a guard against such intimacy when it was Melchior and I together in San Diego? I remembered his tentative reaching as he searched through photos on the couch that day as we overlooked the city from the Palisades. I had thought it nostalgia of a kind that wished for reclamation, that needed, as I felt I now did, to discover something hidden in the past, something to right the present. Now I saw that it was not that at all. It was discomfort born only of the desire to connect up with me in the present. It was a way *into* the present, begun from our only common ground at first. Had it been I that had asked him to bring the pictures out in the first place? Wasn't it I who had lingered too long in the past?

Once we had started out for The Heat's trophy, it had gotten easier. Once we had things to do together in the here and now, our references to the past were centered, for Melchior at least, though I was not at all sure about myself. Taking me into his life had been sane for him, but I had kept noting the changes in his body, his developed vocabulary, referring them constantly back to another time. I think it was Barbara who had brought me completely forward finally, brought me to that place where I could accurately see him as he was, now, in the present, and not as some aberration or mutant development of a truer self that I had known before. Did I think of myself as truer also? What could I be now, then? I was torturing the syntax again, but I held underneath that twisting the feel of the quickly relaxing sinews of Barbara's body under my oily hands the night before. I had felt I'd touched her in a perfect present then, that she had trusted fully in the knowledge that though the touch had sexuality in it, it was itself that completion. It led to nothing other than what it was. She had spread her legs to my touch not as an invitation, but for fulfillment. Her deep, quiet moans had been orgasms in a present and finished event.

We had some trouble getting our caravan around the tight turns that would take us beyond the immediate enclosure of those rock towers among which we had spent the night. At places the rock came up tight against the trail-like road again; there were no shoulders at all, and the road seemed even narrower than it was because the rock tended to taper in, hanging over us, until in places there was no more than a sliver of light entering a hundred or more feet above us.

Melchior drove, and Barbara and I walked to the rear of the caravan, calling out and directing as Melchior got too close to the rock. He had to back up at times, which was difficult with my car as a second trailer, and once we had to jack up the rear of the car and push it off the jack to shift it away from a protruding bulge of rock at a turn. The trailer had a long, dusty scrape along one side of it by the time we had gotten through. When Melchior wiped it with an old piece of toweling, we found it was superficial, something that could be feathered out easily and spot-painted; it had not gotten below primer to metal.

The road straightened enough then, though rocks still came to the edge of it in places, and

Barbara and I were able to get into the Jeep beside Melchior. By ten o'clock we were back into relatively open spaces and were beginning to climb slightly. There was still nothing but red rock, scrub of pinon, yucca, occasional juniper, sand and dry soil all around us. The sun was high, and it beat down brightly on the hood of the Jeep. We wore sunglasses, and Melchior wore a visor. It was a little too small for him, and we joked about the way he looked in it, though we all kept our eyes on the road and the strange landscape, the dead and primitive moonscape through which we slowly traveled.

"They say there's wildlife here in the brochures, bobcats, coyotes, even black bears, but I can't imagine it," Barbara said. "It's so brutal and barren."

"Maybe high, where the trees start," Melchior said.

There were plenty of birds though. We could see them when we leaned forward in the cab. They soared and roosted high up at the top of the rock slabs that we passed among, and some drifted down, almost to our level at times, in search of living things on the canyon floor.

Barbara had marked up maps, and she held them in a ragged pile in her lap, fingering through them, opening and folding them back on themselves, studying and reconnoitering as we moved slowly along. The roadway had widened slightly, was twisting again, and when we came to spaces where we could see for some distance, we noted that the rock slabs and obelisks a long way off seemed to be sinking down into the earth as we rose to elevations that were almost as high as they were. The air cooled a fraction as we ascended, and I could feel it on my arm where it rested on the sill of the open window. Melchior was in four-wheel drive now, had downshifted as the pitch of the incline increased. We made a turn around a pile of large red boulders and saw the first trees, greener than they really were, seen against the barrenness of the landscape that still surrounded us. They were mostly fir trees, tall and sinewy, growing very close together, sun filtering through their branches, making them look a little dusty.

"This is Manti-La Sal, maybe," Barbara said.

"I don't think so yet." Melchior glanced over at her lap, then back at the road.

"Could be it's beginning," I said. "I don't know."

"The Beehive State," Melchior said, gesturing to both sides of the Jeep. We were passing through a miniature meadow, no more than a brief dip in the road, a place of scrub growth, but with scraggly flowers, wild roses I thought, in places at the road's edge. There were hundreds of bees, drifting and dipping into the flowers' cups. The petals were pale pink, washed-out, but the bees were bright in their banded colors.

"Could those be gardenias?" Barbara said, pointing away from the roadside to a gathering beside a low rock formation.

"I wouldn't bet on it," Melchior laughed. "But they do look like our sheets."

"They *are,*" Barbara said. "Imagine!"

It was one o'clock now and we were still climbing. The red rock formations had given way completely, and we could see trees and other green growth in every direction. In the distance, in some places, the rock slabs were still visible, but our view of them was most often cut off by the tall firs. The sun was still overhead, but much of it was caught by the trees, softening it, and there was a cool breeze. I'd brought my arm inside the cab, and Barbara had dropped a thin sweater over her shoulders. It was not cold, but our mild sunburns made our skin a little sensitive to the touch of air.

In two more hours, by three o'clock, we had reached leveler ground, but at a high altitude this time; the firs had shrunk in size, were thinner, fuller as the spaces between them increased. We had come across a few other roads intersecting our own, raw new roads that headed off through the sparse terrain, then dipped and turned and disappeared. There was rock and moss on the ground now, patches of wildflowers here and there. We moved through small meadows that had trickling streams meandering through them. There were low rock formations in the distance, but they were white and gray now, no longer red and dusty. Barbara exclaimed at one point, calling out "sheep!" but by the time Melchior and I had looked where she pointed there was nothing there.

It was after a tight turn in the road, a slight dip as we moved down into a broad meadow where the road straightened for a few hundred yards, that we came upon the car. It was the first sign of anything man-made that we had encountered since leaving the town two days before, the first thing other than beer cans and rifle casings, and I felt the Jeep lurch, the weight of the Airstream and car behind us push ahead for a moment, when Melchior pulled his foot back from the pedal. He didn't touch the brake, but let us coast down the slight decline.

The car was to the side of the road. The hood was up, and as we approached we saw the figure of a slight man leaning against the right front fender, facing the road. He heard us before he saw us. His head turned our way. Then he moved quickly around the front of the car and out of sight, blocked off from our vision by the raised hood. Before we got there he was back in sight again, this time edging out into the roadway tentatively, raising his arm and hailing us. Melchior pumped at the brakes, slowly bringing the Jeep and the weight pushing behind it to a crawl. We came to a full stop to the rear of the car, and Melchior engaged the hand brake and got out. We watched him walk slowly to where the man stood, then the two of them went around to the front of the car, out of our sight. We could hear some talking and some tinkering, then we could hear nothing. We waited a few moments, and then I opened the door on my side, climbed down from the Jeep, and headed for the raised hood. Before I got there, Melchior and the small man rounded the car's front again, and a third man, larger and behind them, came into sight as well.

He was wearing bib overalls, dark blue, stiff and brandnew, and under them a white short-sleeved dress shirt. His hair was silver, combed back from his forehead in a tight pompadour. The legs of his overalls had ironed creases, razor sharp, down the front, and they were slightly belled and a little short where they approached the tops of his shoes. A good two inches of white sock showed. The shoes were black low-cuts, dress shoes with plain toes, and before my eyes traveled up from them and back to his round, flushed face, I knew, even as the thought of it disoriented me, that the Bishop had returned to Utah.

"David, my son!" he called out as I approached him. The flesh at the corners of his eyes creased as his mouth moved into a broad smile.

"This *is* chance!" he said, and he reached to the shoulder of the smaller man, urging him forward ahead of him. Melchior shifted to the side to let them pass.

"This is my friend Burl," the Bishop said when he reached me. He put his free hand on my shoulder, pressed both of us, turning us toward each other, formalizing our introduction. "Burl, you remember, I told you about David?"

If it was chance that had brought me together with the Bishop again, chance of the same quality that had brought me to Melchior in the graveyard earlier, there was nothing to be wondered at in it. But I knew it was not that, knew that the precipitator in our meetings had been myself, my own sad meanderings, and that they were growing away from that sadness as we had come together again, at least insofar as attitude was concerned. I was feeling better, at least in the new community of our traveling, though the quality and direction toward destination were still in question. I had not thought of Anson, or even Lorca, in many hours of the days now, and the oddness of that struck me fully as we worked on the Bishop's car. I had headed into Utah for answers to both relationships, but once there it had become not future revelations that held me but the quality of immediate ones, relationships that in this place had a way of remaining jettisoned from the past.

There was nothing for it but to leave the car. The coil had failed, and wires running from it had been burned away. We spoke jokingly of the possibility of extending our caravan, of hooking the Bishop's car to the rear of my own, then we pushed it off into the meadow, transferred the Bishop's and Burl's belongings to the backseat of my car, and locked theirs up and left it.

"It's a rental," the Bishop said. "Let *them* come and get it."

The Bishop and Burl climbed into the Airstream. It was five o'clock and the sun was beginning to sink. Melchior pulled away slowly. We'd decided we would drive on for only a little while, would look for a place where there was water, hopefully another meadow, a good place to spend the night. We drove on for a half hour, then found our meadow, one smaller and more cozy than the one in which we had discovered the Bishop, this one with a narrow stream running through it, fir trees at its perimeter, level ground covered with moss and occasional stones, larger boulders lining the stream's edge in places. The road was level where the meadow's terrain began, and it was a simple matter to pull our caravan out into the mossy surface. We got fifty yards from the roadway, among a stand of tall, thin aspens, before we stopped.

The Bishop and I sat together, I on the ground, he in a folding director's chair, among the aspens, no more than twenty feet from the Airstream. He had brought out a bottle, a full liter of the best Martell, from a leather case in which he carried quite a few of them. There was a place for large snifters in the case as well, and he had passed them around to all of us. Melchior, Barbara and Burl were sitting at a card table a good distance from us, playing canasta. Melchior had gotten the oil lamps ready, and one rested beside the leg of his chair, the other on a rock where the Bishop and I sat. Neither was lit. There was still light, though the sun was very low, only a faint red wash now among the aspens and firs.

We had barbequed some steaks. Burl had soaked French mushrooms, then sauteed them with onion in oil, and while Melchior was tending the grate, wearing a blue butcher's apron and a white chef's hat, Barbara had made a salad from the one remaining head of lettuce, romaine, a Caesar salad, with egg yolk and packaged croutons. The Bishop had bottles of fine red wine in another case, and we had finished two of them among us. Burl brought out some mints when we were finished, handing them out like a waiter might, bowing and smiling.

"Burl's my boy now," the Bishop said softly. "Well, long lost to me, not really a boy as we were once, but I've given in to what was right with us. I might have lost it forever had I not returned."

He spoke softly, but there was a deep quiver in his voice, and I recognized the gravity of what he was saying, though he said it casually.

"Will you go back?" I said.

"No, I think not, my boy. No, I won't. I'll call in, in a while. I'm sixty-three now, David. Soon enough for retirement in my order and position. They'll not like it much, having to work things out with so little advance notice. But I've kept my affairs in good order, and there's nothing really that they can do about it. No. I won't go back."

"How did it happen?" We could hear Burl's high chuckle, Barbara joshing him as he made his bid.

"Not really too long a story," the Bishop said. He still wore his overalls, but he had put leather slippers on and had changed from the starched white shirt to a light-blue chamois one with long sleeves. His hair shone in the filtered light, and I could see the touch of redness at the edge of his eyebrows where he had recently plucked them.

When he received the letter from Cora's daughter, the whole thing lit up for him in his mind again, and he was shocked at the depth of his immediate sadness and disorientation. Cora was dead, and with the end of her life that strain of his past that had revealed and changed the way he saw himself years ago was now in its way permanent in its alteration. The diorama might turn—there was still Burl— but its turning could only be attenuated now, creaky, and difficult. He could no longer entertain, even in that small recess below thought, the going back, the reseeing of things again; it had been his secret wish, revealed to him and then denied forcefully after he had rehearsed the story, for the first time in close to ten years, that evening under my hands in the grotto.

Dead in her sleep. And her illegitimate daughter, Patty, who had remarkably been in New York City only a few months earlier and had taken the body of a dead one back with her to Utah (fulfilling a last wish of her grandmother from years before), had found his name many times in Cora's diary, his address in her slim book. They would bury her near Nativity. The town had changed, but this was her desire: to rest in the old cemetery near the school. He recognized in the letter the name Anson, remembered its source in a while. Would *he* be buried in the same cemetery? What was the connection to Cora's mother? *Worlds within worlds,* he had thought, but the torquing irony of that glibness could not save him from anxiety and wonder. It was Burl only now, and he was twisted again into thoughts of possible reclamation. He would be going to Utah again. He would visit Cora's grave, he would look for Anson's, and though he did not note it, he knew too that he would try to search out Burl.

"I made my way to Nativity uneventfully. The state of the place was of course shocking. They had beshitted the exterior walls of the school with graffiti, and there was evidence of crude home-steading in classrooms and chapel. The town itself was like another place entirely. But you can imagine my shock. All those tall dead trees, boarded up houses, a wasted environment. It was once thriving, a decent enough town.

"I found Burl at the seminary. It is not too far from the town, and though it too is merely a shadow of what it once was, there's still a kind of skeleton crew there, a few priests, some workers to keep the grounds in reasonable shape. Burl kept the financial accounts up. It was really makework for him. He had been living there for ten years, having given up the secular life shortly after our encounter upon my return to Nativity, the one I told you about that evening in the city, in my grotto. He had drifted for a while after that, selling things still, but slowly extricating himself from his accounts. Then he had just walked away from it, begged entrance to the seminary. It's a sad tale all around, but it's over now."

"What was it that he sold?"

"Oh, high fashion clothing. Things to buyers in expensive department stores and such."

Burl was dressed in loose slacks and a flowing satin shirt of the same color. He wore tan Italian shoes, a silver identification bracelet loose at his wrist, and a purple scarf to the side of his neck, the broad tails draped over his shoulder. I followed the Bishop's eyes as he looked over at him while speaking. He saw us watching and lifted his arm and hand in a wave. We waved back, and we could see his teeth shine as he smiled.

"He seems relaxed enough," I said. "Not at all as I remember from your story."

"*Now* he is," the Bishop said. "I'm more relaxed too, David."

I recognized that that was true. Creases that I remembered in his face, a certain tightness in speech and movement, a slight slump in posture even in his severe clerical clothing, all these were gone now. His vocabulary remained the same, full of words that seemed gleaned from reading, but he now used them with more comfort and a certain irony. They were parts of another language, one that he was giving up as the growing awareness of his new freedom became part of him.

"Is he your lover?" I asked, lifting the snifter to my lips and lowering my eyes, giving him time.

There was a pause, an extended moment in which we could hear the twitter of the first night birds, just a few notes, distinct, with spaces of silence all around them. "Ah, David," he said. "We may be too old for that. I don't know. But I admit, I hope not. Time will have to tell. That I have found him again, can possibly right something—that is my measure, at least for now."

I felt that itch in my fingers, hearing him say these things. Intimacy, and so I yearned to touch flesh again, knowing that the itch may well have been my exact pathology, the desire for possession that was control and not possibly intimacy at all. I thought of Anson and what might have been my own missed chance. There was nothing possible where he was concerned now. Could there be a chance with Lorca should I find her? What would I be finding if I did so? She had left me so long ago, and I was not sure I had any real idea of what she had been then or would be now. But it was the same, I supposed, with the Bishop and Burl. The Bishop too had felt he'd lost him beyond reclamation. He'd said, as I remembered, that he'd forgotten him completely until he'd gone back and at the reunion come upon him. Maybe I had still a ways to go before discovery. It came to me that I was already discovering things. I could give no names to them yet, but I was learning. First

Melchior and Barbara, now the Bishop and Burl—possibly the old story of the journey itself being the arrival. Still my fingers stretched and began sweating, though the Bishop was going on now with the details of his story without my touching him.

"So we had lunch together at a picnic table under a ragged old awning in the yard of the seminary. And we talked, and before we knew it Burl was packing his things. I found this clothing in the one open shop in the town when we got there. I changed out of my clerical garments in the car. What Burl has on are things he has had for years, but he has never before worn them beyond the privacy of his rooms.

"We went to the cemetery and stood at the foot of Cora's grave there. The earth still had that fresh turned look to it. I tried in what phone booths I could find in the town, but all the books had been ripped free of their chains. When I did find one, back in the store where I had purchased this clothing, Patty's name was not in it. We searched the cemetery for your Anson's grave, but we could not find it there. We left the town, uncertain wanderers really. We were going nowhere, just getting placed in the new somewhere of our being together again. Then our car broke down and you came upon us. We must have traveled by another road. Surely we would have met earlier otherwise. And the terrain your friends spoke about was nothing at all like what we passed through on our way."

The revelations of the connection between Anson and the Bishop, the fact of the three women, grandmother, mother, and daughter, came to me with less shock than I would have imagined after I heard it. The Bishop was talking loosely and freely, and when the facts came, they came as just part of a gathering of details, of equal value with the rest mentioned. He said that Patty had noted in her letter that she'd had no trouble keeping up with Anson, had traced him easily through fashion magazines. She'd been in the city on some business when she'd seen the obituary, a prominent one, in the *Times*. She had held on to her grandmother's wish for many years. She was the only other family that she had. And so she had come and taken Anson away, returned him again to Utah.

There was a hint, the Bishop said, of a rift between Cora and her mother. It had been Patty who had held the tenuous family together.

"She wrote a lot," I said. "As much about her grandmother as her mother?"

"That's true, actually. I suspect with both of them gone she needed to hold them together, hold herself together."

"Is it possible that she still lives in that town? The place seems very wrong for that."

"Well, I doubt it," he said. "I suspect that she only buried Cora there because it was home, home for her mother that is. The letter was postmarked elsewhere, another town that I did not recognize, though also in Utah. I found no evidence of the grandmother's grave either, but then I had no name to go by."

"It was Maudie," I said.

He lifted the snifter to his lips and tipped it back. Then he rested it on the rock between us, took up the bottle, and refilled both of our glasses. The game at the card table had grown quiet and more casual. Melchior had lit his lantern, and its glow washed across the players' arms and the fans of their cards. I took a match and lit our own, placing it on the rock to the side of our glasses and the brandy bottle.

"What will you do now?" I said.

"Go with you for a while, if you'll have us. We're in no rush to get elsewhere. We're just getting used to each other in this new way. It's lovely here, not at all as it was below in that red rock. If you have room for us, that would be good."

We set the camp up almost as we had the previous night. The bed and cot came out, and we unhooked two of the other bunks for the Bishop and Burl, putting them next to each other, no more than a few feet from our own. Barbara and Melchior went to the river to bathe, and then the Bishop and Burl did the same, separately. I heard the Bishop laughing to himself when he came back. There was a twinkle in his eyes and a certain shyness. He had a large white Turkish towel wrapped around his girth and he wore only his leather slippers.

"David," he said. "It has been a considerable length of time, my boy. Do you think I could prevail upon you?" I knew what he meant, and I smiled as he approached me.

"Burl, too?"

"No, no, I don't think so. Too modest for that. Am I right, Burl?"

He was sitting on the edge of his cot, a few feet away. Melchior and Barbara were in the Airstream, getting ready for bed.

"Yes, yes, you're right, Father," he said in a high, shy laugh. "My time will come though, I assure you."

The Bishop laughed and nodded.

"You don't know what you're missing, Burl!" It was Barbara, standing in the narrow doorway of the Airstream. We saw Melchior's smiling moon-face over her shoulder.

"She's right about that, my man," Melchior said, and then we were all laughing.

It had grown dark now, and only the lights of the lanterns lit up our encampment. They gave a bright glow, and it was easy to find our way among rocks and trees. The moss was soft and spongy under our slippers, and in the lantern light it looked like a thick green carpet. Melchior and Barbara went to their bed and sat down on it in their matching pajamas, gray ones with narrow white stripes and little emblems on the pockets. They still held their snifters in their hands. Melchior had put a tape on the recorder in the Airstream and had opened the windows on our side of the trailer. The music was turned down softly, Miles Davis's "Sketches of Spain." Burl lay on his cot with his arms over his head on the pillow, looking up through branches of the trees, into the bright stars that were just beginning to come out. His snifter sat on a low rock within easy reach. The Bishop lay on his stomach, the bright white towel, shining in the lantern's glow, covering his hips and buttocks. And I was astride him, bending forward slightly, my hands slick with oil again, my fingers beginning that push into tissue, those movements that would take him to a kind of recovery, but only that right and inconsequential one, the one of refreshed muscle and sinew, after a day of bodily movement and long periods of sitting that he was unaccustomed to.

We rose quite early in the morning, washed in the river at first light, then packed up the bedding and other gear. The Bishop was his new, jovial self, which was like the old one, but touched with a new freedom of gesture, a loose informality. He joked with Burl, and Burl was more talkative then the day before, giving back to the Bishop in equal measure. It was good to see them together, the one robust and bold, the other still a bit tentative in the wilds, but smiling and enthusiastic in his willingness to learn as he helped with the packing up. Melchior taught him the turns that the mattress needed to get through the narrow door, and it was Burl who helped Barbara with the light breakfast she was preparing and who set the table. I watched the Bishop help Melchior check out the vehicles oil, tires, hitches, and various other inspections— in preparation for our departure, and I was warmed to see the pairings that were bringing us together as a community. We were five wanderers out of multiple pasts now, but connected together for me because of my own singular decision to reenter mine. I felt some affirmation in being able to introduce them to the pleasures of each other's company.

By seven we were back on the road. Melchior had moved gear from the small backseat of the Jeep to the Airstream, and though it was crowded, there was room for Burl and Barbara there. Melchior, the Bishop, and I sat abreast in the front. Barbara kept most of the maps, and she and Burl examined them with their heads together, pointing, tracing out faint, broken road-lines, naming places. The Bishop had one in his hands in the front.

"This is quite useless," he said after studying it for a while.

"You're right about that," Barbara said. "Where we are just isn't there."

"We'll go along," Melchior said. "This one seems pretty good. It got us together anyway."

"But just where is it that we're going?" Burl said.

Barbara laughed. "I'm not sure we've figured that out yet."

The road *was* pretty good, relatively gentle in its climbing turns, enough shoulder, and growth far enough back from its edges to let the width of the Airstream through without too much brushing and scraping. But then, as we continued to climb and the sun reached up to the tips of the low trees, ruts began to develop, with good-sized stones and rocks in them, and the road itself narrowed; larger boulders and trees began to creep to the edges of it. There were tight turns and twists again, and we heard the dull thuds of things shifting in the Airstream.

"Is it secure?" Burl said, a note of concern in his voice.

"Oh, sure," said Melchior. "It's all tied down or in locked drawers and cabinets." Just then we heard the distinct sound of something falling and clattering.

"Dishes from the shelves, I bet," Barbara said. "Thank God they're plastic. We better check it."

Melchior pumped the brakes until we came to a stop, and then we all piled out. The road was now in a cut between large boulders and trees, and

328

Barbara had to sidestep to get to the door of the Airstream. Burl went with her while the three of us stood at the hood of the Jeep, bending and stretching. They were back in a short time. It had been just the dishes, a loose latch. Everything else seemed in order.

"I think I better check up ahead," Melchior said. We all looked up the road as he stepped away from us. There was a tight turn about fifty yards away and we could not see beyond it, but we could see that the road got even narrower there, trees leaning in over it, one large rock formation extending a bit out into it. The Bishop and I moved after Melchior, walking quickly until we caught up with him.

"You'd better think about changing shoes," I said as we moved along. The Bishop was still wearing his overalls and I could see the black leather cleric's shoes he had on. He slipped a bit in ruts. Leather soles, I thought.

"I know it," he said. "These are good only on carpets and city streets. I've a pair of roughhouse ones among my belongings. They'll need breaking in."

Beyond the turn, the road ascended at an acute angle, disappearing over a ridge in the distance. The ruts were rougher and deeper in its climb. It looked difficult and I was not sure that we could make it.

"I don't think we can make that," Melchior said, shaking his head. He had his hands on his hips, looking up the road, then to the left and right. "What's that up there?" he said, "on the left." There was what looked like a break in the trees where he pointed.

"Another road, I suspect," the Bishop said.

"Let's check it." And Melchior moved off again.

Even on foot it was hard going, and we recognized before we reached the break in the trees that we would have some real trouble negotiating the climb to the turn and beyond. The ruts grew deeper as we climbed; there were rounded rocks the size of a man's head at various places in them. Rock protruded out into the roadway, hard and with sharp edges.

The break was indeed another road, broader and in better shape than the one we were now on. It ascended, but its climb was gradual and we could see up it for a good distance. There seemed to be no rock overhangs, no trees of consequence. Melchior stood at the entrance, checking the angle of turn into it. He nodded after a while, indicating that he thought we could make the turn.

It took us an hour to get up as far as the entrance onto the road. We got caught in deep ruts, had to back up, remove large rocks, and twice we had to use Melchior's old folding army-shovel to dig our way out. The turn itself was no difficulty once we reached it, and once we had made the turn and had all of our twelve wheels on the new roadway, we stopped and took turns at the Airstream bathroom to wash up. The Bishop went to my car and changed his shoes, and Burl got into rougher clothing.

We were silent for the next hour, worn out from the effort of getting our caravan onto the new roadway. We watched as Melchior constantly moved his hands, steering, shifting down, negotiating sharp turns. The road had begun to climb along a developing ridge. Where there had been meadows and forest to our left, the land had begun to fall away, had become a steep decline of rock and brush, the floor of a valley in the far distance below us. To our right there was only rock now, rising sheer and vertical to a height we could not see or measure.

"We're in a little trouble," Melchior said softly. I thought he meant the terrain, for we had rounded a turn to find that the decline on our left had suddenly become as sheer as the rise to our right, the road now even narrower, with no shoulder at all, only the drop-off no more than a few feet from our tires.

"Gas," he said. "It's reading empty. We'll have to siphon. I hope to hell there's some in yours, David." He opened the door to get out, looked down, then closed it again. "I don't think that way's good." Even from my side of the cab, I had seen nothing but empty space when the door was open. I tried opening my own door, but it hit the rock and there was no room to slide through.

"The back window," Burl said. "I'll go."

"Wait, Burl!" But it was only a reflex of concern. The Bishop could see as well as the rest of us how narrow the window was. Only Burl was thin enough, small enough, to squeeze through. Barbara helped him and we watched him go, up the ladder to the roof of the Airstream and out of sight. He came back in ten minutes with the gas can. It wouldn't fit through the rear window, and he had to climb to the roof of the Jeep and pass it down the side to Melchior's extended hand. Melchior got it adjusted, turning it in the air outside the window, and Burl climbed back in. Then, with the Bishop holding his belt and I holding my arms around the Bishop's ample waist, Melchior opened the door and got the can in position at the gas cap. He had to lean well out to get it to Barbara. She had kneeled on the rear seat cushion and had her arms out the window. She removed the cap and reached even further out, taking the bottom rim of the can, elevating it as Melchior held its handle. It was tricky, and some spilled. We could smell it vaporize in the air. But she managed to get most of the two gallons in. It would take us a few more miles at least. When the operation was finished, the can sat on the seat in the back between Burl and Barbara.

The drop to our left remained constant as we

climbed, and after a while Melchior remarked that we must be very high up now. He could see clouds over the cliff edge at our left, a good distance down, hanging over and obliterating what might be there. Barbara could see them too, from her place in the backseat, on Melchior's side of the Jeep.

"I see them," Burl said, leaning over Barbara to look out the window, his hand on her shoulder. There was nothing but sheer rock on both sides now. The road was serpentine, with constant turns that prevented us from seeing very far as we ascended.

Melchior drove at a snail's pace. The air was still, but it was crisp and dry. We knew by the sharp shadows the sun made on the rock around us that we were very high up; it was bright where the sun lay, but there was no heat shimmer at the shadows' edges. We watched the gas gauge. It had moved only a fraction when we'd added the fuel, and we saw it slipping back into the red zone. Melchior kept the Jeep in low gears. The engine was laboring, the valves pinging a little in our steep ascent. We were alert to the possibility that was now becoming a certainty. There would be no gas stations ahead. There was nowhere to turn around, no road had led off this one since we had entered it.

"I hope you care for a little stroll, Burl," the Bishop said, and though we laughed at his dry humor, our laughs were hollow. From our vantage in the Jeep, we felt both the openness and the enclosure, the sheer rock on either side, the slight giddiness of being so high up and on the brink of a fall into the tops of clouds over the precipice no more than a yard from the Jeep's side. If we lost my car at some turn, it could pull the Airstream with it. We could wind up like the whip of a small train dragged from some high trestle. My imagination played with such things, and I was really wishing that the Jeep would begin to cough soon.

Then it did cough, a brief choking sound and a lurch. Then nothing. Melchior set the hand brake, looked over at me, shrugged, and gave the key a turn. The starter ground, but there was no hint of a spark at all.

"Sooner than I would have thought," he said. "Can you get out that side, David?"

I was able to get the door open this time. With luck, we had stopped at a place where a shallow crevice in the rock face allowed for it. We were able to stand together outside the door, but we had to make our way up the ladder to the roof of the Airstream to get back to my car. We hugged to the rock incline as we walked along in our tight line; we felt the pull of the open air to the other side, that strange beckoning of the fall down hundreds of feet to the tops of the clouds. I tried to look out, rather than down, but the clouds kept drawing me. The roof of the Airstream was slick and slightly curved, and even though we inched along close to the rock rise, our hands extended and touching it, we could see hundreds of feet below the cliff's edge. The clouds were thick and bluish, storm clouds, and I thought it must be raining under them. We were in clear, crisp air, and the earth far below us seemed like another, stormy, world entirely.

Barbara was behind me. I felt her touch my back from time to time. I could hear brief sounds in the throats of the others. We didn't lift our feet, but slid them along the slick roof.

There was room on the rock-wall side of my car, and when we reached the ground again, we were able to sidestep between the car and the rock rise.

I got the pack I had from the trunk, and Burl and the Bishop gathered the things that they had that could be of use. I saw the Bishop slip a fresh bottle of Martell into the one canvas shoulder bag that they had between them.

"It will be good to have this evening," he said. "Even out of the bottle."

We made our way back to the Airstream, and Melchior broke one of the rear windows, got the latch open, and carefully hoisted Barbara in. She was gone for a while; we saw the trailer shift a little with her movements. Then she returned to the window and began handing things down. When she was finished, Melchior helped her out, and we all went to the rear of my car again and packed the three knapsacks that we had between us. The Bishop's canvas shoulder bag was small, but he was able to press clothing and some cooking implements into it. When we were ready, we crossed the top of the trailer again and started up the road.

After fifteen minutes of climbing, stumbling, and huffing in the thin air, we began to notice the flowers.

It was Barbara who saw them first, just a few, growing out of crevices in the rock face itself.

"What can those *be?*" she said, but they were too high above us to get to easily and we continued on.

"City flowers they look like to me," Burl said, and the Bishop nodded in agreement. He had his roughhouse shoes on now, high-top climbing boots with a fresh shine on their new leather.

Then we turned a corner in the road and came upon more of them. They were growing in what soil there was on either side of us now, and in profusion, and there were numerous bees gathered around them, flying lazily, dipping into cups, loading their feet with pollen. On the cliff side of the road, the flowers leaned out over the edge, moving a little in the downdraft, and even the bees there dipped out of sight, and then fought back from below the cliff to grab at petals and buds.

"Like the sheets," Melchior said.

"God, yes. It's unbelievable!" Barbara said, going over to a pair at the rock wall. "They're gardenias for sure. Blue ones!"

"Look over there!" Melchior said. He was pointing ahead of us and to the right, to a place no more than fifty yards in the distance where the sun shone in flowers on the bare rock face. There were thousands of flowers. They covered the sheer incline in the shape of a large arch that was close to twenty feet high at its peak. I could not imagine how they could have grown wild there. The ragged flower-lined edges of the arch were too symmetrical and intentional.

We moved quickly on, and when we reached within a few feet of the arch, we saw that the road we were on ended a few yards beyond it. It ended oddly and abruptly. The sheer face of rock simply turned into its path, closing it off, ending and climbing to a great perpendicular height at the cliff's edge to our left. We turned from it, standing in front of the flower wall now, and then we saw that it was indeed an archway, an entrance into the rock face. The flowers hung out into the opening, and one would have to brush against them to get through. The petals that edged out into the space were translucent at their tips. There was light emanating from within them, a faint glow from a source far beyond us, something deep in the very rock itself. Burl squatted down a little and peered in.

"I can't see the end," he said. "But it's a tunnel." He turned on his haunches and looked up at us. "Let's go," he said.

"Right. There's nothing else for it," the Bishop said, and we all nodded to one another. There were smiles on Barbara's and Melchior's faces, and I realized that they were responses to my own. I was not sure what I was smiling about, but I was the first one to squat down a little and creep into the low entrance of the archway.

The going was easy, the floor of the tunnel level and clear of large stones, the walls smooth and without protuberances, and in only a few feet I was able to stand up to my full height. The tunnel turned, but gradually, and I could hear the four others, breathing easily now, as they moved in behind me.

We went on for a full twenty minutes. The walls

remained lit with the glow we had seen at the entrance, and there was nothing to make us pause or consider. Melchior whistled a few random notes at one point, hearing the echo come back to him, but the sound was inappropriately loud, and he left off immediately. Then the tunnel made its final turn, and we could see the duplicate of the archway where we had entered in the distance in front of us. The glow was soft there, the light vacant and empty of objects—nothing but a wash of blue. Then something white and soft-looking passed from one side to the other, and we realized it was a cloud and that we were looking into the sky.

When I arrived at the archway, I stepped out on what proved to be a broad stone ledge at its entrance and waited for the others to join me, looking back into the tunnel. It was only after we were together, in a tight gathering on the ledge, that we looked downward.

"God!" Barbara said. "What can this be *about?*"

There was a small valley below us, no more than fifty acres in size, I judged, surrounded on all sides by the steep rock face in which the tunnel had made

341

its exit. We were high up above the valley, but the air was so clear that the cabins that formed a rough circle around the perimeter seemed much closer than they really were. We could see the burls in the logs, the bright glint of skylights, the textures in limbs of fir and aspen growing around them. At places, the steep surrounding wall of rock had cut-backs in it, deep cul-de-sacs of miniature meadows in which there were other cabins, set deeply back. We could see bits of roof ridges, places where trees had been cut down, small cultivated paths. At the very end of the valley, directly across from us, there was a thick stand of fir trees, the beginning of a small forest. The sun cut a broad stripe of light across the valley's empty center, but the forest was in complete shadow. I thought I saw the symmetrical edge of a structure deep among the forest trees, well back into them, but I couldn't be sure of it.

"Here's a pathway," Burl said. And we all moved to the side of the ledge and saw the cuts in the rock, the foot places, and then the dirt trail that meandered back and forth as it descended down the rock face.

I went ahead, keeping my eyes on the ground and rock; the trail was narrow and steep, but the decline was less severe in its pitch as we descended, and the going got easier. In no more than ten minutes we reached the edge of the valley floor, coming out onto it at the side of a cabin. I glanced in a window as we passed, seeing furniture edges, but no human movement. Then we got beyond its side and moved out into the valley proper. We came closer together as we reached open space, becoming a tight little crowd. I felt shoulders touch my own, hands brush against fabric. The place seemed peaceful enough, but there was something vaguely ominous in its complete emptiness of human activity. A few songbirds sounded, but there was no other animation at all.

Then I heard a tentative scraping sound in the distance to my left. I looked that way, squinting in the sun, and caught a brief flash of light from a window in one of the cabins. The light blinked as a figure moved on the cabin porch in front of the window, then it shone brightly again. I raised my hand to my brow and peered into the light. I saw a woman standing beside the cabin door, something familiar in her posture, then saw the smaller figure emerge from behind her long skirts, pause for a moment, leaning forward tentatively, then step and bound from the porch and run toward me.

"Look there!" Melchior whispered at my shoulder, and I pulled my eyes from the porch and the running figure and looked across the valley to the darkened forest. The trees were waving slightly, a breeze had come up, and the figure seemed to materialize from deep within their moving branches.

She came out of them, half shimmering and obscure, washed in mottled shadow figures the branches cast over her garments at first, then emerging whole and distinct in the bright sunlight, yards beyond the small forest. I somehow knew she was Lorca, though there was nothing recognizable yet in her movements. She had a long staff in her hand, at arm's length and held upright. She carried it without effort, though I could see a thick, heavy gathering at its top, well above her head, a moving mass of some sort, a swelling and pulsing ball that was clearly alive.

"What *is* it?" Barbara said behind me.

"Sweet Jesus," the Bishop said. "Those are bees!"

"They are! They are!"

The swarm moved thick on the staff, elevating itself to the tip, then descending slightly, thinning as it swelled out, thickening in recession. Small figures bounced from it at times, sparks in the light, atomic elements thrust out from the energy of its center, then pulled back in as others replaced them, a constant, shifting aura of hot droplets that seemed to evaporate as they reentered, renewed, then sparked out whole around it in the air again. The whole had a rhythm, up and down on the shaft, like a piston containing its own power. We could hear nothing, but I felt a deep drone in my chest, the rumble, at idle, of some massive engine.

She came forward, moving out from under the darker shadows of extended limbs, then stepped into the lighter, simpler shadows at the valley's brink. Then she was in the sunlight and we could see her clearly, could see the grain of the upright staff, the shimmers in the pulsing ball of bees, her clothing, and the distinct movements of her body.

She came forward until she was no more than fifty yards from us, and then she stopped. Her hair was long, tied with a ribbon, the length of it draped over her shoulder, extending to where it fanned out at its tips, covering her right breast. She wore a long paisley skirt, heavy climbing boots below it, and a loose blue blouse.

I felt hands grip at my belt, small arms encompass my waist tightly. I looked down into Coppie's smiling and upturned face. I put my hand over his brow and pressed his head into my hip. Then I looked back at her, saw the jaunty blue gardenia she wore in her hair over her right ear. She was smiling, but I could not otherwise read her expression. I could hear the deep drone of the bees for real now. The engine was no longer in my chest.

Pretty dramatic, wasn't it?" Anne said. "I mean the staff and bees, that flower in her hair and all."

"How long have you been here?" I said.

"Oh, about a week, week and a half, I guess."

We were sitting near the end of the long table, Coppie at the very end of it. He needed to sit straight in order to reach his food, which he was just toying with, small bites on the end of his fork occasionally. His bright eyes were mostly on me. He leaned to the side a little in my direction. Anne was across from me.

Lorca had looked at us for a long time. I'm sure that the others behind me were watching the bees. I could hear them, their deep communal drone over her head on the staff, but I was watching Lorca, trying to manage some sort of smile through my shock. She looked pretty much the same, but more mature, centered in some way, and of course older.

I wondered how my face had changed for her, whether it had changed at all, at least in character.

"Welcome, David," she had said. "I'll need a little time now. You can go with Anne; she'll take care of you."

And then she turned and walked back toward the forest. I watched her go, seeing at least some residual of that swing in her hips that I remembered. Halfway to the forest, she lifted her staff and tapped it once on the ground. She looked up, and though I could not hear her I think she must have said something. The swarm tightened and rose, rotating slightly, until it was in the air above the staff's tip. Then it seemed to swell out a little, elongating into a kind of cylinder as it moved off. When it reached the forest edge ahead of her, it melted into the first branches. She entered among the trees herself then and was gone.

Barbara sat beside Anne, across from me, and down the table from her were the three men, the Bishop holding forth in a soft, jovial voice, commenting on the quality of the food, the wine they had brought us in large carafes. We had been served by three men in white outfits. I could see other men through the doorway leading into the larger dining room. They stood at the elbows of the seated women, offering food from large metal and wooden bowls, pouring wine into glasses. I could see only part of the table around which they moved, the heads and faces of a few women. I guessed there must have been twelve or so there. I had thought I'd seen at least one man in the group when they had entered, but when that figure came into full view I saw it was a woman with short cropped hair, dressed in rough casual clothing. She had delicate features and wore no makeup. The women had come in severally and in pairs, talking vibrantly, dressed in various work clothes, colorful checks and paisleys. I had caught a glimpse of Abbey and Dana, Anne's two girls, among them.

"What is this place exactly?" Barbara said, turning to Anne. "Some kind of art colony? They've certainly fixed old Melchior up."

Someone had seen his altered grave rubbings at that small show in New Jersey years ago. She was a small, compact woman in her thirties, and she had recognized him from the opening. She must have been very young then, but Melchior had a look that was hard to forget. When Lorca left us, and before Anne had managed to get us back to the door of her cabin, the woman had appeared from somewhere and had taken Melchior aside and spoken intently to him. They had then gone off together to one of the other cabins. Melchior had talked briefly to Barbara before going with her.

"She said she had something to show him, is what he said. Now he's got his own studio! He took me to it just before dinner. Do you think they expect us to stay here? "

"I don't think they expect much of anything," Anne said. "They seem very self-contained here. I think it can only be because they liked what he was doing."

"And have you spoken to her?" I said.

"We've talked a little. Quite a bit actually. She's changed, David. Really not the same person at all. She seems to have left most of her past behind her, except for a few important things."

When we were finished with dinner, the men in

white brought dessert in on a large cartlike affair with wheels. There was a tall chocolate cake, a bowl of whipped cream, and strawberries. Coppie didn't seem interested, but Barbara was, and I saw the Bishop carry back two heaping plates, one for himself and one for Burl. Melchior got his own. Then the men poured coffee, brought cream and sugar to the table. In a while there was the tinkle of a little bell.

"That means we're to leave so they can clean up," Anne said.

When we were back in Anne's cabin, I asked her about Carl. Coppie sat on the arm of my chair, his head resting against my shoulder, both hands holding tight to my left arm.

"Daddy's gone," he said sleepily, and Anne came over to him, disengaged his hands, and led him away into a small bedroom at the rear of the cabin.

"It really hasn't been too tough on him," she said. "I know that sounds naive, but it's true. The fact is he's more relaxed now than he's ever been. The girls found a way of handling the situation long ago, pretty well at least, but he never did:

Banyon and Kip, Carl's weirdness and all. He hardly clutches at all since Carl left. I was surprised when he grabbed at you so quickly."

"Something out of the past," I said. "Those days when I was with you in Sharonville."

"I suppose so."

Anne's girls were not in the cabin with us. She had told me at dinner that they were working in the evenings with a photographer, a woman who was showing them how to develop pictures. She'd been showing them how to take them in the last week. When they had arrived and met her, they'd shown her some of the prints that Karla had taken of her daughters. The woman had tightened, flushed a little, and told them she would show them what photography was really all about. They had been photographing rocks, trees and flowers, and would soon get to people.

"How long are you staying here?"

"We're not in any hurry to get anywhere else," she said.

One of the women had met them in a town a good distance away. It had been a long drive to the place, and it was after dark when they arrived. Anne had no idea how they'd entered the colony, but the last few hundred yards had been on foot. There was no tunnel that she remembered. Surely not one of the kind that I described to her.

"They're efficient here. You need not worry about your caravan. I'm sure that'll be taken care of."

"Carl just walked out of the place," she said. "No goodbye, and no note. Nothing at all. I didn't even know for sure that he was gone until three days had passed. Then I got a card from Los Angeles. *Enough,* it said, that was all, just his initials at the bottom. Then the letter from Lorca came, brief and insistent also, and I figured what the hell."

I thought she was finished, and I was searching for some way to press on with the subject, when she continued. She looked away from me as she started talking, but after the first few sentences she began to catch my eye again.

"Kip and Banyon," she said. "I'm sure Karla told you something about that. They were sleeping together with Carl in the house, off and on, together and separately, when they were there. I could handle that. I guess I kidded myself that it was some sort of aberration, and that it would end. But the fact that the kids knew about it—they couldn't help but know—was embittering, though I didn't feel the full force of that for sure until very recently. That I had closed off from him completely. He's really crazy, David. Never violent, though that always seemed a possibility, in any way, with any of us. But that distance in him. I think he had a way of covering up when we first married, but it wasn't really very long before I felt the full force of it. A shell that just could not be cracked. And then he got stranger with us. Little things with the kids. Like laughing at the wrong things, showing physical affection when it wasn't wanted, talking to them about things they couldn't possibly understand. It was the worst with Coppie; the girls had each other, and they had me like another friend, but he had no one. Christ, he had Kip and Banyon! They came and went and were as bad as Carl was. It was all extremely sick.

"Then about two years ago, he started bringing

all that pottery. That, and his fucking cooking (he was obsessed with it) cooled things out for a little while just when they were about to break. He got focused on things that didn't really harm us, and I guess we just all decided to live with it. I did at least. You can live with a lot of things, I guess.

"Karla didn't tell me about the pots, but I could see that there was a problem there. She got strange when she saw them. I looked into it as best I could, in books and such. Anasazi pots. He was making those summer trips to Yosemite for climbing. I knew he was meeting Banyon and Kip there, and I figured that they weren't staying just there either. I figured they were here in Utah, digging that pottery out."

"Do you know of somebody, a young girl, named Luna?"

"Yes. I know of her. Now at least. I didn't know a damn thing about all that until I got here. But I just can't tell you about that, David. It wouldn't be right. You'll see. You'll have to talk with Lorca."

I wanted to press her, but I could tell by the way her lips tightened that she would tell me nothing.

I could sense that their reconnection, even though Lorca had changed for her, was an important one, not only because of the fact of information. Her tightening had what seemed like an edge of loyalty in it. Something to do with the past, but something that was also a product of their reconnection in the present.

"She's got a hold on something now," Anne said. "Her painting. It's a way of life here, and I think that it's been that for a long time with her."

"What's her position?" I said.

"Why, I thought you knew! She runs this place. Has for a while. About five years, I think."

"Can you tell me anything at all?" I said.

"I can tell you that there are answers. Whether or not they'll be what you're after, I can't tell you that."

I woke once to the sound of a bell tinkling, faintly, a long way off in the distance. I thought it was the same one that had been rung at the end of dinner. Sun came in at the window, washing across my chest and stomach, but my face was in the shade. I rose to my elbows, feeling a certain stiffness in my arms and legs. I could see the edge of a fir limb and rock a few feet away from the sill. I sank back again, turned over, and went to sleep.

"You've missed breakfast, my boy," the Bishop said. "But there's plenty of coffee brewing. Burl, get him a cup, will you?"

I was sitting on the porch of their cabin, in the shade. The Bishop still wore his pajamas, white cotton ones with a small gold monogram and emblem on his pocket. He had a cup in his hand. Bits of unruly hair poked up at his ears, small twisted curls. His eyes were bright.

"We did it last night, my boy," he said in a whisper, not looking at me. "Is that the way you put it? I don't know." He laughed tentatively, his voice breaking a bit in the high register.

"That's good enough," I said, leaning toward him. "How was it?"

He shifted in his rocking chair, taking his coffee cup in his palms. "Oh, my. Well, I don't know exactly. These are old bones, you know. Burl had some experience. He guided me. That was new for

357

me, being guided, you know. This morning I feel glorious!"

"Then it was good," I said. "Regrets?"

"Oh, shit no! Not a single damn bit of it." He was rocking in his chair. "Only that it took so long to get here. And even that's not a bother. Not now."

Burl came out with a cup for me and in his other hand the pot. He poured more for the Bishop and filled up his own cup where it rested on the small redwood table beside his chair.

"Did you tell him, Johnny?" he said. He too was shy at first, but when the Bishop nodded, his face broke into a broad smile, and when he took his seat he looked directly at me.

"Two good old boys!" he said, somewhat whimsically, and the three of us laughed together.

"This seems a perfect place," the Bishop said. "For most anything."

We drank our coffee and talked, and I noted, in the pauses in our conversation, that there was a certain complete silence in the air. I looked around. There was no one at all in sight. All the doors of the other cabins were shut tight. It was as if the place were deserted, a ghost town but for the fact that all the structures were in such good repair, well-tended flowers in pots at the corners of porches, frames freshly painted, windows washed, and not a dead limb or leaf on any tree.

"Where are they all?" I said.

"Why, working," the Bishop said. "It seems this is a place where people get things done! You should have seen them disperse after breakfast. By the time Burl and I had sauntered out of the dining room, they had all disappeared."

"You went there in your pajamas?"

"Well, no, not exactly. A little late morning nap, you know?"

"Oh," I said. "Of course. What about Barbara and Melchior? Where's Anne and the kids?"

"Barbara's with Anne and Coppie somewhere, I think," Burl said. "Melchior's at his studio."

"I take it the little girls are developing now," the Bishop said.

Burl and I glanced at each other and laughed.

"Film! I mean film! You two lads know what I'm talking about!"

"Everyone seems quite busy here," I said.

"And what's for us to do?" the Bishop said, smiling over at Burl.

I saw the glance they gave each other. "Well, for me it's time to shower and clean up," I said. Then I left them on their porch, looking at each other with a fresh, new wonder, and headed back to my cabin.

Lorca did not appear at our table the next two evenings, nor did she eat with the other colonists in the larger room. I was getting itchy and feeling offended. I recognized the latter as an odd and almost humorous feeling, as if no time had intervened and Lorca owed me at least civility. If she owed me anything, it was much larger than that, and I knew my feelings were petty ones, given the circumstances. What could an explanation of her having left me over ten years ago mean to me now? Save that I could alter my sense of myself, rotate the diorama, it could mean very little.

"She's very into something," Anne said to me on the second evening. She had placed her hand on my arm and spoken privately. "A series of paintings, she told me. Don't take it amiss. She belongs to her art now, not to anything else." She said the last with seriousness and conviction, and though the words were arch and overdone, I could tell she meant them quite literally. Who was I to make a judgment, who knew nothing of her anymore?

The first two days seemed to last a week. I had absolutely nothing to do and everyone else had. Everyone but Anne and Coppie, that is. Barbara divided her time between Melchior, when he wasn't working, and Abbey and Dana, at the photographic lab and near them on the grounds while they were taking pictures. The girls seemed not to want their mother or brother with them, wanted to be treated as adults involved in adult enterprise. And indeed they acted that way, like adults, measured and serious in their endeavors, acute in their observations and involvements with light, color, and subject as they selected places for shots and adjusted f-stops and filters. I noted that they had removed their earrings and now kept their hair tight and tied back. "It got in their way," Anne told me. "They're streamlined now, for work. Looks are beside the point." They had indeed developed and were developing.

"I'm getting itchy," Anne said as we sat on my porch in the afternoon. Coppie was somewhere deep in Anne's cabin, reading a book that he had been at with ferocity for most of the last two days. He had come and clung to me, appearing out of nowhere, from time to time. But he had held on for only a short while, and had needed no urging to disengage himself.

"He's found books, ever since Carl left. I don't know how good it is for him, but he can't leave them alone. He seems much more relaxed in the evenings after a day of reading them. I think it's a good thing. He's come out with the most startling facts and figures, bits about geography and populations."

In the morning after breakfast I had strolled around, getting a better sense of the place. I stayed away from Lorca's forest but walked as close to the cabins and studios that I discovered set back in deep declivities in the rock facing surrounding the valley as seemed appropriate. I could hear the peck, peck sounds of typewriters faintly behind some cabin walls, the click of paint cans and the scrap of tools on canvas behind studio walls. At one place the repetitious sound of piano notes came to me on the breeze, occasional brief snatches of melody from a source I couldn't pinpoint.

"She's a composer, working on the beginnings of a new piece," Anne said when I asked her about it. "Keeps pretty much to herself. She's not always at meals. Works into the night most of the time."

"We need to be doing something too," I said.

"Like the Bishop and Burl?" She winked at me, shifting provocatively in her chair. It was no seductive comment, but a joke in intimacy that I valued highly right then. We had both been left by those we had thought of as in the position of lovers. I believed a knowledge passed between us; whoever had been the cause of the failing, neither had been lovers to us for a long time before their leaving. Burl and the Bishop were on the brink of the new, and in their glances we had both seen those flushes of our own beginnings, so many years ago for both of us. We had been looking deeply into ourselves, to test that thoroughly for a part of the explanation. Neither of us had found anything conclusive there at all. But we *had* been looking, and we smiled at each other with a certain feeling we held in common.

"It's all like dreamwork."

"What do you mean by that?" I said.

"The memory. To ferret facts out of that mire, to draw conclusions, as if the vividness of the facts could make them real events and not just colorful constructions that remain constantly suspect. Like with dreams, the whole mire seems so often circular and only reflexive. Brings me back to this naughty, conniving self, this possible conner. I can't seem to be sure of anything at all, you know? And now, with Lorca, some new information, it's like the figures in some dream have shifted, the memory torqued, wholesale—not events, but perspective that has changed."

"Like one of those dioramas at the Museum of Natural History? The ones with the platforms, that turn?"

"I wouldn't say it that way. Where did you get that image? "

"From the Bishop. It seems a very long time ago now. I'll bet it does to him too."

"Do you think we could have made it together in L.A., David? I mean, slept together, possibly gone off together?"

"I think we could have easily," I said. "But only were we the same as we are now. What is it that Lorca told you?"

"Many things." She reached out and put her hand on my knee. "You really just have to hear it from her."

Barbara took us all to Melchior's studio after dinner that evening. He had not come to the dining room himself.

"He's really into it," she said. "But he wants you all to see what he's been up to these past few days."

We forced outselves to eat slowly, to hold back our anticipation. It must have been a weekend night or a holiday of some sort. I realized as I ate the turkey, the good corn, that I had lost track of the days. The serving men were still dressed in white, but now they wore small chef's hats as they served us. There was a bowl of fresh cut flowers as a centerpiece. The talk and laughter we could hear from the other dining room was celebratory.

"What's going on?" I said.

"Somebody came this morning," Barbara said. "I saw them usher her into one of the cabins after breakfast."

"Which one is she?"

Barbara touched my arm and leaned against me. She was by my side at the table. Coppie was on the other side of me this evening. He'd touched my shoulder with his head, my waist with his hand, only a few times during the meal. He had brought a thick book with him to the table, and he snuck occasional glimpses into it at times.

"The one to the far left. Can you see her from where you are? "

I had to lean against Coppie a little to see the whole face through the doorway leading into the other dining room. He looked up at me as I pressed him, blinking a few times.

"Right. I see her now." It was Patty, the woman who had taken Anson to Utah for burial, the one who had written to the Bishop about her mother's death.

Melchior's studio was in one of the small cabins back close to the rock wall of the valley. It was around one of the many slightly extending walls of rock that jutted out into the valley a little, so that from most places it was out of sight. It was set behind a small stand of pine, a kind of yard of trees in front of it. He appeared at the door as we approached, waving, a broad smile on his face.

"Looks pleased with himself, doesn't he?" Barbara laughed.

Anne was walking beside me, and Burl and the Bishop brought up the rear. The sun had sunk down behind the high escarpments around the valley, and though there was still plenty of light at the valley's center, Melchior's studio was completely in shadow and there was light beaming from all the windows and the large skylights in its roof. Though the place was rough hewn on the outside, its interior walls were modern, sharp angles, bone-white Sheetrock with track lighting overhead, a few drafting tables and others, two easy chairs resting on the paint-spattered hardwood floor.

"I wonder just how they got lights here," the Bishop said.

"They've their own generator," Barbara answered.

Melchior had laid his rubbings out on the broad table that stood in the very center of the room. There were numerous large sheets, most curling just a bit at their edges. There must have been ten or more. The Bishop and Burl moved up close to the table, and Anne moved to the head of it. Melchior was shuffling through the large sheets, looking for the first ones he wanted to show.

"Are these ones he brought along when we came here?" I whispered to Barbara beside me. "He can't have carried all of those."

"Oh, no," she whispered, bending toward me. "They all come from here."

I'd no idea that there might be a cemetery, and I moved up behind Burl and looked down over his shoulder.

"My dearest Christ!" the Bishop said. "Where in

the world did you find that?" He was looking down at a rubbing, set to the left of the pile. It was a finished one—the full arch of the stone stood out clear in its outline. Melchior had added small angels in watercolor at the corners above the legend and had worked in scrolling where there had been none before. The angels, though small and with wings, were in no way sweet. They had a robustness about them that was sexual, serious, and womanly at the same time. Their garments were not diaphanous but a mixture of tight girdings. They seemed ready for serious activity, and I could see implements, a chisel and a paintbrush, in their small hands. There was nothing else that Melchior had added, though he had applied a bronze wash to the entire surface and had lightened and rendered three-dimensional the angels, scrollwork, and the legend itself. The whole looked like a kind of emblem, or a seal, something that if reduced could be put on a patch to be worn on a uniform, or left as it was could be bolted to the side of some building, over a cornerstone. The work was careful, exact, and beautiful. The legend read *Maudie*, with dates of birth and death under it.

"This is something," the Bishop said, turning his head and looking for me. I was close to his shoulder, behind him, and he couldn't find me right then.

Anson's Maudie, I thought. Then I thought back to that image of the house as I had seen it only a few days before, and then further back to Anson's talk about the place, about Maudie and his time with her. I could see in my mind the renderings that Anson had done of the house, his talent with the ancient historical. And I could remember some details of what Anson had told me. How they had worked with cutouts of people from her past, had altered family relationships and gatherings. She had taught him the way to his art, he'd told me, and here her name stood out in a beautiful emblem, one that was the clear product of Melchior's.

"It's back behind Lorca's cabin," Anne said. "A little way into the woods there. Just a few honored graves. This one, a woman who died here in residency, and some others, friends of this Maudie, I think."

"And there's this one, David," Melchior said, shuffling among his rubbings. "It was the first one I noticed, right beside hers."

He lifted the rubbing up and let it hang down for a moment, then spread it beside the other, working it into alignment, just a few inches from the other's edge. The words came boldly out at me, the stone's impression isolate in the middle of the empty outline: *My Anson,* the dates under the words, and nothing else.

"I didn't want to begin work on it until I talked with you, David, until you saw it."

"Good," I said, the word coming quickly and easily to me. "We can talk about it in a while, I guess."

I didn't know what to think or what else was possible at that moment. But I knew that the word *My* on the stone impression did not hurt me as I thought it might, and knowing that released me from any vestige of desire for possession of Anson that I might still have carried with me. He had *never* really been mine, nor had I ever asked that of him. What I had never felt about him was jealousy.

I had not known that, before this moment, or at least had never put it into words. But I knew it now, in the way I gave him over to her possession in their deaths with such ease. There was some shock in knowing that both were here, and some anticipation in knowing that there was more to learn about that. But what I felt most was a kind of release in giving in, in giving everything up that I might have thought I'd wanted to hold. I was affirmed at last that I could let him go, had probably already done so with his death. I hadn't been sure of myself, and how I thought and felt; I'd mistrusted that, thinking that what I felt must not be true feeling. Now I knew that it was.

"Has the diorama begun to turn for you?" the Bishop said. Burl looked up at him quizzically.

"Not that," I said. "I think it's tilting a bit though. I'll have to tell you how it stands in a few days."

There was some shuffling of feet and coughing, some brief discomfort in the others at our exchange. Melchior lifted Maudie's rubbing and put it on top of Anson's. Then he slid both to the side. He had a few more to show us. He had been working hard and had finished four of the seven he'd gotten. He revealed them to us one by one, only commenting briefly and unassumingly when we asked him questions. Each of the rubbings that he'd finished had its own feel and integrity, and this in spite of the fact that the stones themselves seemed to be very similar in size and content. Even the cutting in of names and dates was in the same calligraphy. There were some figures, angel wings and skull heads, but they were small and perfunctory, as was the dressing of occasional scrollwork under names and at some edges. The work he'd done was careful and quite exquisite; the colors, unlike the ones I'd seen in his work earlier, ran together in delicate streams of complement. In places it looked like paisley or madras fabric.

"These are the best I've ever done," he said at one point. He said it quietly and without arrogance. It was only a matter of fact.

The path that began after the first few trees at the very brink of the small forest was a shaded and narrow one. At breakfast, at seven-thirty, the rain had come, pounding so loud on the dining room roof that we could barely hear the talk of those beside us. Anne had to put her lips to my ear to pass the message. "Lorca would like to see you around ten."

Now the sky was clear and bright again, but in the shade on the path the green needles were still sodden, dampening my wrists and the sleeves of my shirt as I passed among them. Even as I entered the forest I could see parts of her cabin in the distance. It got lost at times as the path turned, but reappeared in its parts, closer at each step as I moved on. The path was marked in places by blue gardenias, and I could imagine her plucking one out that first day, placing it in her hair behind her ear before she emerged from the forest edge, her staff in her hand, those bees gathered on the pole, above her head.

As I got closer I could see the five white huts. They were set close together in a cluster to the left of the cabin, a little back from it on a small open rise, the miniature houses of the bees, a diminutive version of the larger colony. When I reached the last trees and entered the clearing in which her cabin sat, I could see that it was larger than the others. There were skylights on a sloping roof, a broad porch, and to the rear a lower, flat-roofed section. I guessed that this was studio and living quarters all together in the same building and that she need not leave the place for any reason.

She was waiting. I did not see her at first as I approached; the porch had pillars and was lined with hanging plants at various elevations, and only when she moved from behind a drooping fern did I see the stir of her hair, the ripple of fabric at her sleeve.

She came down to the first step of the porch and stood and waited. She had not changed so dramatically. Her hair was longer and had lightened a few tones where the gray streaked it, but her face looked very much the same to me, her broad forehead, lined a little now, still lovely and vulnerable at the temples. She stood very straight. She had always had good posture, and though I saw her now in heavy boots below her long skirt, I could imagine her delicate ankles under the leather, could picture the red dust of the clay court on her legs above her white socks.

"David, you've changed." She smiled as I reached the porch. "You've gotten older, better looking."

She touched me briefly on the shoulder, then turned and took me to a chair, then left and got a pot of tea and cups and put them on the small wicker table between us. I watched her move, trying in some way to get back to her, to connect these first moments up with our past moments together, to find some thread of continuity to span that empty space of years since I had last seen her. I wanted something that I could not understand. I wasn't here nor there yet, and I wanted something— before I heard her tell me things, whatever they might be—that would explain the past. I wasn't even quite sure what needed explanation any more.

"You're wondering why I left you, David." She had turned her chair toward me but was looking to the side of my face, up a little into the planters hanging behind me along the porch roof.

"There are certainly many things to be said about

that," she said. "But first, before we get into it, let me show you something."

She put her teacup down and stood up and reached for my hand, then let it go when I had risen. She led me down the porch steps again and then went ahead of me. We passed the five white huts. I thought I could hear a deep drone in them, but I wasn't sure of it. Beyond them, guarded from sight by another small rise and a gathering of aspen, was the cemetery, a low wrought-iron fence surrounding the few graves with their stone markers. In the center, at the head of plots that had been tended and outlined with various planted flowers, were the stones of Maudie and Anson. They were very close together, intimate, as if two lovers lying beside each other in the middle of a bed. Lorca stepped to the side, so I could see them clearly. *My Anson,* the stone read, clearer and sharper in its cuts than in Melchior's rubbing of it.

"I believe you know this Anson," she said softly. She was beside me now, and I thought I could smell something of her that I remembered, a faint scent of gardenias.

"I knew him, yes. We spent many years together. I'm not sure how well I knew him."

"Maudie did," she said. "He was her son."

I turned quickly to her. She was too close to me, and I stepped to the side slightly. Again she was not looking at me but was gazing down at the stones. "What do you mean?" I said.

"She adopted him. Didn't you know that?"

"No," I said. "When?"

"Oh, I believe it happened early on. When he was a very young man. When he lived in the same town she did. It was nothing really to do with money, inheritance and such. She didn't have any. What she did, she did through her willpower. She did a lot. It was more to fuse their relationship is what she told me, to formalize it. They meant a lot to each other."

"I know that," I said. "He spoke of her intently." I was searching my mind for a hint of it, for something Anson might have told me in talking of her, but I could remember nothing. Then suddenly, I remembered his very words: *Things developed between us and became a pact. We made it official, but insisted on no responsibility in any way.* That was it, I guessed. His talk had not been so much a sharing with me as a display of a very important thing for him, something that he told me because it had meaning for him, his art, and the directions his life had taken. I realized that it didn't make any difference. It had been a private thing, appropriately, and I had not been diminished through lack of his sharing it with me. Maybe he had wanted me to know the facts but could not bring himself to say them outright. Now I could never know, but that was all right.

"It was at the dress shop," she said, her voice quiet at my elbow. I was not looking at her now, but above the stones to where the trees started again.

"She was an old woman, then, but had just begun this place. Somewhere she had seen that work of mine, those flower drawings, you remember, that the bank took and sent around the country with all those others. I was flattered of course that she had come to see me. She said this place was open to me should I want to come. She wanted me to come. She introduced me to other artists that she knew, other women, there in L.A. I went places with them. We spent time together. You of course knew nothing about this, David. I was torn then about my place with art and I guess too, because of that, about our being together. Maudie must have been in her eighties then, but she was a very forceful and vibrant woman. She had a way of getting her point across.

I turned and looked at her. I wanted to see the way she looked as she told these things. Her head was down as she remembered how it was, but when I turned she looked up at me. She brushed her hair back, keeping her eyes on mine, and then she continued.

"It wasn't any cause in you, I don't think, David. You remember I stole those dresses? I was a little crazy then. All those vibrant women and their art, and my own struggle with my own—should I give in to it? I knew if I did, it would make problems for both of us. I'd have to put just about everything into it. That's why I never told you about what I was doing."

I had a brief urge to ask her more about the dresses. But more troubling to me was what I heard as a lack of logic in what she was telling me. I couldn't figure how her coming to her art could be a problem for us. It was clear, though, that she was sure of it, and I began to feel that that itself was the logic. Still, I knew that I wanted to hear more. I needed details.

"Then it was that Maudie left L.A. She had only been there a few weeks, gathering slides, looking in on artists and such. She left me her address and said I was always welcome. More than welcome, is what she said. She told me—honestly, David—that my work was very, very good. What did I know then? I was flattered, drawn to her, and a little suspicious at the same time. I don't know now if I would have followed her then. The other thing intervened, and I never found out."

She shifted a little where she stood, turned her head and glanced at the aspen trees, then she took an audible breath and looked back at me again.

"We only did it three times, Carl and I, but almost right away I found out I was pregnant. I think that tipped the scales. I might have been ready to go anyway, but it was that that pushed me to it.

I knew it would hurt you, be a general problem all around. My parents, Anne and all. And so I did the easy thing, I guess. I just left. I know I would have been leaving anyway, in time. But to tell about the child, and *then* to leave, that just seemed a little too much to handle. So I just left. I went to Santa Fe. That's where I had Luna. I had plans to come here when she was old enough. I kept in touch with Maudie, sent her things I'd done. Then when Luna was six years old, Carl came and snatched her. He'll be coming here soon. I've put out bait for him. Things will be settled up before too long."

She turned and walked slowly away, still talking, and I followed at her side. I was a little shaky, but I managed to remain attentive, to get the whole story. What I saw as her cruelty to her mother is what struck me most at the time. I remembered the way she'd looked, standing at the door.

She told me things about her life in Santa Fe, her daughter, and her painting. The painting kept getting the upper hand. She would be talking about Luna, her pleasure in her and the difficulties, mostly logistical, in having to raise her without help. Then she would mention a particular difficulty and would date it with the nature of the work she was involved in at the time, work with the figure or with color. Then it would be all about the painting for a while. She'd turn to Santa Fe again then, the weather and the community, but soon she'd be into light and color in the place and how that had influenced her work.

Nothing she said seemed egocentric. The work was not her, but something she could do and therefore had to do. Nor did I have the feeling that she slighted her daughter, that she was a faulty mother in some way. She tended to speak of her with much respect, but I didn't feel that she had much room for love. I wondered if she ever had, with me or with anyone else. I did not feel that she was the person I had thought I'd known before. Not so much that she had changed over the years, but rather that I had probably never known her in the first place, not that part of her that now revealed itself. Probably she hadn't known of it herself then, when we were married. It struck me that we might still be married, and I asked her about that.

She told me she had taken care of it, something in Mexico had been worked out. She said that had been a hard thing for her, but that after she had done it, it had seemed right. When she spoke of Mexico and Santa Fe, of schools and her daughter, her friends, her painting, the details of her life began to accumulate for me, their foreignness to my own experience coming upon me finally in a rush that firmly separated us, properly. Whatever lingering desire for vague reconciliation that I might have felt went away, as it should have for me much earlier. We were finally together again, and now I could be free of her. And I was free of Anson too; he lay where he belonged now, only a few feet behind me, next to his proper love, his mother, the one who had given him his art.

"There's one other thing," she said. "One very important thing."

We were in her studio now, a large room beyond the porch. She had taken work she was currently involved in and laid it out on large wooden tables, pinning a few finished pieces to composition board that lined the walls. The three large paintings stood on easels in their stretchers at the far end of the room. She had me stand back so I could see them properly, and I thought she was going to tell me something about them.

"Luna is your daughter too," she said.

I wasn't sure I understood what she was saying, thought she might be talking about a kind of fellowship that was still between us after all these years.

"Right," I said, a little embarrassed in seeing it that way, as a kind of intimacy that she might be pushing on me.

"I mean it literally," she said. "There was a blood test. She couldn't have been Carl's."

Finally the diorama made its turn, and I was rushing back to get my past and hold it fixed, to search within whatever sense could remain of it and find those clues I might have missed. There was a wooden kitchen chair, paint spattered, within reach, and I put two fingers on its back to hold myself steady and in the present.

"Couldn't you have gotten to me somehow?"

"I couldn't do that. I'd wrecked it for you already. I didn't find out until she was five."

"What do you mean?" I said.

"The antigen," she said. "Carl had one and we didn't. There was a rash or something. When Carl and I were doing it. I don't remember. But we were tested, he and I. Type and cross-match, all of that. And then, when she was five, the school tested her. It was routine I guess. She wasn't his type."

She laughed a little, with no energy, and turned her face away for a moment.

"He wasn't my type either, not ever."

"Not mine either," I said. "But I think I've just recently learned that."

"And then Carl took her, and I couldn't bring you into that. I didn't even know that it was he who'd done it for two years. Oh, I figured it was, but I wasn't sure. But as I searched for her, through rumor and vague bits of news, I got wind of him with her in Yosemite. I'd traced Carl and Anne to Sharonville, and even called once, but he was cool, said he didn't even know that I had a child, let alone anything about her whereabouts. I never did talk to Anne, not until very recently.

"They took her from school in Santa Fe, Carl

and two others. One of them was probably named Kip, Anne told me, and another one. She was only in the first grade. They were seen, but there was nothing suspicious and nobody had a description of them. But Carl was always strange, and I just figured it. I looked hard in the beginning, even had the police involved, but there was nothing. I even thought to call home at one point, but I was well past that and I didn't do it. What could my mother have known anyway? I never gave up of course, and recently I found out for sure that it was Carl."

There was little left to say. I couldn't ask her much about the girl without hurting her. She hadn't seen her in years now, had missed all of her growing up since she was six, and I couldn't ask her either about those early years. I could have asked her more about her leaving me, but I realized now that the mystery of it would for me always remain so. What I would need to solve that was impossible. The mystery was in the nature of her feelings about things then, not in any facts, and those feelings were over now. Anything she could tell me would only be a kind of fictional reconstruction from the events as she remembered them. That we had not seen each other and the world in the same way at all then was clear to me now. The only thing that wasn't was my part in it. She'd told me I had no part. I thought I knew better. I remembered the photograph of Luna that Karla had shown us that evening, those vacant eyes and white hair. I wondered how Lorca would feel, seeing her that way. It was a cruel thought, all the more in that I suspected that the sight would not really crush her. It was as if her art had brought her into an absolute present, as if nothing in the past could ever really touch her, not me, not her lost daughter. How different we were, I thought, symmetrically so. I was still in bondage to the past, to memory and the righting of it. She was perfectly free in the present.

"Sex was never quite right with us, was it?" I said.

"Oh, well, how could it have been, David? We were both somewhere else entirely."

I took her hand, then pulled her to me and held her for a moment. She yielded to my touch, but only with her body. I suspected that her eyes were open, that she was looking at the large paintings over my shoulder. I was looking at the ones she'd pinned to the wall. Each was a rendering of a bee in a stage of some kind of metamorphosis: abstract figures suggestive of cocoons, shed casings like translucent snake skins, gardenia petals twisted into the host shells of hermit crabs. Each rendering shone with a kind of deep light that seemed to come from within the paint. The sun that streamed in the window had no effect on it. It was the same in shadow as it was in light. They were paintings of a tortured self, but the self was *in* them, totally. They told me absolutely nothing about her.

The three large ones that I could see over her shoulder as we turned slightly were different from the others, very close to photo-realism. Every inch of each of the canvases was covered with figures of life-sized bees. The light in these made the bees shimmer as if they had swarmed to the canvas and were alive there. In places the bees were in tighter clusters than in others, their wings and bodies overlapping, pulling those from other places on the canvas toward them. There were many such clusters, large and small, and the tensions they provided to the paintings were various. It was these tensions, drawing in, pushing apart, that gave the work such animation. Photo-realism it may have been, but the photos were moving. The bees, in their mass and thickness, even seemed to have real weight. I thought the canvases were sagging slightly, concave, the bees ready to spring from them, to drain them of their color and let them come taut again. I thought the paintings must be finished, but I could see no signature, nothing that could define bottom and top. They were very large and square, and gravity seemed to play no part in them at all.

"These are really something," I said, still holding her.

"I've a thing for bees," she said. "I imagine you could tell that right off." She pushed herself away from me, smiling and laughing lightly. Her eyes were brighter now than I had yet seen them, either here or in the past. The subject was her painting now, and there seemed to be no memory in her, at least none that could touch her. Her look was invulnerable.

"They've been here since the beginning, since Maudie died and I came to take her place. She must have trained them in some ways herself. It's been easy for me to get them to do things."

I remembered Anson speaking of the bees at Maudie's house in the story he told me about her so long ago. He had seen them through the windows and a few inside. She had touched them and painted them. I thought I remembered that he said she had not been concerned at all.

"There's one last thing," Lorca said. "It's beautiful and it won't shock you in the way the other did. But it's something that can tie up the last few threads possibly. We'll have to go out again."

We left the studio and went to the porch, but this time we headed from it to the other end of her cabin, where the kitchen and bedroom were. I could see her dresser, a bowl of fresh cut gardenias resting on it, through the window as we passed. We started up into the woods again. I followed her and could see through the trees over her shoulder that the rock wall surrounding the small valley was closer on this side of the cabin. We only had a few yards to go to reach it. The trees came almost up to its face. I watched her push a limb away. It brushed against the rock, and there to the side where she was stepping was the opening to a cave.

The mouth of the cave was low, and I followed her in, ducking down as she did at the entrance. After a few feet I saw her rise up, and when I got to her side I was able to stand straight also. There was light coming from above, and when I looked up I could see places in the cave's ceiling where fixtures had been set into the rock. The lights were dim, but they illuminated the whole interior. It was bright enough so that we could see everything.

To the back and on both sides of the cave room, wooden shelves rose from the dirt floor, halfway to the ceiling. There were hangers bolted to the rock itself to support them. The shelves were covered with objects, pots and shards. In the middle of the domed, rock room was a circular hole in the floor. Lorca took my arm and moved us forward to the lip of it. The hole was large enough for a man to get through with ease, and its edges had been lined with stone. There was a ladder leaning against its lip, going down to yet another floor a good twelve feet below us, and I could see that another room had been excavated under us. A few objects were visible from the edge— a bright-colored wooden box, a shovel and pick leaning against it. The lower floor on which they stood was smooth, hard-packed dirt, and when I squatted down and looked I could see the foot of the stone wall where the floor met it. I thought I saw marks on the stone, scrapings and chisel cuts. The teeth of a rake were visible, off toward the rounded corner of the room.

"That's the burial site," she said. "Seven hundred years ago, David, the Anasazi. Very little is known about them. But they made beautiful things."

She tugged my arm a little, and I rose to my feet and looked up from the hole and at the shelves. Then she tugged again and took me around the edge of the hole to the back of the cave.

The shelves were thick with objects, some stone, but mostly whole and close-to-unblemished clay pots and urns. Lorca moved to a shelf at the side and took something down. I heard a sharp click, a loose rattle. She brought the thing back and handed it to me.

"Carefully," she said as she rested it in my hands.

It was a jug of some kind, and I remembered holding its twin as I took it from her. It had the same thin, curved handle, and there was something in the handle, a loose pebble or bit of flint. It was painted with various figures: that fat flute-player again, people and animals dancing, holding hands, going around the pot's surface.

"Kokopelli," she said. "He's on a lot of them." She raised her hand up, indicating the shelves with a sweep of her arm. "There's a lot to look at. This was Maudie's find. She kept it close, and so have I. It supports this place: a few pieces sold to museums, through middlemen, over the years. It supports the art itself. There's something about having the ancients here, some kind of energy, I guess. Maudie told me the bees were here, inside this cave, when she found it. She had a way with bees, and a better way with these than with any others when she came upon them. Her telling me that was a trust, given when I came here once from Santa Fe to visit her. I knew then that I'd be taking over here when she died. She was extremely old then, in her mid-nineties. She was still very strong, but we both knew she couldn't last much longer.

"Patty, Maudie's granddaughter, got the word out about this place, as rumor, to Carl. That's the bait. We did it carefully so that no one else would hear. I knew it wouldn't go beyond him. He'd keep it for himself, wouldn't let it out to other pot hunters. There was enough in the rumor so that he could find us without too much trouble. Patty's an artist too, did you know that? She's been here the past few days."

"How did you know of Carl's interest?"

"Oh, that goes way back," she said. "He was into it even in L.A. He'd heard about it from somebody in Yosemite when he was climbing there. He had pictures from museums that he showed me back then. He kept it mostly to himself. Then when I called him in Sharonville that time, trying to find out about Luna, he brought it up, said only that he had found some things. I remember because I thought it odd that he should speak of it. Really, he wanted to get off the phone. He was extremely cool and guarded with me, and yet he found a way to mention it. He's strange—always was, I guess—but that was very strange. I didn't forget it. He's obsessed with these pots. I know that for sure now, from Anne. We'll have our daughter back soon."

The cave and the ancient presence in it; the screwy talk of bees that made her eyes shine; the way she said, so coldly, "our daughter"; and the strangely formal, visionary quality in her voice—all made me feel that in a different place and time it might come to me that she was crazy, at least on another level of perception, seeing and knowing things that I couldn't see or know. But in this situation it was I who felt the odd man out. I had seen that staff with the bees gathered on it, the colony as a measure of her efficiency, and now I saw this magic cave, the lighting and the care of excavation. I felt I had seen only just the tip of her resources. Deeper down were probably things no one had seen, no one but Maudie that is, who had seen things of force also in Anson. Only the product, those paintings that were strangely separated from her, stood as possible evidence of it. They were powerful enough, I thought, and I thought too that they were instances of complete closure. Whoever she might be, I'd never know her. Then I thought that of course she had never known me much better either. Maybe I had a power too. Maybe neither of us recognized what we had within ourselves very well at all.

We sat on the porch again, drinking coffee this time. There were long pauses, silences in which we seemed to be searching ourselves within our conversation. She had her legs crossed, was sitting in a rocker as I was. We rocked only a little, sporadically. The light shone through the trees, fractured, touching the hanging pots that moved just a little in the gentle breeze. She asked me about her mother, and after I had told her of my brief visit with her, she was silent. It was as if she were trying to remember herself as a daughter, to recapture what it had been like to be a child. I saw her shake her head, as if she were freeing herself from strange thoughts.

"My father was not very valuable for me," she said after a while.

"Well, he's gone now," I answered, wondering

at her strange construction. The words were so egocentric, but her tone was matter of fact. Valuable in regard to her art is what I knew she meant. I wondered what value she thought her daughter had, but I dared not ask her.

"I haven't slept with a man, made love to one, in over ten years," she said.

"Neither have I."

She laughed in a tentative way. "Did you ever?"

"No," I said. "I slept with Anson once, in the morning, when he was sick. At least I got into bed with him and held him. That was all."

We were both silent for a while again.

"I tried to burn Carl out of me those last few times with you. But I was already gone away in my mind, I think. The massages had their way with me though." She looked somewhat shyly over at me. "You remember that?"

"It's still in my fingers and hands," I said. "Nothing to forget about there. That hasn't changed at all for me, I guess. I think it's something I'll never quite understand."

"Sure you will."

"Why Carl?" I said. "Is there any way to know about that anymore?"

She turned her head away and looked beyond the hanging plants and up the rise toward the five white huts. "I didn't want a child. Just a little taste of freedom. It was a way to begin to leave, I think. A wrong way as I see it now. I remember nothing specific. He was cold, taken with himself in it, with the *idea* of himself. But I'm not sure really what he wanted. He was insistent about the second and third times. I think I was well out of it before the end of the first. I'm not sure how he found out about Luna, or why he tried to find out, or why he snatched her."

"Can we ever find out?" I said. "His character?"

"I'm not sure what that is," she said. "If he was ever in one. That he wanted a child, can that make any sense?"

"He didn't want his own."

"He wanted something, though. He seemed to be always wanting. He thought he wanted me, I think, a kind of complete possession. It was spooky. It wasn't what he really wanted at all. Maybe that was it. I mean Luna. Having her really to himself. I don't know. Sex can be ridiculous. I don't feel I've missed it."

"I have," I said. "I've wondered if I stayed with Anson all those years in order to avoid it. Do you think it's nothing at all important?"

"The idea of missing it can be. Haven't you just said that?"

"I guess I have. I'm not sure if I just thought of that or not."

She reached and poured more coffee for us from the pot. Then she settled back into her chair, moved her hand in that way of hers, gathering her hair behind her ears. The light had softened in the trees still further. It was getting late. I could see the mottled shadows on the white huts.

"Are they all in there?" I said.

"Oh, most of them are. There are others elsewhere, swarming. I can call them as I please. They'll come to me."

"That's a strange thing," I said.

We talked haltingly for another hour, searching in those details from our pasts, the ones we'd shared together and the ones we held separately, looking for places where we could alter and right things or at least understand them. That's the way I thought about it at least. I wasn't sure about Lorca. There was a certain dreaminess of surface in her, one that I recognized from our time together, but now I saw that there was a tough, hard shell just underneath that drifting surface, something impenetrable that may or may not have been there before. I'd wanted something in finding her, and though I'd never understood what it was, and still didn't, I knew that what was happening between us now was not it. What I'd wanted was a revelation of some kind, and though I'd had many of them in the hours we'd been together, I hadn't had the one that I felt could settle things and send me back, wherever that might be, renewed.

I had a daughter now, and that was sinking in. Maybe if I actively pursued that in some way, the thing, whatever it was, would get settled. But I couldn't ask Lorca any more about Luna. It was clearly something she didn't wish to go into further. Neither did I, I realized. Not right then at least. I knew what Luna looked like now, something that Lorca didn't know. I was afraid to find out what it would be like when she did see her, fearing that even that sight wouldn't move her sufficiently. I began to feel that I was holding on to a wish without an object.

I think we could have made love then. There were times when she looked at me in a certain way, and I know I did a similar thing at times, a thing that needed no more than a little pursuing, a word or gesture. And there was a place in me, I thought in both of us, a little fantasy hint, that to make love together might this time be correct, might after all these years and changes be the way it ought to have been and in being that solve something. But it was fantasy only. I thought she recognized that too. It wouldn't do anything really. It would be a disappointment, another failure between us, and knowing this so certainly made even the vague anticipation of it a little exhausting.

How much we were inside ourselves, I thought. Our words are fairly exact and certain when they come, but there's too much tortured cooking in our minds between them. I began to get bored with that looking into myself, that blind and circuitous searching. There we were in the real world of Utah, and all I could think about was past memories and present meaning.

"I'm sorry," I said. "Not that I found you again and that we've reconnected, but that I've dragged you back to things."

"You really haven't, you know. It's been another life and series of concerns entirely. I said she was your child, but that's only genetic. She was a child of love at least, as far as we could manage that. That's why I told you. But there is nothing else, no kinds of responsibilities or ties. No events that intersected where you were or went those years. There's nothing of value to reclaim."

Her words were spoken kindly, but they were cold. And she was right, I knew. There was nothing left to search for. I had gathered my past up in this place, the living and the dead, the ones I could be with rightly and wholesomely because of their altered selves, alterations that had very little to do with my past or my sense of it, and the ones like

Lorca (and Carl, should he come here) who had changed or become themselves in ways that could yield no connection, love or even friendship whatsoever. Even Anson was here, and about him I felt a certain peace. I thought now only about the textures of our years together, their permanent realities, and had no wish anymore that I could change them.

"We can't even be friends," she said. "If that means getting together, talking and sharing things. We've got a few days left though, and we can talk and reminisce some if you'd like, when you feel like it. I've talked with Anne. It's been pretty much the same for us. We'll have to see about Luna when she comes."

"I guess we'll have to see about that," I said.

That evening we ate together with the artists in the larger dining room. Connections and early friendships had been made, through Melchior and his rubbings and Anne's girls and their intensity with the photography, and even the Bishop and Burl, in their interest and joviality when they visited various studios, had made a mark with the artists. The Bishop knew a thing or two about religious music, and he had had some good talks with the composer. Anne and I had stayed back from things a little, but we were accepted through the good graces of the others.

The room was similar to the one we had been eating in, only it was quite a bit larger. The table seated twenty-five, and with the nine of us present it was full. I looked for Patty as we entered, thinking that I might speak to her about Anson and her mother and grandmother, but she was nowhere in sight.

"She left this morning," Anne told me when we were seated. "She was only here to look things over, a thing Lorca says she does occasionally."

Melchior and Barbara sat among the artists at the far end of the table. Anne's girls were there too. Halfway down from us, the Bishop and Burl spoke with the composer and a sculptor. The artists were mostly in their thirties and forties, very robust women for the most part; the thinner ones were wiry and looked strong. I was drawn to them and had, just for a fleeting moment, a regret that I was sitting beside Anne and that we were probably thought of as paired. They would tell more things to the Bishop and Burl, harmless as they were to them in their joining. I shook my head to clear the thoughts away. That's all over now, I said to myself.

Coppie's hands crept up around my arm at the elbow. He had a book on the table, beside his plate, and though he held tight to me he released his grip from time to time to turn the pages. His head pressed against my upper arm at times, but the pressure no longer felt smothering. The book seemed to be taking care of things a little for him. I could read bits of its prose on occasion, as he turned it. Something about Utah, geography and Indians.

Barbara laughed, holding onto Melchior's arm as Coppie did mine. Melchior gestured in the air over his plate, outlining figures, his fingers moving in ways I did not recognize, in delicate pantomime. Anne's girls sat up straight in their seats. They had dressed up a little for the occasion, our eating all together in the same place, and they looked older than they were, sophisticated in their intensity and conversation. It was not the kind of false sophistication that I remembered in Karla's girls those days in Sharonville. This was earned, possessed of real power, wholesome and certain.

"They're looking good, aren't they?" Anne said softly from her place beside me. "They're growing up. Fuck that bastard Carl. They're better off without him."

"Can that really be true?" I said, turning to her.

"Look at them," she said. "Why, even Coppie's better."

I felt his hand lurch at my elbow when he heard his name spoken, but then his grip left me as he reached to turn another page.

"I guess you're right," I said.

"I'm not, really. You know that, David. It'll take time, probably a lot of it. But they *are* relieved a little. Ours was a painful house for a long time."

"I'm sorry," I said. "If there is anything…"

"Shush now, David. We'll see, when the time comes." She touched me lightly on the elbow.

It was a good and simple meal: meatloaf, mashed

potatoes and braised carrots. Bottles of jug wine stood on a cart to the side, and people rose and poured for each other as the eating progressed. About halfway through, when we were starting second helpings, Anne touched me again and I turned to her.

"I'm getting itchy, David," she said, a corner of her mouth twisting into a half-lurid smile. My eyes must have widened, because she laughed and shook her head a little.

"Not that, David; it's my fingers." She waved them in front of her breasts for a moment and laughed again. "I've found a very nifty place where we could do it. We could make a party out of it for all this kindness, later, after the kids have gone to bed. What do you think, babe?"

I laughed to hear her call me that, and nodded and grinned.

She made the announcement when the dessert came, cake again, with a large bowl of whipped cream and fresh strawberries. She was awkward when she rose in her place and tapped her spoon against her wine glass for attention, but she was also excited and pleased with herself, and her words were bright and clear.

The artists turned to each other when they heard the offer. I saw smiles and heads nodding, saw the Bishop's bright flush as he squeezed Burl's arm. Barbara had her head on Melchior's shoulder, and he turned his own head a little and kissed her on the temple through his broad grin. Everyone chattered as the dessert was eaten, glancing down the table occasionally at Anne and me. When they were finished they rose quickly, gathering light wraps and shawls from the coat tree in the corner. Some waved lightly as they were leaving, nodded, or smiled. They knew they would be seeing us in a little while. Anne's girls left with the photographer. They had a few minutes of cleanup work to do in the darkroom. She said she'd have them back at the cabin in a very short time. Coppie folded his page down and closed his book. He rose and put his mouth to Anne's ear and spoke privately. She nodded and he left the room.

"Going back to the cabin to read in earnest," she chuckled. "It's another obsession, but better than the other, I'd say."

I agreed with her, a little embarrassed to admit that I was missing his clinging attention just a little.

"Well, here we are," the Bishop said, looking for a moment at each of us.

Here we are indeed, I thought. The Bishop and Burl, Barbara and Melchior, Anne and I. The right pairings, though I had made a pair of sorts with three of them at least at other times. I had made other pairings too, with ones who were not here. Still, as I smiled in turn at each of them, I felt that there was no one who was missing.

Anne held my hand as we went to the place, a low, sprawling structure in the same woods where Lorca's house was, but well to the side and out of sight of it. This was Anne's idea, and she was excited as she pulled me along, telling me it was an old bath house, a place where residents used to shower and wash together before facilities were installed in each of the artist's cabins. When we got inside, entering by a door in the building's end, Barbara and Melchior were already there and so were the Bishop and Burl. Barbara had gathered sheets and towels and whatever oils, lotions and creams the artists had on hand and had placed them on a low wooden table at the end of the large open room. It must have been the Bishop, Burl and Melchior who had brought the other tables, for they were busy positioning them in careful lines, with spaces between them. There must have been twenty-five of them at least, filling the whole room, reaching almost to the walls.

"There were some here already," Barbara said. "Stored in that little place in the back." She pointed to a space that had been partitioned off from the rest of the room, a sheetrock enclosure with untaped seams. The tables were all close to the same height, and I thought I recognized one as the table we had eaten at in the smaller dining room.

There was an open doorway to one side of the large rectangular space we were standing in, and as I looked at it Anne went over and threw a switch on the wall beside it. The interior lit up brightly, and I could see the first few open stalls.

"The showers," she said. "There's a line of ten of them in there."

"Well, let's turn them on," I said. "Is there enough hot water? "

"I've checked it out," Melchior said. "It's an old wood burner outfit, a big one."

"We've stoked it," Burl said, with a grin on his face.

"I believe it's up to snuff," the Bishop said, grinning in turn at Burl.

While Anne and I covered all the tables with sheets, not folding them under but letting their edges hang down almost to the floor, Burl and the Bishop went into the shower room and turned the hot water on full in each of the stalls. By the time Anne and I were finished, the beginning drifts of steam were coming out through the open doorway, floating up to the ceiling, and spreading across it. The first few artists came in then, smiling as they saw the clouds developing, thickening, and pressing down into the room. Anne and I went to a dressing area at the end of the row of showers. We were damp with steam when we got there, and Anne stripped and put on a pair of white shorts and a halter. I caught the look of that familiar body, the one I had seen in that other steam in Sharonville, as I stripped to the waist and rolled my pants legs to my calves.

There were two tables set up at the other end of the shower stalls. These had no sheets on them, and the wood was already wet with a thin layer of moisture when we got to them. I looked through the doorway as I passed it, seeing that the larger room was almost full now. The Bishop, Barbara and Burl were passing among the artists, instructing them. There was laughter and a lot of motion and looking around.

"I found this whole barrel of salts," Anne said, pointing to it where it rested at the side of the two tables. "It's old and caked up some, but it breaks and powders easily in the hands."

Melchior came in the door at the end of the row of showers, a soft breeze following him from the outside, creating a space of clear air behind him that was filled again with steam soon after he had closed the door. He was stripped to the waist as I was, and I could see the heavy sweat streaming down the slabs of muscle to his belly and matting the hair on his chest.

"I've stoked it up," he said. "It ought to last for a good while now."

When the first two artists appeared in the steam clouds at the doorway, Anne sent them down to the dressing area, telling them to grab towels from the table just inside as they went. The first two were the small composer and the photographer who had been working with Anne's girls. The latter seemed a little tentative, but Anne was very businesslike, and she took a towel and followed the composer, feeling along the walls in the now thickening steam as she went after her. Anne then went to the open doorway and called out, "Another two in about five minutes!" I saw Barbara's disembodied face emerge from the steam for a moment. Her head nodded, and then she disappeared.

By the time the two had returned from the dressing area, Anne and I had spread damp sheets over the wooden tables. There was a deep sink near the head of each of them, and someone had attached hoses to their spigots.

"I hope these tables'll hold up," Anne said. "They're old ones the guys found in storage." I had to laugh a little in the steam, hearing the Bishop and Burl called guys. But they *are* guys, I thought; just two old guys now, out for a permanent romp.

"They look sturdy enough," I said.

We each took a hose and soaked the tables. Anne stuck the end of hers in a bucket that held a large dipper, and when I looked to the side of my sink, I saw there was a bucket ready there too. The floor was wooden, slates of decking with spaces between them, and the water ran through to the concrete slab below, flowing to what I guessed was a drain a few yards away under our feet.

"You've thought of everything!" I said, leaning toward her in the steam. Her halter was quite wet now, and I could see her nipples through the thin fabric. She laughed and nodded with pleasure.

The composer arrived first. Anne took her, and

I took the photographer when she emerged from the steam. She had her dampened towel wrapped around her body as best she could, but when I got her on her back on my table, she let me pull it away with no resistance; she even rolled her hips so I could get it easily out from under her. She was small and muscular. She let her head rest to the side a little, not meeting my eyes. I felt a hint of faint embarrassment in her, that I was above her and looking down upon her naked body. It won't last, I thought; it never does.

I took a good handful of the salts and saw Anne, a few feet away from me in the steam, do the same. Then I broke the chunks into powder in my palms, dropped little piles of it in places on the photographer's body, and began to rub. The salts were a good abrasive, a little like sugar melting on her sweaty and steam-dampened flesh as I rubbed it in. I did her stomach, the creases under her breasts, was more vigorous with her legs and the soles of her feet. I pushed her legs apart a little to get the flesh between them. As I worked, I saw her head turn. There was a smile now on her face. She could see I was into the job at hand, and it felt good to her. As I did the sides of her muscular hips, I saw her mouth move into an O of pleasure.

Then I got the hose, told her to close her eyes, and washed her down, running the thick, gentle stream of hot water over her face and breasts. I remembered washing down newborn infants in this way, years ago in the Navy. Her face had the same spacey look in it, transported as she was in a brand-new experience. I got her on her stomach then and went to work with the salts again, digging vigorously into her calves, her upper legs, and then her buttocks. I had wedged her soaked towel into the groove, to keep the salts from stinging her. I heard her grunt in the distance, muffled, as I worked her hips and lower back. I glanced over at Anne, who was doing the composer's wiry torso, and she smiled and winked. When the melting salts had covered her, I got a sheet and draped her from head to foot, pressing the sheet into her body until it formed a kind of second skin. Then I filled the bucket with hot water and began to ladle scoops of it out, letting it flow gently over and through the sheet, to heat and soothe her body.

Anne was finished before I was, and I saw the composer move by me, wrapped in the wet sheet, the end of it gathered around her face and over her head like a monk's cowling. Someone met her at the steamy doorway and took her away. After I had ladled the hot water slowly out for a few minutes, constantly filling the bucket with hotter water until it was almost too hot for my touch, I took the hose again and flowed a vigorous steam of warm water over the sheet-covered body. She was perfectly still under the flow, and when I was finished I had to help her to a sitting position on the table, to let her stay there for a moment and gather herself before I got her to her feet, wrapped in the sheet, and pointed her to the doorway. By the time I got back to my table Anne had begun a sculptor, and there was a beautiful, blond painter lying naked on her back, waiting for me.

I don't know how long it took us to do the salts and sheets for all of them. After a while I could feel a grit of salt at my belt line, and between treatments I opened my fly, let my pants fall sodden to the wooden floor, and kicked them away under the sink. Anne had by that time taken her shorts off. She kept her halter on, but like her brief, cotton bikinis and my own undershorts, it was nothing but a transparent covering of thin, filmy fabric. Our hair was soaked and plastered against our brows and necks, and we were dripping with sweat, water, and glistening remnants of salt. The showers beat down in a constant rush, steam billowing from their stalls, and once I noticed Melchior pass by again, go out the door quickly, and then return.

I was fingering the salts carefully along the creases close to the dark hair near a woman's pubis, when I heard the familiar voice above it. "Hey, it's me David! Don't get *too* lost in it now." When I looked up, I saw Barbara. I looked down a little at her breasts and smiled.

"It's you!" I said. "I remember now!" She laughed, throwing her head back a little. "Getting near the end, I guess?"

"Old, chunky Melchior's next," she said.

Then it was Melchior, then Anne taking Burl and I the Bishop.

"David, my boy!" he said, his gray hair curling at the temples, drops of sweat at the end of his nose. "We've never done *this* before. You've held out on me!"

"I guess I have," I said, grinning at him through strands of my own wet hair as I worked the salts into his arms and chest. "I'll never do it again."

"Oh, but you must!"

"I mean, hold out." He got it then, and turned his head to look at the other table, to watch Anne's hands move along Burl's hairless chest and legs.

When we had finished these last two and they had left the room, Anne and I stood for a moment, smiling at each other.

"This is something special," I said, and she dipped her head at my appreciation.

"Come on," she said. "We're just getting started."

She threw the last sheet in the deep sink, and I did the same with mine. Then she went to the row of showers and turned a few of them off. The steam cleared a little, and at the far end near the dressing area I could see that it was almost gone. She took my hand and led me down that way, and when she got to the last stall, she slipped her halter off and peeled her panties from her legs.

"Come on," she said.

She turned the water on and tested it, and we got into the shower stall together. There was a fresh bar of soap there, and she took it in her hand and began to wash me down. I turned so she could get at my back, and I felt the touch of her damp hair against my buttocks as she got to her knees under the steam and washed my legs. Then while I was rinsing off, I did the same for her, soaping and washing remnants of salt and sweat out of all her creases. The stall was small, and we touched against each other, it seemed to me, just about everywhere in our movements. I felt myself rise up a bit at times, but then I fell back again as the washing became more vigorous. When we were finished and had stepped from the shower stall, I felt the cooler air outside against my skin for a moment. But there was still steam in the passageway, and a light, clean sweat coated my body almost immediately. Anne got a dry towel from somewhere, had me lower my head, and dried my hair a little. I did the same for her. Then she went away again, and came back in a moment with a pair of dry white shorts for each of us and a white T-shirt, much too large, for herself.

"Big boy Melchior's," she said.

We dressed then, and barefoot headed out through the open doorway into the larger room.

A few feet beyond the doorway, the steam began to thin out. Wispy trails of it floated at our level in various places, but it was thickest where it clung to the ceiling, churning slowly, a cloud layer three feet thick extending down into the room. The light from the long fluorescent tubes, invisible in the ceiling, was refracted by the steam, making the whole cloud layer glow as if the sun were shining through, as if there were no roof on the building and it was a foggy day, sunlight above the fog, just beginning to burn it off.

My mouth was open as I gazed into that sky; then I felt Anne's hand on my elbow and lowered my head to the rows of tables. Each one had a body on it. The sheets that had hung down to the floor had been brought up to cover each, and they were like corpses in burial wraps or wrapped obelisks of some kind. They were still. Most had the sheets covering their faces. As I gazed down at them I could see the faint movement in the sheets, chests and stomachs rising and falling as they breathed. There was the sound of quiet snoring from various places. Some of the sheets rippled slightly across the contours of the bodies; the black squares of the windows across the room must have had little leaks around their frames. The jettisoned, miniature clouds of steam that drifted down from the ceiling were pushed and moved slowly through the room by a light breeze. At the end of the room, at the head of the rows of white cocoons, was the bare wooden table on which the oils, powders, lotions and creams had been gathered. It was a large table, and its entire surface was covered with bottles, cans, and tubes. Anne and I went to it and began to select things. I found a large bottle of eucalyptus oil and one of rubbing alcohol. Then I glanced among the bodies and selected a sheet-wrapped figure close to the center of the room. I moved among the rows then and headed for it.

When I reached the table, I rested my bottles on the floor. Then I stood beside it for a moment, looking down at the quiet figure. I could see the push of breath, the gentle rising in the chest. I reached out and unpeeled the covering from her, letting the sheet ripple out and fall down until its edges brushed the floor.

She was a tall blond woman, a painter as I remember, with large breasts and delicate waist, tight curls at her pubis. She was sleeping. Her body glowed from the salt rubbing. She was extremely white, her lips and cheeks touched with a natural red flush. I saw her long blond eyelashes flutter slightly when I revealed her, her mouth twist up a little in an unconscious smile.

I got the oil and poured some in my palms, smelling the ripe eucalyptus as it rose in the air to my nostrils. I saw her own expand a little, flair out slightly as the scent reached her. Then I put my oily hands on her, very gently, starting at the rise of her hips, moving across her thighs and down to her knees, spreading the oil to her lower legs and feet, running my fingers carefully between her toes. Then I came back up again and worked at her arms, her pits, then along her clavicles, under her breasts, and across her belly. I began to massage then, using only the tips of my fingers at first, running them in long, rhythmic movements from her ankles, along the sides of her legs and hips, over the edges of her flattened buttocks to where the curve dipped quickly to her waist.

She came awake very gradually. I saw the arch of her small foot flex when my fingers were at her ankle, heard the first deep groan, almost inaudible, and saw her breasts rise as her breathing became quicker. I took her toes in my oily hands as she came back to herself, bent them gently forward, then ran my fingers between each of them, taking each toe individually, pulling it slightly, feeling the thin ligaments, the pads at the knuckles and tips. "Oh, my God," she said, her voice dreamy and breaking a little on the last word as she came awake. "That's so fucking *good,*" she said, almost losing her language as it crumbled into another groan. "Do it," she said as I pressed my thumbs into her arch. I watched her face, her twisted smile, and then her eyes slowly opening, showing only the whites for a moment, and then the irises rolling into view, the pupils slowly contracting until she had me in focus. I saw her teeth then, as her lips drew back from them, her nostrils flaring and opening again. Then I held handfuls of her hips, had my oily knuckles in her armpits. I searched in the muscle sheath of her flat stomach. Her hair was between my fingers as I touched her temples.

The night went by as if its quantities had an aim that could lead us into satiation. But the quality of it, for Anne and me, had things within it that prevented that. At times she was at the other end of the room from me, bending over a figure I could not see clearly. Both got lost in a steam cloud, then reappeared. At other times, she was right beside me. She had stripped the T-shirt away at some point, and her lovely, sweat-glistening breasts hung down and swayed in the air rhythmically as she rocked, digging her hands and fingers into the shoulders and neck of one of the artists. Then she was behind me somewhere and I could not see her. I could tell that she was close though, could hear her heavy breathing, the creak of the table as she moved someone's flesh and muscle. When we could see each other, we watched each other for long moments, watched the ways our hands moved, the way we used our fingers. We smiled at each other, blinking through our sweat. As we finished each body, each shape and set of possibilities, we pulled the tails of the sheet up, covering them again, left them to sleep or dreaming. Someone had placed a large glass bowl of gardenias floating in water on the table that held the lotions, and as we finished each body and covered it we placed one of the flowers between spread knees or at the edges of the table near head or foot to keep track of our progress.

I took on Burl and Melchior, the latter with familiar slabs of muscle groups that were an anchor, a kind of interlude deep in the sea of an unfamiliar story. Burl had lost all vestiges of that concern and modesty that I had seen the night I'd moved the Bishop underneath the stars near the Airstream.

He gave into me completely. He was so thin, yet compact and defined, that I could get my oily hands almost completely around his thighs, could feel the shape and pulsing of his muscle bulges in my palms.

I moved from eucalyptus to peanut oil, rose and lilac. There were thick, hot oils that warmed the flesh with friction, cool, thinner ones that made for almost no transition to the splash of alcohol that I used to finish when they seemed to need it. Waves of rumpled white towels grew on the floor, little fallen clouds or shards from broken ice floes as the night was turning. Scents rose in vertical columns in the drifts of steam. We passed through them, as if through various lush and invisible gardens, as we moved among the tables.

My concentration waxed and waned in intensity over the course of hours, but when I began to feel it slip profoundly, my thoughts and memories taking me elsewhere, I would look up from leg, the creases of buttocks, arm or shoulder, and watch the rows of white-draped bodies, the few lazy movements—breath or turning in sleep or mild stretching—and I would hear the piecemeal drone of talking, stories told to Anne or me while we were rubbing, continued in many cases afterward, a quiet talk that moved to mumbling, then to the sounds of breath only, as sleep or other driftings came upon them.

Language rose, both fractured and extended, carried with the rising scents up into the glowing cloud layer of the ceiling. It seemed to gather there, light up in various combinations, and become a single story. I knew it was only the slight electric drone of fluorescents, but it sounded more complex than that, more various. There were stories about childhood, anecdotes that dealt with loving parents, released lovers, friends that died by drifting gently into oblivion. There was a story about a movement through watercolor to gouache, one about lost wax, a tale in which the importance of drawing was discovered. Some of the stories would have had hard edges in another time and situation, stories of painful memories of life-changing decisions, ones brought up from the deep well of memory, forgotten for good reasons. One was about a lost child, divorce, and competition. But there were no edges here, and I realized as I had done before, the more profoundly given the scope of things this night, that what I held was specific catalytic power, one that I was distanced in, a power that gave release of memory to others, release too, through perfect relaxation, of the knowledge that it could not hurt them.

It came to me that this was not so far from, was a perfect analogue to, that quality of intimate conversation I had had with women while I was with Anson and they thought me harmless and gave in to me. I wasn't harmless though, and that had been a cheat. I had cheated myself really, as well as them. But here the power was an honest one. I was sure it was that for Anne too; I was sure I saw that certain quality in her eyes across the tables. Distanced in it, but together in it. Had I been able to aid myself, the way I'd aided the Bishop and Anson into their pasts so long ago, I thought, that would have been something: distanced and within it at the same time. My route had been so faltering, tentative, but it had burgeoned—not its destination, not with Lorca, but the route itself. And not memory. The diorama had indeed shifted, I knew now, permanently. The route had not been a trail into the facts of memory, but a fresh path entirely, passage into a new and different world.

I had the flesh of a woman in my hands near morning. The black squares of the vacant windows had lightened, and I could see the outlines of trees through them, thick and fleshy shadow-branches at first, silhouettes, then outlines of the needles, pine cones, even the movements of a bird or two. Anne had shut down all but two of the showers. The rush of water now seemed very far in the distance. The drone of talk, the sleepy articulation of stories and bits of memory had tailed off, almost ended. Each body seemed in complete repose, sleeping or on the edge of sleep or waking.

The woman under my hands was a potter. In her story she had come here trailing the Anasazi artifacts for their beauty. It was a strange beauty to her, a mix of sophistication, humor and simplicity. She had chalked that up to the fact that it was seven hundred years from her, was out of a different memory than hers entirely. Maybe she didn't understand what she had been seeing, in museums and picture books; maybe its qualities were only a strange kind of nostalgia of her own, strange because there was no question of reattainment of that past at all.

She had gotten here and seen the real thing, without lighting or posing. She had taken a water jug out into the center of the small valley, out under a clear sky. She had taken a chair with her and had sat with the jug, had lifted it and turned it, had put it on the ground beside her, had just stayed out there with it for the whole day. She had tried to know it completely, each shade of color, each hairline crack, each movement in the dance of figures. She had tried to bring it, really, into the present, into *her* present. But she found that she herself couldn't stay there. She kept drifting as the day turned, into memories, into her own past, her years of imitation, of shaping and firing, mixing earth colors, her father's certain disregard of her craft, her mother's smoldering anger that she had not married.

Then she had begun to think about her marriage, the one she realized she had been forced into. He had been a baker, of all things, a man older than she was, who left her alone each morning at three AM, so that when she woke the other side of the bed was empty. She could never get used to that. Not his absence so much, but his sleeping presence when she went to bed and then his absence when she awoke. She remembered that vacancy quite vividly, his smell still there, drawing her every morning to a kind of nostalgia, a desire for something that had never really been.

The pot rested at her feet. She realized she had not thought of it for a long time; the sun had started to move down and the pot was now in shadow. She took it back before dinnertime. That had been three years ago. Now she was working on shapes that resembled bread, loaves that had only half risen and ones at the edge of mold or staleness. These were objects of no utilitarian value. Things to look at. She was after something about transition. Then she was talking about transition.

Her eyes were closed, her voice losing the train gradually as she drifted off. She was in transition. I held her hands in my own hands, moving my fingers over the pads at the base of her knuckles, then pressing my thumbs deeply into her palms. The tendons and ligaments there were vibrant and heavy, and it was taking a while to relax them. Her hands had grown into power through kneading also, chunks of clay pressed into shapes that looked like bread, bread in transition, at the brink of rising or of decay. I was kneading too, taking her into the wholesomeness of untroubled sleep. When she got there, she would be like the rest, dreamless and without bother. I was not shaping her as she shaped clay. I was only gently urging her to something in her, that uncensored place where there was no thought or dreaming because there was no holding on, wishing things had been otherwise or still here. I saw her eyelids flutter as she let loose. Her garbled words still came for a moment, the last remnant of any intention in her. Then her lids relaxed and lost their tiny creases. Her lips parted, and the breath that passed over them was empty.

Then I smelled the coffee. Anne had finished before I had and had gone to her cabin to make it. I hadn't noticed her absence or her return. I was deeply into the coda that was the potter's body, feeling my arms and shoulders begin to relax as the last of my energy left them. I looked up as I covered her. Anne was perched on the table at the head of the rows of sleeping bodies, the place that held the oils and ointments. She had cleared a place for herself and one for me beside her. She had combed the snarls from her sweaty hair, had put on a fresh shirt and fresh white shorts.

"I brought one of yours," she whispered to me over the sheet-covered figures, holding the shirt up for a moment. I could see the way her panties clung to her inner thighs, through the cotton of her shorts, the outline of her pubis between her legs. She had her legs up on the table, sitting in a lotus position. She handed me the shirt when I got to her, and when I had it over my head, she handed me a cup of coffee. I sat beside her on the table then, both of us watching the sleeping figures, each now with a gardenia somewhere on the table beside them. Anne had turned the last two showers off, and the steam was almost completely dissipated. The light was brighter now at the windows.

"It's five AM," she said, anticipating my question.

"This has been something else," I said. "Just look at them."

"I know, David," she said. "This was your present."

I leaned over and took her damp head in my hands, turned her face toward me, and kissed her long and fully on the lips. We smiled at each other as we parted, and she laughed quietly and lightly. I looked down at the bulge in her wet crotch with no embarrassment, then back at her face again.

"If we had energy," I said, "we could do each other."

She laughed again. "Haven't you had enough yet?"

"Yes. Oh, yes."

"What'll we do now, David?"

"Have breakfast, I guess, get some sleep."

"I mean staying here. Or going. Is there anything for you and Lorca?"

"No. Not a thing. There may never have been."

"But there's the child," she said. "You know about that now."

"But I don't know what that can mean yet."

"I know what *Carl* means," she said.

"That may be Lorca's business now."

"It's all of ours, David. Nothing has ended yet."

"You're right of course," I said. "I'm just tired."

"Give me another kiss," she said, "a nice long one," and leaned over for it.

We sat silently then and watched the sleeping figures. We were not lost in thought. We wanted to hold onto the peace that we saw before us, a peace that we had had a part in making, a major part in it. There was the deep silence of early morning in the room. The only movement now was the gentle and rhythmic rising of chests and stomachs as the artists and our friends breathed. There was nothing in the air now above them, just open and clear space to the ceiling. There seemed to be no energy at all under the sheets, nothing but that slowly moving evidence of breath that showed they were alive.

"Have you ever been so peaceful?"

"Not that I remember," I said. "Maybe that's the problem, the memory, I mean."

She didn't answer, but she didn't seem confused. We just sat there, watching.

I wasn't sure how long the bell had been tinkling when I heard it. It was very faint and in the distance. I think it must have come from the woods where Lorca's cabin was, been muted by the dew on the branches, then released to a slightly higher volume as the rising sun's heat dried them. A moment after I heard it, I felt Anne's hand on my arm.

"Look there," she said. "They're stirring."

I saw a body lift up a little, a sheet fall from a head, another figure roll over slowly on its side, gardenias drop silently to the floor. Then all around the room, in certain places, sheets were rising as limbs moved under them. Sheets slid from bodies, their long lengths billowing, then dropping down to sway and hang free to the floor at tables' sides, where the light breeze leaking in at the window frames rippled them lightly like sails. White bodies rested for moments like alabaster sculptures, half reclining beside the still-covered figures. Then those too were moving, turning. Then all the naked, white bodies of artists and friends were revealed, sitting at the edges of the tables, their legs hanging down, reaching out, or standing beside tables now, bending and stretching, limbs shining in the new sun that came in through skylights and windows. I saw Melchior, Burl, the broad Pan-like haunches of the Bishop, breasts of blonds and brunettes, buttocks flexing, thin-waisted forms bending.

Then they were all standing, and some were moving. I could see their gnarled hair, the crystal brightness in the fresh, half-opened eyes, their smiles. They were talking to one another, reaching out and touching one another in first waking gestures. Some called quietly across the room, nodding and grinning, others moved among tables to meet and embrace friends. They were waking up, discovering each other naked, as if newborn—were watching each other's limbs move, laughing lightly now. Some twisted in slow, mock dancing. Burl moved to the side of the Bishop. Barbara found Melchior, reached up and tousled his hair and pressed her breasts into his arm. I turned to Anne. She was still in her lotus position on the table beside me. She reached her arms up in the air before her, stretching. Then she moved her left arm over, put her hand on my head and patted me. We looked back. They were all still now, standing naked at the sides of the tables in small new gatherings. They were looking at us, their eyes clear and completely open now. They smiled and grinned. We could hear the dry, muted tinkle of the small bell coming from a distant place in the forest.

Then I saw the hands of the small photographer come up, saw her breasts rise and jiggle. Her palms came together in gesture only at first, silently. Then I heard the singular clapping, then more, spaced out, from other places in the room. Anne unfolded her legs and got down from the table. I pushed up from my half-sitting and stood beside her. Now they were all clapping, their arms raised, shining in the bright sunlight, their hands, rings and bright nails sparkling in the room. The bell's faint tinkle was lost under the fresh new certainty of their applause.

We smiled back at them. Anne took my hand then, nudging me, and we bowed deeply to them. The volume of their clapping rose up, filling every space in the room. When we were standing erect again, we looked a last time at them, their naked bodies at the sheet-covered tables, their bright eyes and smiles, their sweet vigorous gestures. Then we turned from them, hand in hand, and walked slowly from the room.

I cannot be sure that I remember in authentic detail all the things that happened after that. Memory can be a poor servant, twisted as it is by self-deception, nostalgia, and its own natural decay. I had discovered all I thought I could discover at the colony and on the way there, and that had its culmination with the massages and with Anne that morning and through the sleepy day. What followed was a dream world, I think, even as it happened. It is certainly that now, something that comes back to me on occasion only, when it is thrust up by something accidental, seen or heard. I think about it a little then, but really don't trust my memories of it at all.

When we got back to Anne's cabin that morning it was six AM, but her children had already risen, the girls getting themselves, their prints, cameras and materials ready for the day's work, Coppie, still in pajamas, tucked in the corner of the couch with a bowl of cereal and a book. We were exhausted, Anne still in her wet shorts and I feeling the oil on my arms under the fresh shirt she had brought me. The girls looked quizzically at us for a moment as we entered, then their heads disappeared as they hurried to get jumpers over their underclothing so they could hit the road. Coppie put his cereal and book down and drifted slowly over to us, his eyes still only half awake, and put his arm around my waist, his head into my hip.

"Not now, Cop," Anne said softly.

"Hurry up, Coppie!" Dana urged. "You said you were coming with us."

He seemed reluctant to release me, but it was clear that he wanted to go with them.

"Come *on*, Coppie."

When they had left, Anne went dreamily through the room, picking up pajamas, book and bowl, straightening cushions, while I saw to the coffee, warming what was left from earlier on the stove. I watched her move slowly around in her exhaustion, her gnarled hair, the shine of the oil still on her wrists and forearms.

"Could you hold up under a shower?" she said after a while. She was standing beside me as I looked down at the boil of coffee in the uncovered pot for a moment before I could connect to it and shut it off.

"I really doubt it," I said. "It's getting to me now."

"Me too. Shit, are my arms ever *heavy!* Let's go to bed."

She was moving toward me a moment after our heads touched the pillows. She came lazily and seemingly without conscious intention. The light was coming in the windows as the sun climbed. There was still the glisten of dew in the few trees we could see in the distance from our positions. She was on top of me, thin and light, but it was all I could do to get the large, wet T-shirt out from between our chests and up over her head. She sat up on me as she slipped from it, the collar catching in her teeth for a moment, her breasts lifting and separating when her hands came up. I had my slick, oily palms at her thin waist, and I slid them down and out to her buttocks where she sat, taking whole handfuls of flesh, kneading it deeply, then ran my hands up to the small of her back. She arched down over me. I reached her shoulders, dug into the tight muscles, kneading, pressing, searching with my fingertips. My hands had already begun to tighten up, and massaging her was difficult and awkward at first. She smiled at that, but as I pressed my heels in and flexed my wrists, my hands began to loosen a little, to come back again to that old knowledge.

"Get my neck," she whispered, her words half muffled as she bit gently into my shoulder. I was in her, and she squeezed me as she bit. Then her hands moved to my biceps and began massaging them, long oily finger-strokes at first, then knuckles rolling in a little deeper. I could smell her, the whole wash of the previous night's activity flooding from her armpits, from the creases below her breasts: salts, the various body lotions, alcohol, the sweat of the other women and men, perfume, peanut oil, glycerin.

We fell asleep at some point, and I awoke, I think, to the sound of some bird singing, not knowing exactly where I was. I felt skin and wet fabric on my cheek, and when I turned my head a little and lifted it I was looking into the gentle and soft rise of flesh high up in her thighs. The thin band of her panties at her crotch was inches from my face. Strands of damp hair feathered out under the elastic band. Her legs were widespread, and when I lifted and looked up her body, I could see her head turned to the side of the pillow. She was sleeping, and I took the bulge of flesh to the side of her covered pubis into my mouth, moving it with my teeth, sucking and tongue. Her panties had small flower remnants running down that thin band. I think they were gardenias. She moaned in sleep, her legs falling even wider. I heard the muffled sound of her head turning on the pillow as she came half awake. I brought my hands up to my face and took those sweet small bulges in them, pressing slowly and deeply for her tendons. A hand came to my cheek then, and I smelled eucalyptus. I moved a finger under the elastic, pulling the thin band aside, then took the edge of her lip into my mouth, sucked the sweat from her hair, still massaging those sweet rises with my fingers and palms.

"David, that's so good and relaxing," she said, her voice only the faintest whisper of a voice, though specifically familiar now, not from my past at all, but from this recent present. She hesitated to say more, to possibly begin telling me something. Maybe she did continue. I had turned my head back, resting my cheek again on that soft flesh, and had fallen asleep.

I saw the dark wood beams, the light high on the walls now, heard the soft whisper of a breeze. The window was raised a little, and I could feel the air stirring in the hair on my arms, feel its cool wash on my penis for a moment, then a wetness. I lifted my head from the pillow and looked down. She was sucking me, lazily. She must have felt or heard my movement. Her eyes came up to my eyes. Hers had creases at the corners. I was deep in her mouth, and she was smiling up at me. I felt her tongue move. She was saying something. It sounded like *vid,* but I was not sure of it.

Singing then, a song of unfamiliar melody and lyric, not words really, but half-animal sounds, a drone somewhere, deeply, like bees in the chest or throat. I swallowed. It was my own sounds that brought me to consciousness. She sat upon me

447

again, and I felt her hands on my testicles, on the tendons to the sides of them. I was deep inside of her, and I was talking.

"I'm so fucking tired," I said, and she laughed and lifted her head up from my shoulder and smiled and nodded. She touched her nose against the tip of my own, stared into my eyes, and gently squeezed me. Then she lowered her face and pressed her forehead against my cheek, and I was looking into her matted hair, and my eyes were closing.

Again I woke, this time to a distant rushing of water. I reached over, but she wasn't there. When I looked up, she was standing in the doorway naked. She brought her hands up, cupped them under her breasts, and lifted them slightly. I looked at her large aureoles beside her fingertips, saw the shadow bisecting her chin. She was moving toward the bed, weaving a little, her arms hanging down at her sides, when I lost the image.

She was asleep beside me, facing away from me, tucked in a half-fetal position, naked on top of the coverlet. I lay on my back with elbows out, palms cupped behind my head. I thought it must be noon or later. I remember the faint tinkling of a bell in the distance. The birds weren't singing. The morning ones were gone, and it was too early for the night ones. I brought my left arm down and put my hand on the rise of her hip beside me. My legs were aching and I shifted them, spread them a little, bringing my toes up to stretch the tendons. She stirred, and I gripped the flesh under my hand. Then she unfolded and rolled over and turned, and we moved our arms and bodies into new positions and went to sleep.

Behind her then, kneeling, she on her knees, her legs spread and hips elevated, arms extended, fists of sheet, arch of her back and neck. Facing the headboard, like a figurehead. To face into the board and the wall behind it as I pushed up into her, flare of buttocks, to break through and leave me. Her head turned. The long, dark column of her neck. Her face over her shoulder then, quick words of urging. Lifting then and stretching, reaching to kiss each other. Then a pinwheel, coming to rest on top and in her deeply. Then sleep again.

The day continued on like this, in lazy

beginnings and endings, small cameos in which there was some closure, some finishing of what was begun. But mostly there was a waking to specific touches and postures, to actions I found myself in the middle of coming awake and that did not end, because we fell asleep before that, only to wake again somewhere else, holding a foot or breast, tasting salt, awakened by the tickle of hair against the cheek. We were coming to know each other as if brought to it without any care for it, half hypnotized by exhaustion, sweaty, scented and oilwashed. I think I touched each part of her body and she mine, massaging each other, pausing in sight of the flesh we attended to only when those slight rises came upon us, of passion we knew was there but could not, in our exhaustion, rise up to in any significant way. The past drained away from me. The day, in our constant deep sleeping and waking, was like a multitude of days. Somewhere in the middle of it, it felt like the one day. I had forgotten how it had gotten started, and I knew if I fell asleep again I would wake again, would have her somewhere new and very distinct, for a few moments at least, until we fell asleep again, in increasing anticipation, as the day passed, of yet another awakening.

I woke up hungry. The sun had passed our window and what breeze there was was cooler in the room. She was under the cover now, on her back, and breathing deeply. I pulled carefully away from her, so as not to wake her, and when I was standing at the bedside, I moved slowly, watching where I put my feet. I must have stiffened in the last small day of our sleeping, but I could feel that good elasticity below the surface and around the joints, and by the time I reached the bedroom doorway the superficial kinks were gone and I moved easily on the balls of my bare feet.

In the kitchen there was evidence of the children's return, probably at midday: a loaf of bread, a butter dish uncovered on the table. A bowl of fruit rested in the shade on the kitchen counter near the curtained window, and I took a banana and peeled it. Its skin was cool to the touch. I was thinking of nothing as I stood there and ate it, only anticipating finishing and going back to her, getting under the covers and moving against her. I pulled the curtain back and looked out into the late afternoon, at the large open spaces of the compound that the cabins surrounded. I could see the dark edge of Lorca's forest to the left, the rock wall a good distance across from me, the place where we had come down from the tunnel and the ledge well back in the growing shadows to my right. No one was stirring. They're all still working, I thought, making their art. It must have been around four o'clock, still over two hours until dinner. Night birds had begun to sing, just a few of them, off in the distance in the trees. I dropped the peel on the counter and turned. I could still feel a weight of exhaustion in my arms and shoulders.

When I reached the bedroom doorway, I saw she was awake and waiting. She was on her back, the covers pulled up to her chin. Her eyelids fluttered and her mouth twisted slightly when she saw me. I was naked and could feel the soft breeze on my legs and stomach. I moved to the bed and sat down and looked at her face. Then I reached for the cover and pulled it slowly down, revealing her breasts. Her smile grew slightly serious. "Fuck me again, David," she said. And I did, and then we went to sleep.

I don't think I was dreaming, but something like a dream was bothering me. It was a sound I could not place in the room exactly or identify. I heard what I thought was a catch of breath, then a faint scratching somewhere above me. A brief knock then, like a piece of furniture being pushed or struck against, a muffled voice, somebody moving. I turned and saw the bulge of Anne's leg beside me under the covers. She was sitting up straight in the bed, looking in front of her. The catch of breath had been hers.

"What are you *doing?*" she said.

I rose up and saw the man leave the chair, heard the chair legs scrape on the wood floor as he released the arms. He crossed in front of another man, who stood to the side of the window, holding a rifle at the ready across his chest. Then I saw Carl in another chair, and behind him, in shadows in the corner, the girl with the white hair that I had seen in Karla's photograph.

"What the fuck *is* that?" the man said as he

reached the window. The other stepped away from the wall a little, keeping us in clear sight. The one at the window put his hands on the sill, squatted a little, and looked out and up.

"What are you *doing?*" Anne said.

"I've business here," Carl said somewhat vacantly, leaning back in the chair and running his hands along the arms.

I was sitting beside Anne in the bed now, but he didn't look at me. She had the covers held at her neck, covering her nakedness. I could see no movement in the girl standing in the corner beside him. She was thin and she stood very straight. Her hair was bone white, and though she was deep in shadow I thought I could see the same dead whiteness in her brows above her invisible eyes. I couldn't see her eyes, but I knew she was looking at us.

"Hey, man, don't get the wrong idea," I said, hearing my voice breaking a little. "You left her." It was a foolish thing to have said, and I regretted it immediately.

"I don't *have* any ideas," Carl said. "It's overhead, Kip." He looked up into the rafters, then brought his head back down and looked at Anne again. The man pushed back from the window and left the bedroom. I heard the front door open, then the screen.

"You bastard!" Anne said, and I moved my fist on the cover and pressed it into the side of her knee.

"It's the way it is," Carl said. The girl remained still in the shadows, but I thought I saw her head turn slightly, looking over at him.

"Can we get our clothes on?" I said.

"Soon. Not just yet."

The man with the rifle, who I guessed now was Banyon, smiled faintly. He was taller than the other one, dressed in tight jeans and a cheap flowered shirt with a leather vest over it. I could see the glitter of an earring in his lobe.

"This is Luna," Carl said, nodding his head almost imperceptibly to where she stood behind him. She came forward only slightly, and I saw again those burned-out hazel eyes. Even her lashes were white. Her cheeks were a little sunken, but not from physical weakness. She was thin, but she looked hard and fit. I saw her torn fingernails, but when I looked down at her feet, I saw she had boots on and could only imagine what her toenails must be like. She made no gesture at all, nothing appropriate even to his weirdly casual introduction of her. My daughter, I thought, trying very hard to see something, anything at all, in her eyes and mouth. As in the photograph, there seemed nothing of mistrust in her. She was beyond the possibility of trust completely. I wanted to raise a hand, smile or nod to her, but I could manage nothing. I saw Anne's head move, but the girl did not acknowledge it. She only stayed where she was, out of the shadows now, in the half-light, still in the corner, as if she were guarding her back from some assault.

"We've got to talk about..." but Carl raised his arm, silencing me, and I heard the screen door open again, movement in the rooms beyond us. Then Kip was at the doorway. He was dressed in a less studied way than was Banyon. His hair was long, almost to his shoulders, but receding, the front half of his skull a smooth dome.

"It's only birds. There must be six of them up there. Big fuckers on the roof."

"There's something else," Banyon said. He gestured with his rifle barrel. "There, at the window." Kip went to the sill again and looked out. Carl gestured, and Banyon stayed where he was. Then Carl was at the window beside Kip.

"There!" he said. "At the tree side."

It took them a few moments to pick it out and understand it. There was another window in the same wall where they stood, and Anne and I knew what it was when we saw it. I felt her hand move to my leg and take firm hold of my flesh under the cover.

"Jesus!" she whispered.

It seemed solid, stationary, only moved by the light breeze, a woody bark accretion on the trunk of a lone tree that stood out by itself only fifty yards or so from the window. But it was beside the trunk and not on it, and it was moving, up and down a little, swelling out sideways slightly, and when we all had a fix on it for what it was, we found we could hear it, even through the glass—a drone, like a deep, powerful motor at idle.

"The Beehive State," Luna murmured.

We looked from the window when we heard her voice. It was deeper than I thought it should have been, totally void of inflection, matter of fact. She was moving behind Carl and Kip, staying back from them, as if to come even within a few feet would contaminate her. When she could see between their heads at the window, she stopped, erect and rigid. Her hair was a twisted castoff of albino straw. Her boots looked too big and sadly heavy on her feet. I thought she must have her hands gripped at her stomach. We could see her back and the sharp points of her elbows, but we could no longer see her wasted face. Her shirt was the same muted check I had seen in the photograph. Her cracked white belt had more shine than her hair.

"They're fucking *bees!*" Kip said. "Is everything shut?" He pushed back from the sill again and moved quickly from the room. We heard the door close, the scrape of windows being lowered. When he returned, Banyon was behind Luna, bobbing to get a view, forcing himself to keep his eyes on us in the bed. I tightened beside Anne, but I knew it would take too much time to get my legs out from under the cover, my feet on the floor. I would never make it. When I looked back out the window, I saw they were moving.

They swelled out a little, brushing the tree's trunk. Bits of bark flaked and fell, and some was taken into the swarm, lightening its color for a moment, then spewing out in a tan sawdust aura around it. Then it elongated itself, thickened, becoming a black obelisk standing in the air beside the trunk, and the top of the column formed a kind of entablature, then separated from the main body and began to turn and rise. When it reached near the higher branches of the tree, it paused, and then it moved forward a little, getting beyond the limbs' reach. Then it seemed to tip downward, then paused again, and when we looked back at the main body of the swarm we saw it rising.

It was like a pulsing ball. It moved slowly, then quicker, and when it reached its satellite, it swallowed it. It was louder now, its sound beginning to fracture. We could see distinct figures bounding out of it a few inches, then returning, as if some dynamo that was not it, but was at its center, thrust them away from it, then pulled them in again, atomic, as if there were a matrix of energy that was not them but between them.

The two pulled back involuntarily from their window. Banyon's mouth was open, but he was not speaking. He no longer looked at us in the bed at all. I saw Luna's right hand come up and touch vacantly at her hair.

Then I looked back and saw the swarm thicken and tighten again. Its edges became almost distinct. The air around it was crystal clear now. The sun had gone down behind the far escarpment, but dusk was hesitating. The drone of the motor now seemed singular, deep and pulsing. Then the ball rotated, wobbled slightly, paused again, seemed to swell out from its center, to be gathering a kind of force. Then it shot forward, rising above the roofline of Anne's cabin, and we could no longer see it.

They stepped back from the window in unison—the three men moving to the center of the room, Luna turning but staying where she was—and looked up, as if they could see among the dark rafters, through the roof and shingles.

Anne and I looked up also. We could see nothing, not even the places where the wood joined. There was still light outside, but none came in at the windows. We could hear nothing.

Then I heard that same scraping that had woken me, the birds, then a kind of rumble, something very deep, as if in the wood of the cabin itself, in the walls and floor. A thud then, a heavy rapping, the sound of wings beating, then nothing again.

Anne brought her hand out from under the cover and put her fist on my leg, the index finger extended and pointing. I turned to the window and saw, high up over the valley, the birds flapping. They were above the lone tree now, at a height where I had seen them soaring earlier in Dark Canyon, and heading for the summit of the stone rise that surrounded the valley. But they were not soaring. Their wings were pumping, their long necks stretching out, their hooked beaks pointing forward, cutting into the air. They flew close together, almost in formation, five of them, each reaching for the lead as if they were racing. I watched them go, still pumping, until they reached

461

the rock summit and disappeared. I lowered my eyes then and saw the swarm.

It was close, between the window and tree where we had first seen it. It had moved down from the roof and was seething in the air no more than thirty feet from the ground. Carl had seen it too, and he and Kip were back at the window; Banyon had given up his guard and was close behind them, looking over their shoulders. I heard a whisper of fabric, and when I looked away from the window I saw Luna. She had moved to the foot of the bed and had rested one knee upon it, leaning over slightly so that she could see out the other window with us. Her torso was stiff as a rod, her new posture had nothing relaxing in it. I moved slightly, hoping she would feel or see me, that she would turn and I could catch her eye. I had no plan at all, didn't know what I might do should I get free of the bed and rise. I was naked under the covers. But if anything developed, I wanted her in it with me, wanted the chance to free her, to find something deep in those vacant eyes. She was my daughter, beaten down and wasted somehow by these three men. I shifted again under the covers and saw the mattress quiver a little at her knee. But she seemed not to notice and didn't look at me. Then Anne grasped my leg again, and I turned back to the window.

The vulture hung in the center of the swarm, a claw and thin yellow leg and its neck and hook-beaked head protruding into the clear air of the evening. The swarm rotated. It was almost perfectly round now, showing the bird, its head turning in a kind of dreamy delirium, its claw opening and closing, a tip of wing now, fanning out for a moment, then swallowed up again. Its eyes were vacant. I could hear nothing of the motorlike drone anymore, only a deep pulsing I imagined at the swarm's center and couldn't separate from the rumbling I was feeling now in ankles and wrists.

Then the swarm began to swell out, to take in first the still-flexing claw, then the long neck, the wing tip, and finally the bobbing, delirious head. As it encompassed them it took on a certain transparency. I could not see the bird's distinct figure clearly anymore, but as light began to show through the swarm, I could see the outline, then the contours, then even the feathered textures, the shining eyes and slick, curved beak. The vulture was now an emblem, a figure fashioned and hammered onto some soft metal, copper or silver, the swarm, backlighted, now like a large circular disk, an elegant serving plate, a shield or gravestone. It was like still, dead art.

Then the disk was rising, the light shining brighter behind and in it as it reached the top branches of the tree. I saw Banyon turn from the window, pulling his rifle back into a ready position, and start for the door. Carl must have felt or heard him. He turned also and spoke sharply. Banyon stopped and lowered his weapon. When we looked back to the window and out it, the swarm was gone. Then we heard the distant tinkling of the bell.

"What is that?" Carl said. He had moved from the window to the foot of our bed and was looking between us into the headboard as he spoke. Kip had turned from the window also, and Banyon was in the center of the room with his rifle. All three were looking at us now. I was naked in bed with Carl's wife, and though I knew his actions had released all claims on her, I felt a touch of guilt, as if I had been caught out in conventional adultery.

"It's Lorca," Anne said. Luna had moved from the bed when Carl approached it. She stood back in her corner again, in the shadows, but I saw her body lurch slightly when the name was spoken.

"I think I see something," Kip said. He had turned back and was looking down the valley toward Lorca's forest. "I can't make it out."

"It's where the pots are," Anne said. I was shocked at her statement, not that she was telling them but that the tone of her voice was so certain. I thought she knew what she was doing, something that I knew nothing about. She must have noticed something in me. She squeezed my leg. "It's okay," she said.

"Oh, it's fucking okay, is it?" Carl said, still looking between us, his eyes strangely unfocused. He smiled then, and I saw that his lips were moving, forming some language that was private. Banyon shifted. There was a creak from his leather vest, and Carl's head lurched, his lips tightening. Then he turned from us. When he spoke, he talked into some place in the center of the room.

"We'll leave them. There's nothing they can do." Then he was heading for the bedroom door, the two others gathering in behind him. Only after they had passed through did Luna step forward from the shadows. She looked at us in the bed for a moment, and I thought I saw a slight slump in her shoulders. I caught her eyes briefly, finding only that dead resignation in them. Then she turned and followed the men.

We sat in the bed, looking into the empty room. I felt I had wakened from one dream into another. There were things I should have done, should have said, but I had no idea what they might be. Everything had been so intense that I had no sense of how much time had passed. They were there, and then they were gone.

"Get up," I said. "We have to do something." And I threw the covers back and slipped my feet to the floor. I was around the foot of the bed by the time Anne got out.

"Not there," she said, moving beside me and taking my arm. "The window."

We went to it, and when we got there we put

our hands on the sill and leaned against each other. We could see down the vacant compound to the wall of thick trees where the forest began. There was still light there, though shadows had lengthened in front of it, large distinct stripes of darkness cutting across the whole open space from side to side. I was shivering slightly in my nakedness, and I went quickly back to the bed and pulled the blanket free and took it to the window and draped it around Anne's shoulders and my own. I could feel her warmth, the softness of her breasts and stomach against my arm and hip.

The three men were in sight in the valley now. Carl was in the center, Banyon on our side, and Kip on the other. I saw Carl gesture, and the two moved further away from him. Luna was to Carl's rear, a good thirty yards behind him. The three men moved slowly but methodically. She, on the other hand, seemed awkward in her progress. She would move closer to Carl, then pull up and linger back a little. I thought I saw her head turn, judging distances and directions. Her white hair was a dull flame in the increasing dusk. Her passage through

467

the shadow stripes seemed to make no difference. Her hair sucked up the sun and did not reflect it. In shadow, her head was a white orb, drained of color.

We watched their progress. They had a long way to go, and they were moving slowly and carefully toward the wall of trees. Then we saw movement at the forest brink, a soft splash of dull color and something angular and hard-edged. The elements came together, and Lorca materialized out of limbs and branches. She was carrying something large and skeletal. It looked light in the way she handled it. She was wearing the same long skirt that we had first seen her in. Her hair was pulled back tight around her head, and I thought I saw the tail of it flick at her shoulder as she moved. I could see a bunching at her ear, and I guessed it was another gardenia.

"It's an easel," Anne whispered below me, moving her elbow tight against my arm.

She set it up, pulling the legs of the tripod base out and fixing them firmly on the ground, shaking the whole structure sharply once as she looked down at where the legs rested in the earth. Then I saw her head come up. She looked down into the valley, then turned and hurried back into the limbs and branches and disappeared.

The four figures were now no more than a hundred yards from the forest. They had moved a little closer together again. Luna was still behind Carl, moving haltingly, lingering back as far as she could, it seemed, without being noticed. Carl turned his head, checking her from time to time. Banyon had brought his weapon up to the crook of his arm, the stock resting at the ready in his left palm.

When I looked back to the forest, I saw a second easel, about ten yards to the side of the first. Lorca was working now with a third one, extending its legs, getting it firmly fixed. When she had it the way she wanted it, she went back into the woods.

"What can she be doing?" I said.

"I can't make it out," Anne said. "But neither can they."

The three men had pulled up. They were no more than fifty yards from the forest wall now. They turned toward each other. I thought I could hear voices, uncertain, then a strong voice, from Carl I think. They fanned out again. Banyon had two hands on the weapon now. They weren't moving forward, but were leaning that way, looking ahead at the trees and the stick figures in front of them.

Then Lorca came out of the woods again. She was carrying something quite large now, something square and flat. Her arms were fully extended, gripping the edges of it. She turned it as she emerged from the trees. I saw the edge of the object brush against a low branch. When she had it fully turned, it was facing down the compound and we could see it distinctly. It was one of the large bee-paintings, the small figures so carefully rendered that even at our distance we could see perfectly, could even make out the individuals, the shine of wings, the light shimmer that made the whole wash of them across the canvas seem to be vibrating. She lifted the painting up and placed it on one of the easels. Then she turned again and disappeared into the trees.

"This has got to end," Anne said. "This is too slow and crazy."

We saw Carl's head turn, heard indistinct talking. I reached for the handles and slid the window open.

"What the fuck's going on?" We could hear clearly now. It was Banyon.

"Move more to the left. Kip, tighten up a little." It was Carl, his voice calmer than I thought it should have been, distanced from the events in a way that I remembered it from very long ago. It was a way I had heard him speak even in Los Angeles. I wondered for a moment why I had not been aware of his madness earlier.

Lorca had carried a second painting out and put it on another easel. Then she went back to the forest and got the last one and set that up also. She moved to the side then. I could see she had that staff in her hand, the one she had carried when she had emerged from the forest to greet us so many long days ago. There were no bees at the top of it now, but there was light there, a brief flicker at the tip. She held it firmly at arm's length, standing straight up from the ground, parallel to her.

I saw a movement behind her, something off to her right, back in the dark trees at the forest's edge. It moved again, and I thought I saw a fragment of sleeve, someone small standing behind a tree. I squinted and peered, and then I saw an arm holding the tree, wrapping around it. It was that tight grip, the fan of white hand on the bark, pressing it, that let me know it was Coppie even before his face came from behind the tree and I could see his hair and the tight line of his mouth. I saw his head move a little, his cheek press into the bark. I heard the dull, concussive sound then, thought I could even feel it deep in my stomach, and when I looked back to Lorca she was raising the staff from the earth. She sent it home again, and then we heard the beginning rumble of the drone.

The three men had started forward, Carl a little in front now, but when Lorca rammed her staff down into the earth, they pulled up again, their legs extended in midstride, leaning forward slightly, peering ahead at the display in front of them. Luna pulled up also, then took a few steps backward. Her arms hung down, her feet were together, and she was swaying slightly from side to side.

"Look," Anne said.

The paintings on the easels seemed to be shaking now, rocking a little, against the still wall of trees behind them. Lorca was standing off to the side of them, as still as the trees were, and to the left of the staff in her hand and behind her I could still see Coppie's face to the side of his tree trunk. Then I saw that it was not the frames and thin wooden legs that were moving. It was the surface of the paintings themselves.

I saw white at the edges, a thin band of it around the square of each canvas at first. Then it widened, its edge ragged, as if the paint were crumbling and flaking, falling into the center of the paintings in defiance of gravity. The centers began to bulge a little as the white space increased, and very soon there was a tight, seething ball of bees on each canvas at the center, pushing out from it, the white space rippling now, catching what light remained near the tree line. I looked to Lorca, who was still standing rigid and holding her staff, then quickly back again, and saw the shapes come free of the canvases, dip toward the ground, then rise, until they were rumbling in the air above the now empty white frames. Then they started toward us.

Banyon was the first to break and run. His

weapon hit the ground with a clatter as the metal on the strap struck against the trigger guard. He headed for a cabin to his left, between his place and the forest. The other two watched him go. They had forgotten Luna, and she was stepping carefully backward, but not turning. She was watching Banyon also. He was only a few feet from the steps rising up to the cabin's porch when the swarm reached him. It thinned out and widened as it approached, interposing itself between him and the porch, forming a broad concave vessel, a large ragged-edged dish of some kind. Then it pushed forward, wrapping itself around him. We lost him completely for a moment. There was only the blanket of bees, a cylinder whirlwind in the still air at the porch steps now, and the drone growing louder. The cylinder expanded, rotated, shuddered a little. It spun like a large, slow top, its center swelling, the bees gathering in tighter at its head and foot. Then it was tipping, falling. It seemed to skip a little, moving the few feet to the cabin's side. Then we saw Banyon's leg come out of it, an arm in front, and one behind. He was like a runner in midstride caught in a quick photographic frame. He was trying to step out of it, to run from it, to stay on his feet and fight it. We saw his head come out of the top of it. It was almost as if he had managed to extend his neck, to stretch it, but it wasn't that. The swarm had tightened and sucked closer to him. I thought I could hear bees bouncing, slapping like rain on his leather vest. The swarm turned him, and we saw his bright eyes for a moment, his lips, the white blocks of his teeth. Then his leg went back into the swarm. His arms flailed out from it. The cylinder teetered, skipped more toward the cabin's side, then fell, hitting the ground with a soft thud. Bees bounced out at its landing, kicking bits of dirt and grass into the air. It was rolling slowly on the ground then, shuddering, bouncing a little like a windblown blanket, moving out of sight toward the cabin's rear.

I looked back to the valley and saw Carl watching. He was facing the cabin. His arms hung at his sides, and he was bent over slightly from the waist, his face pushed out in the air, watching Banyon, the disappearance of the rolling cylinder.

Then he was pulling himself erect and turning, not away, but in the direction of Lorca and the empty white canvases and the forest wall. There was a quick movement to Lorca's right, and Coppie emerged from behind his tree. He hesitated beside it for a moment. I saw what I thought were bits of pine needle stuck to his clothing. His hair was gnarled and spiking out in places, and there was bark and small twigs twisted in it. His mouth opened and moved, and his hands twitched at his sides and then rose up to his chest. Then he was running, past Lorca and the easels, out into the compound in the direction of Carl.

I felt Anne's hand at my thigh and turned slightly. Kip had reached the sheer rock rise on the other side of the valley and was climbing up into crevasses as the second swarm approached him. He was thirty feet from the ground, hanging to the rock, looking back like a man might do before entering his house. The swarm moved in the air over the valley in the shape of a black ribbon. We saw Kip turn and climb higher, then saw him stop and look back again. The ribbon untwisted, becoming a flat rectangle, approaching. Then Kip turned and disappeared into the rock, and the black rectangle sliced into the long, vertical cut behind him.

Carl must have seen Coppie coming. He stepped back, awkwardly, almost tripping, and in the corner of my eye I saw Luna move, take a step back as Carl had. She was fifty yards behind him now and she pulled back quicker than he did, finding her footing and standing still again. I thought Carl might look back at her, but he didn't. He righted himself, leaned ahead toward Lorca again, and then he was running, his arms pumping and his head down in his effort.

The third swarm hung in the air in front of the central canvas. I saw Coppie's arms waving, bees bend away from his progress as he passed the swarm, a few dance along his arms for a moment. Then Lorca stepped slowly to her left, interposing the swarm between herself and Carl. I saw Coppie pass him. They were running in exactly the same manner, intent, knees high and thrusting, and though they passed very close to each other, almost collided, neither seemed aware of the other, nor impeded his progress.

Carl kept going, and as he got closer I saw his right arm come up, his hand form in a fist. He was shaking it. His head had risen and I thought he was yelling something. The swarm opened up, forming a wall of bees before him. He was moving at full speed, leaning forward, his head like a battering ram, when he struck it.

The wall sunk at its center, but its edges rolled forward, came in around him, gathering him, holding on it seemed. He was still running, his whole body covered with bees now, like a garment, like some sort of seething wet suit. His arms waved crazily, small atoms of bees bouncing at his wrists, and his legs shimmered, twisting at odd angles as he passed by the easels and the blank canvases. He hit into a heavy tree trunk at the forest brink, bouncing back from it, reeling, then hit it again, sliding off it this time, passing it. He was in the forest then, stumbling, banging against tree trunks, overhanging branches, thick limbs.

I turned back to the valley in time to see Coppie

approach Luna. She was standing still at the compound's center, leaning forward a little, facing Lorca and the forest wall. Her head was a fixed orb. All else seemed to be moving and seething, and her white hair, that draining of all color, was the only clear focus, a still center in the valley. Then her hair seemed to light up as Coppie slowed down, came to a walk, and approached her. I looked above her, and there over the lip of the high rock rise to the right the moon rose, full and vibrant, flooding the darkened compound with its wash.

They were the same size, and Coppie fell to his knees at her feet when he reached her. I saw his arms come up and surround her, his hands fan out at her hips, his head press deep into her thigh. She bent slightly over then, her shining white hair falling along her cheeks, and looked down at him below her. Then her fingers twitched, her arms moved from her sides, and she gathered his head in her hands.

Lorca had turned. She was looking into the forest now. Carl was still moving, or at least I think it was he. There was motion well back in the trees, limbs shook, bark seemed to be flaking. I think I saw him clearly once. He had paused, still dressed in his living garment. He was standing beside a large tree, his head down as if thinking, his left hand in the air over his head, gripping a branch. But I lost him then, seeing Lorca move, turn, and face back down the valley. In the center of it, in the moonlight, the figures of Coppie and Luna were an emblem, something cut out in the clear air. He was on his knees, holding her. Her body arched out over him. She was looking down into his hair and not at the forest or her mother.

I watched Lorca stand there for a long time, gazing down the valley at them. She held her staff still and upright in her fist. The three white canvases stood vacant on their easels in the moonlight behind her. In a while I thought she was fixed there, like a statue, permanent as they seemed, that she would never move. But she did move. She turned back to the forest, stepped the few feet to its brink, then paused again. I could see her hair hanging straight down the middle of her back, the faint edge of the blue gardenia at her ear. I thought she might turn again but she didn't. She only stiffened, pulling herself upright. Then she stepped forward, dissolving into the branches and limbs. I never saw her again.

Three days later, on a Thursday, I think, we decided that it was time for us to leave the colony. On Friday we were in Anne's cabin, all of us, in the late morning, and Barbara was helping the girls arrange their prints and supplies, packing things away firm and flat to avoid creases in the eight by tens. We had said our good-byes to the artists at dinner the evening before, and someone among them had found candles for the chocolate cake, and they had all toasted us and wished us a good journey. Lorca had not appeared. We knew nothing of the fate of the three men, and it seemed that no one knew anything about the events that evening but Anne, Coppie, Luna and I, and none of us, as far as I knew, had spoken of them, not even to each other. Anne and I had attempted a few words, but we quickly found out that our experiences had been very different and that we were not sure of them at all.

"Let's save it," Anne said. "Maybe at another time."

"Maybe never," I said.

"That may well be a good thing. To just let it go."

Coppie was sitting on the couch beside Luna, pressed tight against her, showing her the books he had. They were talking softly and secretly, Coppie doing most of it. Anne had had a long, private conversation with Luna the day before, and had gone with her into the forest to Lorca's cabin. They had been there for many hours, and I had lingered on the porch, watching them enter the woods, and had waited, sitting in a rocking chair, until they emerged again. Luna and I had passed only a few words. She was attentive and watched my face as I spoke to her, but I could see that she was guarded. She had no trust for anyone yet, except possibly Coppie. He was forcing trust on her, I thought, in his clinging. Maybe that was the quickest way to her.

Anne had taken her to the building where we had done the massages before they went to see Lorca, and had helped her wash, had filed her nails, and had massaged her. Her hair was fresh and ordered now, and Barbara had found some brighter clothes for her. She looked much better, but her eyes hadn't changed. They were set in their deep hollows still, slightly unfocused and totally opaque. But she had a child's face, I thought, even though her white hair and brows fought against it. Her movements were stiff and contained, wary, but she seemed to relax just a little with Coppie.

"End of the road, David, my boy," the Bishop said. He was sitting in one of the overstuffed chairs, Burl lounging on the chair's arm beside him, his arm flung over the back. I nodded and smiled at him.

"Should we not have a little nip then? Just to send us off on our way?"

"It's early," I said. "But why not?"

He reached out, taking the chair's arm and Burl's leg, and pushed up from his sitting. He was quick, getting more agile every day. The brandy was already packed in the knapsack, but it was close to the top and he withdrew it without trouble, held it up and smiled. Melchior helped him find glasses, long-stemmed wineglasses, and he poured a few drops into enough of them for all of us, even the children. He made an occasion out of handing them around;

then he cleared his throat, blinked a few times, and made the toast.

"To the open road!" he said. "To whatever's ahead for us!"

Everyone had risen, even Coppie and Luna, and we all moved around in the room, clicking our glasses against those of the others. It took a while for us to do that, and we found we had to ask forgiveness many times as we got in each other's way. The girls laughed as they made the rounds, and Coppie tucked his hand in my belt as he raised the glass in the other hand to click it against my own. Barbara and Melchior kissed, and Burl was expansive in his gestures as he reached his glass out. The Bishop had a few private words for each one of us, pausing briefly in front of each, as he bent down to click our glasses.

"The diorama won't turn any more now, David," he said to me, a faint, wistful smile on his face when he stood before me.

Then we were back in our places, standing still and looking over at the Bishop, waiting for his signal.

He lifted his glass, looked into the brandy, then rotated his wrist slightly, sloshing it in the bowl. I saw Anne's girls mimic him, heard Dana giggle softly.

"Well, that's it," he said. "Down the hatch!" We all laughed and smiled and drained our glasses.

The way to the tunnel in the rock face was as easy going up as it had been coming down. The path cut back and forth, and the incline was very gradual. It took us some time, but we were all breathing easily when we reached the ledge. Melchior carried the five-gallon gas can that had been provided, and the rest of us split up the remaining knapsacks and bundles among us.

Melchior entered the tunnel first, the four children following, and Anne and Barbara stayed close behind the children, watching their steps. Then came Burl. I paused a moment on the ledge and turned back toward the colony. I could see Lorca's forest, the branches of the trees distinct even at this distance, but I could not see through them to her cabin. I thought I saw a wisp of smoke rising back in the trees, but I could not be sure of it.

"Did you learn anything?" the Bishop said, rather plaintively, from where he stood on the ledge beside me.

"I think so," I said. "At least that it's not anything that can be put into words."

"There's no answer to that, my boy! Best leave it to public speakers and novelists."

I turned from the forest wall and looked over at him. He was smiling, pleased with the joke that was not his words, but was surrounded by them, something I was not sure I understood.

"Let it go!" he said, turning his palms up, as if releasing it from his hands. He touched my sleeve then, and we turned together and entered the tunnel.

The place we had thought was a rock wall where the road ended was really a turn in the road, a sharp right angle where the road rose to the summit. Brush had been piled up, disguising the turning where the road moved away from the sheer cliff. All of us did our part in clearing the brush away. Melchior thought that with a little work we could get the caravan around the tight turning.

When we got to the Jeep and the Airstream, Anne

guarded the children, keeping them back from the cliff edge. Melchior and Barbara climbed in the Jeep's windows and maneuvered the large gas can that Melchior had carried, draining the five gallons into the tank. Burl climbed over the roof of the Airstream to check my car and the hookup. The Bishop and I stood in the roadway, watching.

When we were ready, only Melchior stayed in the Jeep. The rest of us walked up the road in front of it, staying close to the rock wall until we reached the tunnel entrance and past it the turning. We all stayed outside, calling out directions as he worked the caravan around the corners. When the vehicles were in a straight-enough line again, we opened the Jeep doors and started to get in. We were in thick woods now, but we could see, up the steep rise, that the trees thinned quickly near the summit.

"Let's try only the children," Melchior said as we all started to climb in. "This bugger is very steep. Maybe a little less weight would be good."

Abbey climbed in the front, Dana between her and Melchior, and Coppie and Luna sat close together in the back seat. The five of us moved well back of my car, following the caravan's slow, labored movement up the smooth rising road toward the summit. We couldn't see over the Airstream and, given its slow movement in front of us, had very little sense of how much progress we were making. Burl walked beside Barbara, I beside Anne, and the Bishop, laboring a little, brought up the rear.

"Do you think she'll be all right?" I said.

"I think so. Yes. In time," Anne said. "We'll have to give her that. I suppose she'll have to talk sometime about those years. What it must have been like! Christ, I can't imagine."

"But she'll have to," I said.

"I don't think she minded much leaving Lorca. I'm not sure even that she remembered her very well, maybe not at all. Lorca could have changed, though."

"Or come fully to herself."

"That's possible, I guess."

"What about Carl?"

Her face hardened. "He was nothing to her. He was all in himself, the same as with the other

488

children. Is that what you mean? Or do you mean, what happened to him?"

"That's what I mean," I said.

"Well, we'll just have to see."

"But it was Art. And wasn't that strange," I said, half to myself. "A fake of Art."

"Isn't it all?" she said. "Think of Melchior's rubbings. But it can make you feel good."

"Or fuck your life up."

"Or put things back toward a proper order again. Maybe it's done that for us, David."

"We'll just have to see."

Then the back of the Airstream lifted slightly, the rear of my car dipped a little, and Melchior slowed and stopped as we reached the summit. The road widened slightly where he pulled up, and we were able to make our way to the side of the caravan with little trouble. When we got to the Jeep, we saw the broad, open valley below us, extending in rolling hills almost as far as the eye could see. The road down into it was only slightly winding, the descent far more gradual than the rise to the summit had been. There were cows, and I think sheep, small

489

and far down in the distance, and I could see places where the land was cultivated, a white tin roof, half hidden but shining, in a stand of trees. Far out, near the horizon, clouds that were thin and harmless stretched out over the distant hills. There were smoke trails rising up into them, a town or small city I thought, some place to head for.

Melchior and Barbara rode in the Jeep, and Dana and Abbey asked to ride with them. The rest of us climbed into the Airstream, and when we were settled in seats, Melchior started our movement down with only a slight lurch. Once under way, we found that the road was so level and smooth that we could move around with little difficulty.

The Bishop found a deck of cards, and he and Burl sat at the table and dealt out hands of gin. I stood beside Anne, touching her waist and shoulder to keep her steady as she rummaged around in the cabinets for food. There were plenty of canned goods and some packaged goods that were well sealed, and after some brief discussion we agreed upon salmon, boiled canned potatoes, olives, wheat crackers, and coleslaw. There was a can of pâté and a package of beef jerky, and I passed both around as appetizers. Dessert would be fruit salad and pound cake.

While Anne was opening things and cooking at the small stove and counter, I watched Coppie and Luna and listened to the slap of cards on the table, the few bright words that the Bishop spoke, jesting with Burl as the hands were dealt and played.

Coppie sat very close to Luna on the small couch. He had a book in his lap and he was pointing things out to her. She was listening intently, but she seemed just a little uncomfortable when he pressed against her, brushing his head on her shoulder. She had her hands in her lap, her fingers curled under, hiding her ruined nails. Her head was slightly low as she looked into the book, and I could not see her eyes, only the deep shadow places in which they rested, wisps of her colorless white hair along the bones of her cheeks.

Coppie kept talking, telling tales, pointing at pages and turning them, lifting his head up at times, remembering things and relating them. Then in a while his monologue faltered; there were gaps of silence in it, places for entrance, and after a few of these passed by, Luna began to fill them, hesitant at first, offering only nouns and verbs, brief phrases and clauses. Then Coppie left off entirely, and Luna was speaking sentences. I saw her hands stir in her lap, her fingers uncoil, then watched her arms and her head come up. Then, in a while, it was whole paragraphs, her hands forming shapes of ideas in the air in front of her, her still-sunken eyes brightening in their hazel color and focusing. She was looking down at the book, over at Coppie's face, out into the narrow room. Coppie moved away a little, just a few inches, and looked at her face, her hair and eyes, her hand movements as she went on. It was clear that he was very interested, that right now at least he didn't need touching, or expression of affection in clinging, or even re-assurance. What he needed he was getting, ideas and their exciting complexities, that attention to things in a vibrant present.

Anne glanced over at me then, feeling my attention elsewhere. Then she watched the children too.

"Look at that," she whispered, her lips brushing the fabric at my shoulder. "They're good together. This is what he's always needed."

GREEN INTEGER
Pataphysics and Pedantry

Douglas Messerli, *Publisher*

Essays, Manifestos, Statements, Speeches, Maxims,
Epistles, Diaristic Notes, Narratives, Natural Histories,
Poems, Plays, Performances, Ramblings, Revelations
and all such ephemera as may appear necessary
to bring society into a slight tremolo of confusion
and fright at least.

*

Green Integer Books

Green Integer EL-E-PHANT Books (6 x 9 format)